ROBERT FLEGG

Green Wattles

A novel about introversion, faith and accomplishment

Kirk Family Trilogy
Book One

For Michael Robert Flegg
1985-2014
a man of true conviction

Chapter 1

Redcliffe, Queensland. Mid-November 2005.

There I was, sitting at a desk, counting the bricks in the back wall. The ceiling fans turned too gently to make any difference. Only the slightest of warm breezes filtered in through the open windows. A laundry basket full of used football jerseys would have smelled better than this room.

A week ago the walls were stripped bare of any notices, posters and artworks. A near featureless landscape. But at least it revealed variation in the colours of the bricks. The only adornment that remained was a white clock that gave out a faint tick as it counted down the seconds to the week's end.

Then I thought of her being on the other side of that wall. *Maybe she is there. Maybe not.* To get my mind off her I tried to work out how many shades of terracotta were in those bricks. It probably approaches a small infinity. Eventually my mind wandered to weightier issues.

I feel imprisoned. This cannot be what life's all about. Here I am stuck in this room with no prospect of escape for the next two hours. My thirtieth birthday has come and gone. Nothing of any significance is on the horizon. Everything about how the world works fascinates but at present nothing really presents itself as worthy of my deep commitment. I'm wandering purposelessly through life.

I looked up and saw her. Linda. She was walking past the window. The sunlight caught the golden streaks in her beautifully kept shoulder-length brown hair. She wore a figure-hugging yellow V-neck top displaying in profile the most exquisite bustline. Her sensible ear studs coordinated perfectly with her top. *I can only imagine what skirt she's wearing.*

She was heading to the next room, just beyond the bricks. I wished they were transparent. She turned briefly and gave me a smile and a friendly little wave. *Beautiful, fun-loving Linda. The life of any party. My staffroom colleague. I've had a silly crush her for the last three years. But I never had the courage to ask her out. She already has a boyfriend. I've got no chance.*

As she passed by, a primal urge stirred in my loins. I fought to suppress it. *It's strange that a fleeting glimpse of her can be so arousing.* I looked down to check that nothing showed. *Be extra careful. This could be very embarrassing.*

In an effort to suppress the animal within, I returned to my study of the rear wall. A very mundane structure with a great many mathematical surprises. Rectangles with irregular edges. Mortar lines that vary slightly in thickness. I once used a formula to build a brick barbecue. Square metres times sixty and add ten percent for wastage. When I built my barbecue I had enough bricks left over for a curved garden edge by the front door. *The formula is inaccurate. Excessive. Wasteful even.* I thought about my home and family. They mean a lot to me but something in my life is missing. The atmosphere was clammy but peaceful and I drifted off into some mysterious daydream.

Suddenly I sensed movement in front of me. A voice from somewhere whispered "Mr. Kirk. Mr. Kirk."

Snapping out of my trance, I looked across the room until I spotted a smirking sixteen-year-old boy. He said nothing more but made a series of unobtrusive, jerky pointing movements. The atmosphere erupted into muffled chuckles. *Ever had the feeling that everybody is making fun of you?* After a few seconds I discerned that he was directing me to somebody across the room.

It was then that I spotted a young lady silently standing to attention at her desk. Like a sentinel. Brittany Phillips. Her beaming smile was almost certainly an attempt to conceal her laughter at the incongruous situation. On assembly the principal had directed all students taking exams to 'stand quietly in your place if you require help'. Brittany was the first in this two-and-a-half-hour session to do exactly that.

There were little sniggers breaking out.
"Shush!"

I pushed my chair back noiselessly, rose decisively and glanced down momentarily. I would have to sidle between the crowded desks to her place. The manoeuvre had to be accomplished quickly in order to avoid more laughter throughout the room.

No doubt she thought the rule was ridiculous. It

could have even been humiliating for her but she handled it with good humour. *A wonderful character trait. Or was it sarcasm? That's not so commendable.*

I picked my way along to her.

The ruling is a bit over-the-top. I have to enforce it. I want to keep my job. Raising a hand is too easy. It can easily lead to flippant questions or disturb other students. Standing silently may be less disruptive. Maybe not. It's certainly more amusing.

I could see that the students did not care to stand like a penguin in the desert, to be sniggered at.

I don't know whether there can ever be a perfect school procedure. Humans are so unpredictable. Perhaps that's what attracts me to the precision of mathematics? So that's why I'm a maths teacher!

Brittany smiled and sat down gracefully. I bent over with my face next to hers. An aroma something like a cross between roses and frangipanis engulfed me. It was quite a delightful change from dank football gear.

"How can I help you, Brittany?"

"Mr Kirk, how many questions do we have to do from part B?"

"Just three of your own choosing," I whispered, pointing to the instructions at the top of the page.

"Thank you, Sir." She nodded, smiled a little sheepishly and picked up her pen.

What prompted her to ask such an obvious question?

I straightened up slowly to my full one hundred and eighty centimetres and edged my way back along to my desk. Each student looked up briefly and smiled as I passed by. This rapport gave me a sort of contented feeling. *They like me!* I held my breath in an attempt not to disturb them too much.

As quietly as possible I pulled out my chair and sat down facing the class. My thoughts flowed faster than the water over Kondalilla Falls.

These are good students. They don't need much help to complete their final exam. I've got a great relationship with them, I think. I love teaching but by November when we move into exam mode, followed by marking, followed by report writing, followed by end of year games and presentation nights ... why am I doing this? It's not the quantity of work that concerns me. I'm not bored with it. I'm not a fan of some of the inane games we play to babysit the students for the last few days before the Christmas break. But on the whole I love to plan things out and see them happen. It's more about the meaning of my life and where I'm going. I need a plan for that!

The timer on my desk showed eighty-three minutes to go. So, there I sat. Getting lost in yet another reverie.

Who am I really? Donald Ian Kirk, bachelor and daydreamer, mathematician and teacher. Would-be farmer. An introvert who has never been able to make friends. Young eligible ladies just smile sweetly and look away. They must think that either mathematics or teaching or most likely the combination of both is the career for the most boring person on earth. But for me maths is the language of the universe, teeming with practical applications. My students will leave school with a very strong awareness of that.

My thought pattern then took a sudden turn.

Hey wait a moment! I'm a responsible teacher. I take my job very seriously. At this moment it's the most important thing in my life. Perhaps my wandering thoughts are stopping me from carrying out my job as well as I can. I decided something had to change then and there. *The exam supervision is number one. Daydreaming has to give way to vigilance.*

What I had ahead of me was a sticky afternoon of surveillance interspersed with the occasional little toddle around the room to whisper and maybe catch the scent of fresh flowers or, more frequently, unmitigated body odour. *Don't teenage boys know about deodorant?*

You can see how my thoughts wander.

All was quiet for the next twenty minutes. I was more diligent in my supervision but stray imaginings began to sneak in. There is nothing unusual about daydreaming. After all, August Kekulé discovered the structure of benzene while daydreaming back in 1855. That's justification enough for me.

Again my mind wandered to the brick wall. I'm captivated by numbers and patterns. I could have become a statistician. But teaching offered an immediate job. *I might discover a new theorem or solve an enigma that's been around for centuries. How many bricks in that wall?*

I looked around at the students. *Right now I love teaching just as much as maths. Or so I tell myself. I've been at it for eight years. It's never dull, except perhaps for days like this. But that's not so. In the quietness I get the opportunity to think and imagine. So, no, it's never really boring at all. Is that a peculiar line of thought? It makes sense to me.*

Sixty minutes on the timer. The students were all working at their individual desks. Nobody was standing, no hand was raised, nobody was whispering or signing. Feeling unsettled, I began to contemplate the concept of boredom. *What is it exactly? If you have a reasonable level of skills but no challenge, then you will be bored. I need a little challenge. What can I do silently for the next hour? With a good level of supervision? Surely I can think while watching. Nobody can see what goes on in my head.*

Determined that the students must be aware of me looking around, my brain tried to come up with a more accurate formula for calculating the number of bricks in a wall. *But the mortar thickness is a variable I have to deal with. Is there a variation in the size of the bricks? These things need to be investigated. Time to show myself as supervisor!*

I made a circuit of the room carrying a ruler. As I was behind the class, I don't think anybody saw me surreptitiously take measurements of some bricks and mortar. Returning to the teacher's desk I wrote them down and made a few other preliminary jottings. To give the appearance of filling in an attendance sheet, I looked up frequently at the students. They were all arched over their desks solving abstract problems. Just as I was.

Within a few minutes I became immersed in the mathematical universe. *There are quite a few variables to consider. I'll need to calculate on average sizes.*

Another circuit of the room provided some further data. I counted only 976 bricks in the roughly eighteen square metre wall. The half bricks I added together to make one. My inaccurate barbecue formula told me it should be 1060. That left eighty-four bricks over for a garden edge.

As I stared around vacantly I made a breakthrough. I had a formula that I thought would work. I picked up the spare student calculator from my desk and whacko! 980. Not too much wastage there. The most troublesome aspect of my formula however was that it was based on a complex and idealistic equation. *No bricklayer will ever apply it. No builder will be interested but maybe an architect or engineer will one day find the algorithm useful.* I jotted down a few more notes.

Quite suddenly the timer on my desk rang and the exam was over. I forgot to give a five-minute warning. That was also in the principal's policy.

"Okay, guys, pens down. Put all your answer pages in order. Chairs up and bring your work out to me as you leave. I'll staple it. No Talking." *I'm in charge here. Very much to the point with my instructions.*

The bell for the end of the day was already sounding as the students noisily collated their work, scraped their chairs along the floor before slamming them down on the tops of the desks and filing past to hand the papers to me.

Again, a variety of aromas passed by, but I definitely preferred the rose-frangipani. "Thank you, Sir," was frequently whispered. *What are they thanking me for? Probably not for setting such a brilliant question paper. Perhaps it's for accepting their pages. Maybe it's thanks for being their teacher. At least I hope it is.*

Once collected and stapled the student papers were right to go. These were Maths B papers submitted by my own Year 11 class. There was no need to hand them over to a colleague for marking, so I just bundled them up, turned off the lights and fans, locked the door and headed straight to my car.

It's Friday. I don't intend to mark papers during my peak leisure time. That task will definitely have to wait until Sunday night. In the meantime I'll do something much more adventurous.

Chapter 2

I must have been peering down at my shoes as I crossed the verandah. I had a soft collision with Linda as she bounced out of the room next door. Her shoulder glanced off my arm. I came to a sudden halt with my heart fluttering wildly. A slightly fruity scent enveloped me. I noticed her little black leather skirt and sheer black stockings. *That primal urge again. Wow.*

"Oops. Sorry. I didn't see you." I gave a false little chuckle and she laughed along with me.

"That's okay Don, I wasn't looking where I was going. Hey, you've got a pile of marking there."

"Yeah. Maths B. Year 11." I sighed.

"Well I'm free for the weekend. My Biology doesn't come in till Monday."

"Have you got any plans?" I wasn't sure whether this was a good thing to ask. But she didn't respond as if I had evil intentions towards her.

"Not really. Phil and I are probably going to the beach tomorrow and the pub Sunday afternoon but that's about all."

"Yourself?"

"Well. Yes, as a matter of fact. I'm going gold prospecting."

"You're kidding. Wow. That sounds exciting. Where are you going?"

"Near Gympie."

"Wow. That's amazing. I'd love to do that.

Anyway, I have to go. Tell me about it on Monday. See you next week." She leaned in a little. Her hand touched mine. Then she turned.

"See you," I managed in an unusually high-pitched voice. *Her disarming smile had made my vocal cords constrict.*

Don headed off. He had begun to secretly loathe Phil, whoever he was, but he would most certainly tell her about his prospecting come Monday. *Why is she so popular? She's outgoing. Talks to everybody. Do I need to do that?*

The air outside was filled with the warm honey smell of nectar from the abundant trees that surrounded the school. It felt unusually muggy and from the west dark clouds were rapidly approaching. *It's a bit early for a summer thunderstorm. I'd better be off.*

His contemplative afternoon had suddenly dissolved into the turmoil of the end of another school day. As he reached his car, he watched yellow and brown uniformed students streaming out of the school grounds from every exit like bees leaving the hive in search of pollen. A warm breeze had sprung up and was stirring up a bit of dust. The sickly smell of nectar mixed with the dust and exhaust fumes was becoming unpleasant.

Two fourteen-year-old boys bolted past. The chaser was calling out uncomplimentary names. Don wanted to intervene but became lost in his own reflections. At that age he had always referred to himself as Donald and his parents invariably called him that. Following a history lesson on the end of World War 2, certain bullies in his class had contrived a silly game plan. As he entered a room somebody would call out 'Don Kirk, Don Kirk. Evacuate. Evacuate.' All the students present would run to one side away from him and laugh. He never really got over the humiliation, even though the game petered out a year later.

He fumbled for his keys and spotted Peter, one of his teaching colleagues, who was already driving down the road in his grey Mazda. He had a reputation for beating the students out of the school gate every afternoon. And what's more he always had an excuse that could not be refuted. 'My wife rang, frantic. One of the kids has swallowed a stone'. Or something like that. *I kind of envy him having a wife and family. Maybe one day I'd like that. But I'm thirty and I've never had a real girlfriend. What is wrong with me?*

His car was a cream-coloured 1972 Peugeot 504 sedan. Despite considerable research he had never managed to find the French name for the colour so in his mind it was just 'couleur crème'. He loved that car. It was purchased from an old farmer ten years earlier. Don decided some major work needed to be done on it. It had cost him quite a lot. It was now over thirty years old but comfortable, smooth, powerful and economical on fuel. These vehicles were built like a rhinoceros, with a skin of extra thick steel. This one had suffered almost no ill effects when a farm gate swung into it the previous year. He managed to polish out the microscopic scratch. People were either intrigued or somewhat cynical about his choice of such an uncommon vehicle. The car had been unkindly described to him as 'the ugly duckling of the automotive world' and again as 'an old Holden with an Austin 1800 boot'. He really didn't mind. *I relish having good engineering and I like being different. I especially love the comfort.*

For a long time it had been his dream to live on a farm, well away from city noise. That was no longer a figment of his imagination. He actually had the courage to go out and make it a reality. Well, a partial reality and it came with a substantial mortgage. It comprised one hectare of flat pasture with an old timber house and a huge metal shed. No animals or crops, just Don and the 'farm'. He was beginning to wonder why. *I'm not a farmer. Not even a hobby farmer. I only put in a couple of fruit trees. And two of those died of root rot. Why did I buy the 'farm'? To get in touch with nature? More likely to get away from people. Why am I like this?*

So now he was going home to his acreage just north of Brisbane to pick up some camping gear. The town is called Burpengary. It's a funny name. A kind of windy name! Most people laugh at it, except for Don's Head of Department, Garry Willcox. The name actually derives from the local aboriginal language and means 'place of green wattle'. *I like the name. It somehow connects me to the land and its original inhabitants.* So now, in his thoughts, he lived in 'Green Wattles'. He even made a sign for the gate. 'Green Wattles Farm'. Nobody ever commented on it. Maybe because it wasn't really a farm. He decided that one day he would plant some wattle trees around the fence line.

This weekend's little adventure had been playing out in his imagination for at least four months. *I wish I had a young lady to share it with me. But I don't. It's just me on my lonesome.* Shortly he would be heading off towards Gympie, a town located on the Mary River, 138 kilometres north.

Don grew up in Sydney so he was not a Queenslander born and bred. He wasn't even familiar with Gympie but, through reading, he had found out that there was a gold rush there in the 1860s. The alluvial gold that was found apparently saved the state of Queensland from bankruptcy. There had been some very big floods in the area in 1870, 1873, 1893, 1955, 1968, 1974, 1989, 1992 and 1999. Those floods were all after the gold rush so perhaps, he reasoned, some more alluvial gold may have been uncovered. Nobody had been seriously looking for it to his knowledge.

My interest is not primarily in becoming rich through prospecting. I want to experience the thrill of discovery and enjoy the solitude. Fossicking in the streambed will likely see me evaluating density of solids, velocity of stream flow, mineral content of tailings and a myriad of other parameters. So this will, hopefully, be a challenging problem-solving exercise. At the very least it'll give me some anecdotes to share with next year's budding mathematicians!

Don had visited the Gympie region just over two

years before as a guest of John and Pat Myers whose son Rod had been his teaching colleague for five years. With a few other teachers he had been invited for a barbecue to celebrate Rod's twenty-eighth birthday. That was just ten days before his own! But nobody knew that. *We're almost twins! He's close to being what I'd call a friend. But I find him a little too bossy. I didn't get an invite to his thirtieth.* Tonight, Don would be briefly rekindling his acquaintance with Rod's parents and camping by the creek on their property.

With all this excitement firing up his imagination, the old Pug made its way slowly through the school gate, contending with mums, school buses and Grade 12 learner drivers.

The sky was darkening rather quickly. Cumulus clouds were building overhead. There were already light spits of rain on the windscreen. *This is only a storm. It'll pass and it won't interfere with my plans, I hope.* A very quick home stop was all that he needed. His duffle bag, camping quilt, tent, 'morning tea box' of groceries, gas cooker, camera and utensils were all piled up just inside the front door. *They're all waiting to be packed into my spacious boot.* He had crafted plywood partitions in an effort to logically organise his boot. An axe, various tools, a gold pan and a folding shovel were already sitting in their compartments. With the exception of the gold pan, these tools were always carried there, just in case.

The twenty-five-minute drive home was uneventful. A few heavier drops of rain struck the car but gave him no reason to change his plan. Everything checked out at the 'farm'. Doors were locked. Lights and fans were off. The shed padlock was securely fastened. The contents of his boot were neatly stowed. His camera was on the passenger-side floor. Only one thing seemed wrong. Darkness appeared to have prematurely fallen. He went back into the house and brought out his best torch. Again, he dashed back inside for his Driza-Bone coat and an umbrella. *You can't be too careful.*

A gravel track led from the house to the road. Driving out of the property and across the concrete culvert that covered a storm drain, he habitually looked down at his gauges. It was a kind of pre-flight check. This afternoon the fuel level was just above half. To have a positive start to the weekend he thought it best to stop and top up.

The rain was now coming down in torrents and an eerie darkness surrounded him. Visibility was pretty poor on these backroads at night, but this was mid-afternoon. *It'll clear up.* He started to get a feeling of mild claustrophobia. The wipers were small and offered only a tiny window of clarity onto the road ahead. In addition, they wiped in the left-hand drive European direction. *Very annoying. Wipers are not the best part of the Peugeot design folio.*

He turned and headed slowly along the road. *My hopes of solitude and discovery must become a reality. But I know from experience that things do not always go according to...*

Chapter 3

Screech. Instinctively he slammed his foot on the brake pedal. A split second later his brain said 'vary the pressure a little'. The front and rear discs gripped tenaciously. The nose dipped and the car came to a solid halt. The engine stopped with a thud and something in the undercarriage jingled. There it stood, just a metre in front of him and staring straight through the driving rain. A large male grey kangaroo. Bewildered by the lights. Large enough to do damage but not smart enough to work out which way the car was travelling. Once the vehicle was stationary the creature immediately turned and hopped away nonchalantly as if to say 'haha, made you stop!'

Don's first thought was 'is the camera okay'? He glanced down and could see no problem. Something had moved in the boot. He would have to check that later. Rubbing his head, he decided to press on. Slowly reaching forward to restart the engine, he realised he'd lost a little of his enthusiasm for the adventure. It occurred to him to turn back but the prospect of sitting at home marking papers did not have appeal. First gear. He let the clutch out smoothly.

The area to the west of 'Green Wattles' was well known to him. Slightly narrow bitumen country roads passing through bushland dotted with small holdings. The road was comfortable to drive in most conditions but this afternoon was a rare exception. It would be a mild relief to see the lights of his favourite service station further along. It was a small country business. Two bowsers. Unusual in those days. They still offered old-fashioned driveway service. *I like that. Something different.* The visibility was not improving but he pressed on.

Within minutes he sighed audibly as the service station driveway came into view. There was no awning over the forecourt but fortunately he wouldn't have to leave his comfy Peugeot seats or stand in the rain. Pulling up at the bowser, he spotted the lanky youth he had taught in Grade 10. Everyone called him Ikky but Don never knew why. His real name was Joshua. Springing out through the doorway of the tiny shop the lad came running to greet him, soaking wet and grinning wildly.

"Hi, Mr Kirk. It's a wet one. At least it'll flush out the mozzies." He laughed and seemed to relish splashing in puddles and being soaked to the bone. A kind of uncoordinated dancing in the rain!

Ikky was the class clown and did not go on to senior years. Now he was a happy young workingman. Don felt proud of him although his bright personality was none of his doing. *Perhaps I contributed to his work ethic. I'd like to think so.*

"Fill 'er up?"

Not wanting to lower his window too far, he nodded in the affirmative.

Despite the downpour, Ikky washed the windscreen, asked whether he should check the engine oil, to which Don shook his head, filled the tank with standard unleaded petrol and walked around looking at the tyres. Having finished his assessment of the roadworthiness of the vehicle, he turned, gripped some metal protuberance, lifted his feet and energetically swung from the petrol bowser, finally settling with his smiling face at the window. *Perhaps he should have joined a circus!*

The total came to fifteen dollars. Through the window gap Don handed him a twenty-dollar note. He rummaged in the leather bag hanging loosely from his belt and handed back three gold coins. "'n five's twenny" he called out over the drumming of the rain and with an intonation indicating that this was his friendly farewell. *You are now free to drive off.*

Don quietly reflected on the fact that the schooling system may have failed Joshua with regard to literacy but, as his maths teacher, he had obviously imparted a degree of numeracy. *My change is correct. It was all worthwhile.* They both smiled as they waved goodbye. Departing, Don realised that he had not spoken one word to the lad. *Amazing what body language can achieve!*

By now the streetlights had come on and the rain was easing a little. But leaving 'Green Wattles' and driving out onto the Bruce Highway he found himself engulfed by a multitude of orange reflections. *Sodium lights.* The lights were not a problem. But his pulse rate rose and the wheels span a little as the car accelerated to merge into the traffic flow. *The Peugeot 504 may be an excellent rally car but it was never seen on the speedway!* The headlights were on but they didn't seem to accomplish much given the fact that the sun was actually still up, hidden somewhere behind all those black thunderheads.

He was headed north. *I always drive carefully on wet roads. My father's only motor accident was in wet conditions and it still frightens me. Tonight I'll stay ten k's below the speed limit and carefully watch the road markings to make sure I haven't wandered out of my lane.* Lightning flashes occasionally illuminated the countryside, but he stayed focused on the road.

He drove for an hour, averting his eyes from the oncoming glare. The rain was easing to drizzle. Slowing a little as he approached his turn, he began shifting his eyes from the centre line to the road edges. And there they were, the white posts surrounded by a glimmering of wet gravel. He recognised the turn off to Six Mile Creek. There was no road sign but he'd been there once before. *No oncoming traffic.* He indicated and eased the car to the right.

Crunch, crunch, crunch! The wet, stony track was not easy to navigate driving east in the failing afternoon light. The bush closed in and darkness lay ahead. Proceeding cautiously, passing several roadside mailboxes crafted in imaginative shapes, he found himself growing more nervous. The road was becoming treacherously slippery. Twenty kilometres per hour was his self-imposed speed limit.

Almost as quickly as it started, the rain stopped.

In the rear vision mirror there were the most beautiful red sunset colours silhouetting the towering gums on the horizon. Through the now eerie orange light he spotted a small mound in the middle of the track. *Maybe an echidna or a rock?* He carefully navigated the Peugeot to the left a little to avoid it. The camera bag started to slide. He tapped the brakes as he reached for it. *Wrong!* In the loose gravel the brakes didn't even slow the car. It crunched its way toward the bush. *That's inertia!* Before there was a chance to decide what to do his life flashed before him. He had the sensation of falling as the passenger-side dipped down suddenly. The tyres lost traction. His weekend of discovery was sliding helplessly into a ditch!

Chapter 4

Six Mile Creek, Queensland.

The car came to a halt in a second or two. It seemed longer. The crunch of gravel stopped abruptly. No thump. The car just became stationary. Stunned, he found himself sitting for a moment wondering why his expensive European tyres had lost their grip. *The coefficient of friction on the pebbly, wet, clayey surface was insufficient to maintain adhesion. Or perhaps the graded mound on the road edge has collapsed under the weight of such a solid car. This is all purely academic and doesn't solve any immediate problem. Am I hurt? No. Is my camera okay? Yes.* The reality was that the Peugeot had come to rest at an odd angle, he was isolated and didn't know what to do.

He tried first gear and then reverse. The wheels began spinning without moving the car. The daylight was now failing fast. Pulling out his Nokia mobile phone, he wondered whether he still had John and Pat's number. They could bring their tractor and pull the car back onto the road. But the Australian bush is vast and it's not unusual to be out of range for phone reception. That was unfortunately the case.

Opening the heavy door uphill was not easy. He held it open with his foot and somehow clambered out, sliding down onto the road. *What to do? Examine the situation.* He walked around sizing up the predicament. *Driver's side rear wheel up in the air. Passenger's side front bumper in the bottom of the ditch. Only one wheel still in contact with the road.* It was not a pretty sight, especially humbling for such a classic car.

Nothing he could think of would be of any value in getting it back on the road. Help was definitely required. But help was something he never wanted to ask for.

The best course of action would be to walk to the closest farm. They would be neighbours of John and Pat and perhaps they would tow it out with their tractor or at least help him to contact the Myers. He grabbed the camera. After taking a few ad hoc sunset shots, without the usual attention to detail, he set off with torch in hand and out-of-range phone in pocket to walk down the muddy road, or more accurately, slippery, chancy and potentially perilous track. He was both annoyed and anxious. *What a calamity!*

After what seemed like only half a minute of carefully picking his way along with mud clinging to his boots, he heard the hum of an engine. Dazzling car headlights were approaching fast. *I might have to hide behind a tree. Who drives on a country track in these conditions?* Dispelling fears of robbery, kidnapping or murder and hoping for the best, he began to wave.

He could not believe his good fortune. Help had arrived. Hopefully the weekend escapade was about to take a miraculous turn for the better. Again there arose in his mind a worry about who would be driving on this lonely, isolated stretch of road at night.

The car slowed and he recognised the driver. *It's not a serial killer!* In fact he was truly astonished. It couldn't be, but it was his colleague Rod Myers. *He must have beaten Peter out of the school gate today.*

"Is that you Don?" came a cheerful greeting from behind the gradually descending driver's window.

"It sure is. Boy am I glad to see you."

"Yeah. We just called in to my parents' farm to pick up some stuff. We're heading north to the beach for the weekend." *Those were most likely things he'd forgotten to pack earlier. Rod's not generally an organised person.*

"Why are you walking?"

"I slid into a ditch a few hundred metres back. Just looking for some help."

"Hop in." He pointed behind him. In a flash Don opened the door and jumped into the back seat of the gleaming new Honda CR-V. "You know my girlfriend Gracie?"

"I don't think we've met," came the sweet voice from the front. Her pretty face appeared and dutifully he extended his hand and shook hers.

"Don Kirk" he said.

"I'm Grace. Everyone calls me Gracie. Roddy told me you're going to camp at his parents' place."

"Yeah. I'm going to do a bit of gold prospecting."

"Exciting."

"I think so."

The Honda turned slightly and came to a halt askew across the track. The high beam and driving lights were now saturating the old, beleaguered vehicle with light. It was a truly pathetic sight. The three stood pondering the state of the beloved 504.

"One rear wheel is completely off the ground and the diagonally opposite front bumper is touching the ditch bottom." Don reported what they could so obviously see. Indeed, it appeared that the edge of the road had suffered a minor collapse. He was buoyed by the fact that it was the road's fault and not of his doing.

Rod, in his usual jovial but forceful manner, took charge. He installed Grace in the driver's seat. She attempted to reverse the car while Rod and Don pulled upwards with their collective might on the front bumper. The heavy gauge steel of the car now seemed to be somewhat of a disadvantage. They tried to rock it up and down but only succeeded in getting muddy trousers.

"Get the jack," said Rod. Don thought it was time to call in a tractor but Grace had to be impressed by Rod's resourcefulness. Opening the boot he took out a little-used jack and began hoisting the front of the car. The small scissors jack reached its full height but that was not nearly enough.

"Get some rocks," commanded Rod. We two intrepid males headed off into the scrubby bushland, torches in hand and eyes to the ground.

They located, carried and placed flattish rocks under the lower front wheel. That would serve to hold the car at a better angle. Lowering the jack until it was flat, they set it on another pile of stones and Rod began to wind it up once again. The car was beginning to level but Grace was still unable to get any traction in reverse.

"Have you got an axe or a chainsaw?" asked Rod. Don was flummoxed. A tractor was what he wanted at that moment. But without protest he produced a little camping hatchet from the car boot.

Like a frontiersman, his hand over his brow, Rod scanned the nearby bushland. "Cut down that tree," he ordered, pointing to an unfortunate nearby sapling.

Against his better judgment Don did as instructed. The small tree was a tough little customer, probably a wattle. The axe seemed to bounce off it. He had to chop for many minutes before he was able to fell it. About to pass the axe to Rod, the command came to clear the branches. So he chopped wildly while Rod and Grace discussed their plans for the weekend. *Rod is a control freak, a side of him I'm now a little more aware of. But I admire his taste in women.*

Now lathered with sweat in the humid atmosphere Don had everything ready. Rod sauntered around to the front of the car and they began to stack more rocks to make a pivot for a first order lever. He now understood why he had just been ordered to appropriate the four-metre long tree trunk.

The butt of the trunk was wedged up under the Peugeot front end and together the boys pushed down with all their combined weight on the other end of the lever. The bumper rose until the back driver's side wheel was again in contact with the road surface. Grace turned out to be a very astute driver. She gently revved the engine, slipped the clutch and ever so slowly reversed the car out. Don's worries seemed to evaporate. The car was now soundly situated with all four wheels on the track. *I refuse to call this a road.*

Still wondering what had just happened, he found himself being farewelled. There was a slightly awkward moment being hugged by Grace and then having his hand crushed by Rod's macho handshake. He physically winced. *My knuckles just cracked.*

"He could kill you with his grip," joked Grace.

Don smiled but no laughter came out of his mouth.

The whole scenario was totally surreal. It was now dark, and he stood watching Rod reverse and straighten his car ready to depart. The Peugeot motor was still running. With torch in hand, he could see no damage to the car but there was most certainly a big dent in his self-image.

With his window still down Rod slowly drove forward, surveying the scene. Sitting high in his seat, almost triumphantly, he smiled with a kind of oh-well-these-things-happen look on his face. "Well, you'll be right now. Mum and Dad are home. Only three clicks down the road. I'll call them and let them know you're close. Have a good weekend!"

Grace and Rod waved and drove off to have their good weekend. *What will they be doing?* He dismissed such thoughts as he waved forlornly.

"Thanks very much. Bye!" He didn't have time to call out 'hey, there's no mobile reception here'. *I have the feeling that I'm all alone without any human support once again. That's an eerie thought. People who need people...a song with a message for me?*

Chapter 5

Don, in his usual compulsive way, carefully wiped and repacked the jack and the axe. He always made every effort not to muddy the boot. In an attempt to be ecologically responsible he had a strange altruistic brainwave. *I should protect the small creatures.* With this in mind he started to unstack the flat stones and redistribute them throughout the bushland to reinstate microhabitats. The process was actually enjoyable with the scent of the wet bush quite intoxicating.

It was near the end of this operation that one of the stones attracted his attention. He shone the torch onto one face of it. It was unnaturally smooth with a tactile raised vein-like pattern. His sense of touch seemed at that point inadequate, so he carefully placed the flat, greyish stone in the boot for further inspection in the daylight. *It could end up in my rockery, an eclectic arrangement of stones, each with its own story. I think rock samples are the best free souvenirs of any trip*

This whole episode probably took less than an hour but exhaustion was setting in. With everything neatly stowed, he drove off slowly, keeping to the centre of the track. A matter of minutes later there it was, the Myers' driveway, lined with white painted stones. Everything was wet and glistening and as he drove along, the track became less and less distinct. He followed two deep wheel ruts with the tussock grass in the centre brushing the floor of the old Pug. Tall bushes overhung the driveway. With his head forward he carefully navigated the narrow maze of ruts, long grass, tree roots and the tunnel of bushes. It was seemingly only minutes later that he emerged into an open place where there were buildings and lights. *Habitation. Human connection. I never thought I'd want it so badly.*

John and Pat were standing on the verandah waving. Don felt totally relieved to be comfortably back in civilization but a new anguish had started to take hold. He now had to make conversation with people he hardly knew.

"That track's pretty slippery, Mate! Took you a while to get here." John laughed. "Just as well the kids were there to help you'. Council just graded the bloomin' thing last week though it's not much better than it was." Don cringed inwardly at John's nasally strine pronunciation. *Perhaps I'm too nit-picking. Maybe that's why people don't like me.* Bearing up, he made an effort to grin as he opened the door, stepped out and in his best Aussie accent replied "G'day!"

Shaking hands at the foot of the wooden steps, Pat smiled and kindly invited him to come inside. Looking down at his muddy boots and trousers, he suggested they talk on the verandah. *Maybe I should have worn my Driza-Bone.* To the right there was a weathered timber outdoor table and chairs. John reached into his back pocket with his leathery hand and produced what looked like an old blue work singlet. He meticulously wiped every square inch of the wet furniture. The rain had cooled everything down so chatting outside would be relaxing and quite a relief after this afternoon's stuffy classroom. Just a few minutes into the chit-chat Pat disappeared then reappeared in a flash with food and drink on a tray.

Being an introvert is always awkward but for some reason this couple could make a person feel more at ease. They were in their late fifties, grey-haired, tanned and wrinkled from outdoor work. Laid-back country bumpkin types. They only seemed to talk about very mundane things like road conditions and weather. But their hospitality was bewitching. Don tried to steer the conversation onto floods and creeks, but it soon returned to cattle farming and the hardships of living in isolation.

After a long glass of homemade ginger beer, a bowl of hearty stew and retelling the tale of the miraculous appearance of Rod and Grace, he graciously declined their offer of a comfortable bed. This was to be, after all, a camping trip. He preferred to retire to the reclined front passenger seat of the car which would be his sleeping accommodation for the night. *Peugeot seats are very comfortable and versatile.*

Exhausted from the evening's events and possibly dulled by the high alcohol content of John's home brew, sleep came easily. Snuggling up to his warm, old camping quilt he felt an overwhelming sense of security. *The morning will be a fresh beginning.* Thoughts of what tomorrow might bring faded quickly into blackness and silence. The next thing he became aware of was suddenly being awakened by excruciatingly loud noises just as dawn began to light the eastern sky. The new day had begun and he sat straight up.

Chapter 6

Swarms of brightly coloured parrots and white cockatoos came circling overhead. Their raucous squawks were loud enough to raise the dead! Looking out through the fogged car window he saw John pouring seed from a bag into trays nailed to his verandah posts. "He actually feeds these boom boxes?" he grumbled. *I do tend to be irritable in the mornings but living alone I have nobody with whom to share my rancour, so I share it with myself.*

Sleeping in a car does not ensure the most comfortable night. He got up onto all fours. Peeling himself out through the rear passenger door he discovered a degree of stiffness and soreness in his limbs. The car was wet with little beads of dew sitting proudly on the show and shine quality wax finish. They could not stay there. He would have to wipe them away with a chamois once he'd finished his ablutions in the nearby laundry outbuilding. It had a make-shift shower and toilet. A kind of rural ensuite. Very useful for farmer John to clean up before entering the house after a hard day on the land. Don couldn't figure out how to use the jerry-rigged shower, so he had a stand-up strip wash at the laundry tub and a welcome change of clothes. Despite having to make do he felt an exhilarating readiness for the day's experiences.

Walking back to the car his thoughts turned to more serious matters. *It's important to remove the excess water from the car finish before the sun evaporates the drops. It has to be done to avoid blotchy marks.* He wasted no time putting the plan into action. He wiped slowly, examining every drop. Ahead of the chamois the little beads slid off with ease. *I always enjoy doing this. I love to watch them coalesce into larger drops.*

With the duco gleaming once more, he walked away from the car and looked back in admiration. To his horror he could see that mud had caked the underside and wheel arches. No chamois would be up to the task. *I need a pressure cleaner. That's a vital job to be done at home on Sunday afternoon!*

He was abruptly greeted by a very friendly "Good morning. Would you like to come inside for breakfast?" Now clean and presentable he reluctantly accepted Pat's offer and entered the house. *Living alone I'm not one for early morning conversation. I don't like to engage in conversation very much at all. I'm a true introvert, driven by my own thoughts and not by my response to other people.* On this occasion he had to consciously decide to make an exception. *I need a topic of conversation. Quick. There he is, over there.* John was sitting at the dining table. Don walked over and sat across from him. *Now to pick his brain on the best location for gold fossicking.*

"Just follow the track through the top paddock. When you come to the self-closing gate you'll need to go left and follow the fence line down the hill till you come to the creek crossing. That's a beaut spot. Shallow with a stony bottom. You could camp there. Nobody's looked for gold there for years. You might just be lucky."

Finally some useful information. John rambled on about farming as they ate up the scrumptious sausages, grilled tomato and scrambled egg. With a few well-chosen words Don made an attempt to express his gratitude to the Myers for their hospitality. As they walked him out to the car he vowed to call into the house on departure to let them know how the prospecting went.

"We're here if you need anything," offered Pat. He was really starting to like her no-nonsense warmth and conviviality.

The anticipation of an adventurous cross-country car ride and his burgeoning gold fever urged him into action. He took off at a rate of knots down the track. In the rear-view mirror, he caught a glimpse of John running after him, waving wildly. He was heading in exactly the wrong direction. With a guilty smirk and a timid little wave, he wheeled around to go the right way. *Yet another embarrassment.*

Chapter 7

I really delight in the thrill of driving across rough ground in a road car. Achieving something that's not meant to be. The Peugeot 504 is a truly elegant vehicle. It's robust and can comfortably handle the undulations of a pasture paddock. Peugeots were very successful in the Redex reliability trials through the outback in the 1950s. Then the rerun in 1974. The 504 like mine was in that. Wow, this is Redex in 2005! Despite the vehicle's brilliant reputation, he picked his way gingerly along the fence line so as not to risk damage to the underside. There was a certain unease as a wheel dipped into each depression. Then there was the elation as the car rose again without touching bottom. It was like a slow-motion show ride. He was loving every moment.

Reaching a crest, the ground began to dip sharply towards the old, twisted gum trees that lined the creek. Applying the brakes slowed the vehicle a little but it began to skid on the slick grassy surface. Mild panic set in. Another uncontrollable slide. But this time it was in daylight and much less threatening.

He kept touching the brakes and gently maneuvering the wheels. Nothing worked. *What is wrong with these tyres? I might hit a fence post or a tree. On reflection, I do regard this kind of trepidation as an integral part of the experience, heightening the delight of discovery that I know will follow. Anything worthwhile almost always involves a tough grind and a bit of risk.*

There was no collision, just the slightly overwhelming anxiety of not being in complete control. The car came to rest just shy of a pebble beach by a babbling brook. A group of young cattle looked up from their drinking. He thought it best to stay in the car until they began to walk away. With the presence of these beasts a decision had been made for him. No tent would be erected. He would fossick here near the safety of the car and sleep in it again tonight. *Anything to avoid the possibility of being gored by a raging bull.*

The day turned out to be cloudless and the sub-tropical November sun had quite a bite. With a broad-brimmed hat, long sleeves and copious amounts of sunscreen on any exposed skin, he picked up his little shovel and began to wade in, surveying the gravel in the creek bed as he splashed along. The water was moving by quite rapidly. That pleased him. About forty metres upstream these was an old river gum that had been undermined. *Gold nuggets could be trapped in the roots. I'll set up there.*

He scooped up a shovelful of gravel and stumbled back to his folding chair that was now sitting in the stream. He lowered the pan into the water and began shaking it to stratify the material. After twenty seconds he stopped and threw out the larger pebbles from the top. More water was added. With lots of washing and side to side shaking, he was finally down to a teaspoonful of material. That is when he checked and found his first flecks of gold. He was hit by the excitement the old miners must have felt. But it wasn't exactly the mother lode. He lifted them out with his fingertips and placed them in a screw-top jar.

Wading, shoveling and panning for at least five hours he scrounged perhaps a hundred small flakes. Any stones that gave a hint of blue, red or yellow colour, he lifted towards the sun to examine the opacity, as they might be sapphires or zircons. There were a couple of prospective gemstones, which he stored in a ziplock bag. Eventually he moved the chair out of the water and into the shade to take in the pastoral peace and quiet.

Blissfully sitting there under the trees, Don began to examine his own personality. *I grew up in a family that loved me and included me in everything. But being the eldest by several years there was always a feeling of being different. A shyness developed. My brother and sister are not shy. I can't explain where it came from but now I see myself more as a person who is happy in his own company. Then again, I do like people. Last night I just wanted people around. Rod and Grace looked so happy together. John and Pat are so lovely. Could it be that I'm not really a hermit? Is marriage and children a possibility for me? I don't even know my neighbours back at 'Green Wattles'. How will I ever make friends? Linda and Phil? I can't bear to think about them right now.*

All these thoughts were swirling around when he realised that he had not eaten since breakfast. In fact, he had begun to feel rather unwell. He'd been so intent on the quest that he had no awareness of the onset of mild sunstroke. Headachy and nauseous he tried to sit quietly listening to the sound of the water but remaining vigilant in case of a cattle stampede.

Towards sunset he was feeling well enough to pull out his small gas cooker, collect some running water from upstream in a billycan and make tea. A fresh gum leaf was added to the brew to enhance the flavour. *This is truly me getting in touch with nature.* He sipped the black tea but still felt too nauseated to eat anything more than a muesli bar. *Sometimes, in order to pursue one's goal, one has to make concessions. No, my health takes priority over the quest. No more fossicking today.*

In the fading light the sound of a motor could be heard nearby. Headlights appeared on the other side of the creek. It was not a gang of cattle rustlers coming to mug him. It was John waving from his quad bike. Don returned the wave to indicate that all was okay. *Was it pride or shyness that made me withhold any evidence of my sickness? Surely I'll sleep it off.*

Darkness fell crisp and clear. Stars appeared and shone with incredible brightness. His camera was laid out on a rock with the shutter open to capture star trails. He had great expectations of his first digital camera. It had cost nearly a month's salary. The one image after a thirty-minute exposure was not too bad but lacked the colour he was hoping for. *A bit disappointing. I'll take more pictures in the morning, but I might stick to terrestrial objects.*

Despite his initial failure as an astrophotographer, the cool breeze on his face and the glory of the heavens above lifted his spirits after a less than productive day's effort. Retiring to the comfort of the reclined car seat, under his trusty quilt, he went off to sleep quickly. The exertion of the day and the ensuing sunstroke brought about a peaceful slumber. He did wake a couple of times to the sound of the hooting of an owl or the lowing of cattle in the distance. He thought he could make out a few bursts of cicada song, probably the larger species as the frequencies were not all that shrill.

Sunday morning dawned cold and damp. No noisy birds, just the melodic chortling of a magpie. He found himself warmly wrapped in his quilt but his ears and nose were aching a little and there were some small icicles hanging from exposed metal parts of the car. *A cloudless night in the hills results in a sudden drop in temperature just after sunrise.* Without venturing out from under the quilt, he tossed around the idea of heat exchange between the car, the atmosphere and outer space. This was just too abstract, so he exited through the rear door to have a brief standing wash. *I must eat.* The simple menu was eggs for breakfast. His sunstroke had passed but he determined to be more careful.

There was another fallen tree further downstream. He began wading, shoveling and panning but fared no better and seemed to lose interest after a couple of fruitless hours. So, he became a photographer instead. Setting out the little flakes of gold and coloured stones on his shaving mirror, he found that they looked really precious with the reflected blue sky as a background. The camera was brought out and he took a lot of macro shots from different angles. He regarded this as the most productive thing he had achieved all weekend.

After that he spent nearly an hour photographing wet pebbles in the streambed. The variations in size and colour were intriguing. The images would make brilliant computer wallpaper. *How one's focus can suddenly change! I'm more a photographer than a prospector!*

He began to see more value in the beauty of wet rocks than in a quest for gold. Vivid colours and patterns glistening in the sun. *You just have to wet pebbles and their incredible beauty emerges! I don't mind getting my feet wet for this. No cows around?* In the quietness and splendor of the rural surroundings he became a little more conscious that his true aspiration for the future was to discover the extraordinary detail that hides behind everyday things. He had a deep disquiet that his present circumstances were holding him back. *Why do I feel so uneasy? I know. A degree of intellectual anxiety is not necessarily bad. I've read about good stress. It can lead to discovery!*

Then his thoughts turned again to Rod and Grace enjoying their weekend together at the beach. The joy of sharing an experience with a soulmate was something he had yet to discover. *Relationships can be a very challenging field in which I had decidedly low expertise and that causes me a more negative kind of anxiety, so I'll have to learn to put those thoughts aside.*

Around three in the afternoon he packed up all the gear, eased the Peugeot around and picked his way carefully up the hill and across the paddocks back to the house. It was with a mild sense of relief that he found John and Pat were not there. He left a no-luck note offering thanks attached to their screen door and headed off towards home. Within minutes he was driving over the fateful gravel track at a snail's pace and scanning the road for signs of the Friday night slip into the ditch. There was no evidence to be seen. *I can forget that it ever happened!*

Having eaten little, he made the decision to pull into a service station restaurant along the highway where he bought a coffee and a sausage roll. These were not the healthy option but for once he bowed to convenience and quickly consumed them before heading straight for home. Little did he know that something he was carrying was about to cause his rather mundane life to change decisively.

Chapter 8

'Green Wattles'. November 2005.

The mud-spattered Peugeot rolled into the entrance
of the Kirk acreage, 'Green Wattles Farm', late on
Sunday afternoon. Only an hour and a half of usable
daylight remained. Without even entering the house
Don opened the narrow rear door to a little storage
room that housed his garden tools. He pulled out the
pressure washer, attached it to the hose, plugged it
into the outdoor power point and commenced
thoroughly cleaning off the mud from under the car.
That was his first duty. The duco was still
reasonably clean so he decided against a full detail.
The mud dislodged easily onto the grass. After a few
touch-ups to dirty spots with some carnauba wax, he
started to unpack the boot. That's when he picked up
the grey stone he had almost forgotten about. He
examined it in the light of the late afternoon sun and
his heart began to flutter.

This was no ordinary stone. It was a kind of soft
slate or phyllite, uncharacteristic of the alluvial
plains of the Mary River. As he turned it over in his
hands he noticed, among the lichen, a raised design
of some kind. This led him to wash the stone with
the hose and rub off the excess dirt with his
fingertips. It felt as smooth as talc. In the low-angled
sunlight he could just make out what appeared to be
a worn Chinese character standing out in relief
above the surface. *This is a prize!*

Knowing that the light would soon be gone he set

it on the outdoor table and photographed it from all angles. Some parts glistened. He sat down on his garden bench turning the rock over and over, pondering its origin and how best to display it. *Surely it's too precious to use as a garden rock. Perhaps it would look best mounted on a wooden base in the lounge room wall unit.* He hefted the rock in his right hand. *It could possibly be used as an interesting doorstop due to its considerable weight. No, the rock should be mounted on a board.*

He needed to get to work. Hastily he made his way to the big shed – his sanctuary where he could be immersed in things male and some might say arcane. The building was separate from the house, a timber and iron structure, about fifty square metres in area and four metres high. He stood back and slid the door gently open to avoid injuring the geckoes that frequently slept in the track. On many occasions whole or parts of the small creatures had fallen on him as he opened the door. He was now very cautious and had made a humorous sign for the door. 'Beware of Falling Geckoes'. The sign was painted in the standard black on yellow safety colours and showed sections of lizard anatomy tumbling down. *Sometimes I need a reminder.*

These are the common house gecko. If they've been given that name, then they might have lived in houses for a long time, perhaps many centuries. They must have adapted to living with humans. He had thought long and hard about this falling gecko phenomenon. *Why was it that the small reptiles had never learned not to sleep in sliding door tracks?*

How would a serious gecko accident impact the gecko population in the shed? His mind was like a computer clicking through all the permutations and combinations of reasons and strategies for gecko management in a shed.

I have a love-hate relationship with these geckos. I've always admired their ability to hang on to any surface and to keep the insects under control, yet these Asian grey geckoes are feral animals in Australia. They have, bit by bit, displaced the native skinks. Why have the door track episodes preoccupied my thoughts so much? To my analytical way of thinking it's a metaphor for life. I've even typed some thoughts on my laptop computer:

> *Life is tenuous. We think we are in a safe resting position on the track and suddenly an opening door changes everything. We can be quick and change position or fall down injured.*

Entering the shed that day he encountered no falling reptiles, but he knew they were there, watching his every move. He headed over to the old basin in the corner that he had rigged up as a cleaning station. It consisted of cheap black irrigation pipe neatly secured to the wall and a recycled kitchen sink. An old nail scrubbing brush was at hand. As he washed and scrubbed the stone he began to notice something very unusual. In the raised symbol there were flecks of gold. He scrubbed harder and revealed more shiny bits.

Could this be a gold nugget? No. It isn't heavy

enough. It must have been gilded. The work of a craftsman. It's certainly not a natural bush rock.

He placed the perplexing stone on the workbench to dry and walked over to the house. The laptop had to be booted up. He waited for an Internet connection. When this was finally established, he googled 'how to test a stone to see whether it contains gold'. *Thinking about it I could have had the same result by just typing 'test stone gold' but that's not my way. It has to have some sentence structure.*

A determination of density using Archimedes Principle seemed to be the best method, so following the brief Internet search he hurried back to the shed with kitchen scales and a large measuring jug. *Mass.* It weighed 4.3 kilograms. *Displacement.* As he expected, the jug was too small for the rock. He filled a plastic bucket to the brim with water, placed the rock in carefully, catching the overflow in a large, flat developing tray. He was then able to measure the volume of the overflow in the measuring jug. The old calculator came out of a drawer and the findings were written up on a small white board:

      Mass of stone = 4300 g
      Volume of stone = 1439 mL
      Density of stone = 2.99 g/mL

This result was not satisfying. This was not a heavy rock compared with gold which has a density of about 18 g/mL. He had a dilemma. Further investigation might ruin the inscription but he did not want to give up his find to some professional in a museum.

I pondered again my gecko philosophy. Move or drop? Should I offer up the stone to an expert for advice or let the stone drop to become an interesting doorstop? It was now getting quite dark so he locked the shed and returned to the house to sleep on it - the enigma that is, not the stone or the house. Of course, there were exam papers to mark. That would occupy him until bedtime.

Sleep did not come easily but once it did it was light and disturbed. *My overactive brain!*

Monday morning at 'Green Wattles' was bright and sunny, one of those barmy, cloudless late Spring days that are common in southeast Queensland. Don was not feeling well. He had a headache and felt very lethargic. Determined to do the right thing, he phoned the school at 7.00 am to let them know that he would not be in. Having a good deal of accrued sick leave, this was not a problem for him - although it would be for the school!

Finally, getting out of bed around 10.00am he showered, had a light breakfast and sat down on the sun lounge outside the back door. The twittering birds and rustling gum leaves helped him feel relaxed.

After a short rumination he stood up and walked over to the shed and slid the door open. A gecko scuttled away without injury. *In a very strange way, this was the stimulus I needed. Be prepared to move when the time is right. I'm convinced now that I should take the rock to the Queensland Museum. It could turn out to be some kind of national treasure.*

I sort of hope that it is a discovery of great consequence. But I don't want to be famous.

In spite of a rapidly increasing pulse rate, he phoned the Museum. A very patient receptionist put him through to Archaeology. With his ears burning and his heart missing a beat he described the find to another secretary and made an appointment for the following week – after school hours, of course. He then emailed the best images of the stone to 'atauber' in the Archaeology Department whose address had been given to him. Swamped by a mixture of excitement and anxiety, he went to the kitchen and began breathing into a paper bag. He was not hyperventilating but that exercise made him feel more in control.

For Don this was definitely a beginning of something, but what it was exactly he had no notion.

Chapter 9

Brisbane. November 2005.

Tuesday and Wednesday passed slowly with two days of 'fun' maths activities as Don baby-sat junior classes. It was a relief when Wednesday afternoon finally came around.

He arrived at the Queensland Museum for his 4.30pm appointment. He was carrying a shopping bag containing the rock, carefully wrapped in tissue. It had been a stressful drive contending with the city traffic. He made it with minutes to spare and entered via the main public entrance. Hesitantly he walked over to the information counter. Staff members eyed his shopping bag suspiciously. He sputtered out his appointment details. Without hesitation an attractive young staff member rushed out and ushered him through a side door to a private elevator. This took them up to a floor of labs and offices. They swapped awkward smiles but there was no conversation. She directed him to a door that simply said 'Archaeology'. The word 'thanks' was all he could muster. *Why didn't I ask her name? She knew mine.*

He rapped softly on the door and a gruff voice from inside said "come in."

A wild-haired man with a bushranger beard and a white coat was sitting at a large table laden with papers and equipment. The man did not get up. He simply barked "sit down and I'll be with you in a minute." His accent was slightly European.

Donald looked around for a chair. Moments later

a studious looking lady, also wearing a white coat came in smiling. She could have been attractive without the black-rimmed glasses and honey blonde hair pulled back starkly into a bun. She extended her hand and gave him the warmest of smiles.

"Hi, I'm Tanya Pierce. You must be Mr Kirk. I've come to have a look at your artefact with Dr Tauber. Do you have it with you in the bag?"

"Yes, here it is Dr Pierce."

"Oh, please call me Tanya."

"Sorry, Tanya."

He was too slow responding to offer his first name. He experienced weak-knees-anxiety in the presence of attractive women.

"Okay. That's good. Let's go in and have a look."

She motioned for Don to walk with her to the table. The grumpy man stopped what he was doing, stood and extended his hand.

"Mr Kirk?"

"That's right." The nerves were still jittery.

"Arne Tauber, Acting Curator of Archaeology." This sounded a little less grumpy than before. There was a respectful tilt of the head and his handshake was firm. Very formally he motioned towards Tanya, who introduced herself once again.

"Tanya Pierce, Assistant Curator of Pacific and Torres Strait Islander Studies," came her sweeter voice. Her handshake was calming and decidedly more sensual.

"Pleased to meet you". His tension eased slightly as the bag was held up. "Here's the stone I found near Gympie." He had a note of disappointment in his voice. *I'm meeting with an 'acting' and an 'assistant'. Are these people skilled and senior enough to determine the true value of my rock?*

Dr Tauber took it carefully, unwrapped it and commenced his examination. He shuffled around the worktable and placed it under an illuminated magnifier. Tanya peered over his shoulder. Don stood quietly waiting for their expert opinions.

Only grunting sounds emerged as Dr Tauber observed, then he made some notes in an exercise book. Tanya voiced her opinion that it was probably not an aboriginal or Pacific Islander artefact. Without looking up, Dr Tauber enquired about the location where the stone had been found. Tanya observed but did not speak. Donald felt awkward. She was standing very close to him. There was more grunting and inspecting then Tauber finally looked towards Don and spoke in very matter-of-fact tones.

"It's Chinese. The symbol is badly weathered but it is similar to the Hanzi character for "river". The rock is most certainly not native to the area in which it was found. It was probably carved somewhere else, maybe even in China, and left there by a miner in the Gympie gold rush in the 1860s. There were a lot of Chinese miners."

"What should I do with it? Is it valuable?"

"It has only historical value; the gold flecks are remnants of gold leaf that was once hammered over the relief sculpture. It was originally gilded."

Donald had fleeting thoughts of wealth and recognition but they quickly passed. "Wow, a gold sculpture. Would the museum be interested in acquiring this?" *I can't believe I just asked that!*

Dr. Tauber did not speak. He sat down, span around in his chair and reached for the telephone. Don listened while he described the rock to a superior and asked about acquisition.

"The boss will be here in five minutes," said the good doctor.

"Look, this is Arne's area. He's the expert on these sorts of things. I'll leave you with him." Dr Pierce excused herself, smiled, massaged his hand and left discreetly.

Donald waited in silence, not wanting to interrupt due to the man's abruptness. He had now begun leafing through a large folder of documents. They looked important so Don pretended to take no interest. With a heavy thump the door swung open.

"Hello, I'm Helen Peters, the Museum Director," came a voice from near the door. A pompous, rotund woman with two-toned hair and bright clothing bounced into the workroom. *At least now my rock has the attention of the Director.*

"I believe you found an artefact left by the Chinese miners at the time of the Gympie gold rush. That's great! You know, most people wouldn't have given it a second thought. You have an eye for detail. Let's have a look."

Dr Tauber turned on the light in the magnifier. He moved the stone about, pointing at some aspects and mumbling a little, almost whispering. The only identifiable words were 'Chinese' and 'totem'. The Director nodded and peered at the relief for a few moments then turned quickly to Donald.

"Wow! The inscription is very clear but the gold leaf has worn away. It's part of our history. We would love to have this in our collection, Mr. Kirk. We may even consider regilding it. It is a link to the town that saved Queensland financially in our historical past and we want future generations to be able to see it. Come down to my office and we'll chat about it."

Dr. Tauber placed the artefact in a large plastic tray and handed it to Helen. She motioned to Donald to follow her. There was a silent handshake and Tauber turned and became engrossed again in his papers.

They walked along a snaking carpeted hallway that smelled of disinfectant, stopping at an office that bore the plaque 'Administration'. The pair marched straight past a reception counter. A stunningly attractive young secretary wearing headphones looked up from her typing and smiled. In his nervousness Don could only nod in acknowledgment, but he did catch her floral scent. They were headed for a door labelled 'Director'.

Mrs. Peters' office was not decorated with antiquities as one might expect in a museum. It had many nooks and crannies and was very slick with stainless steel industrial fittings and a black, red and white theme. Carefully chosen artefacts and abstract art pieces adorned the walls and crevices. It was stunning. Helen called her secretary to make coffee. She then sat with Donald on a red sixties-style sofa and began to talk, something she was obviously very good at.

"We think it is wonderful that people like yourself are willing to donate significant items. I'm talking historical value of course. That is real altruism. I just have a release form for you to sign and we will have our photographer come in and capture the moment." Donald was dumbfounded that he had not actually been asked whether he would like to donate the item. Still he kept silent and took the pen.

Helen was so enthusiastic and so bubbly that he could only smile and nod his head. He never intended to give away the find but now he was being persuaded to do so without saying a word. It was most probably his deep-seated desire to teach young people that had begun to meld with the museum exhibit idea. He would be contributing to human knowledge.

Minutes later a middle-aged male photographer and the good-looking secretary, now carrying refreshments, entered the room and stood around the coffee table. Donald's attention was so much on the girl that he did not even check the model of the camera. Everything seemed so confused yet somehow very meaningful. Three sets of eyes watched and waited for him to complete the paperwork. Without a word he filled out name and a brief description and signed the donor release form. Helen countersigned. As she did they looked up and smiled for the camera. The pretty young secretary bent forward to set down the coffee tray and snapped up the form as the photographer left.

Over a few sips of coffee Helen asked general questions about his life. Without warning, only ten minutes in, she stood, thanked him profusely and bundled him back to the reception area. The artefact remained in the tray on her coffee table.

At the counter on his way out he gave Helen's secretary his full contact details. She chatted cheerfully as she typed. All he could raise was the occasional 'yes'. But the interaction was most enjoyable. She was lovely. He really knew one important factor that was missing from his life, but he was too timid to pursue it.

"The lift is just over there. Press B for basement and that will take you to the carpark. Thank you for coming in Mr Kirk. Have a great afternoon." Her smile was captivating.

"Thanks. You too." He regretted not having asked her name.

The lift took him to the lowest level. Within minutes he found himself wandering dazed around the underground carpark, searching for the car. *What have I just done? I just gave away my artefact.*

He drove home a little disappointed but also somewhat proud of himself. There was nobody to share his joy or his perplexity. *Maybe I could mention it to Rod at school tomorrow. But he'd show little empathy and just say something like 'no gold hey mate?'. Linda would be more interested. Yes. Linda.*

Chapter 10

'Green Wattles'. Late November 2005.

Over the following few days, Don thought a lot about the artefact. Linda was rarely seen around campus. Somehow his interest in her was waning although she did give him a very sensuous hug at the staff end of year party. But she belonged to Phil and she was not as pretty as Helen Peters' receptionist.

He began a closer examination of his photographs. Each night he pored over them. They were an inferior substitute for the real thing. But it was fun manipulating them on the computer.

There was one little ray of sunshine in his boring end-of-year ritual. He received in his roadside mailbox a small package containing a letter of thanks from the museum director, a copy of the release form and a cardboard-framed photograph of the presentation in Mrs Peters' office. He filed the letter and fastidiously arranged the photograph on his lounge room wall unit beside a print of his own sharpest macro image of the stone. Then it was back to his computer. It was now evident to him that he had indeed found something worthy of his deeper commitment. The research began in earnest.

The internet is a wonderful resource. You can find almost anything there, but search as he might, even on Chinese language websites, there was no exact representation of his particular Chinese symbol. Dr Tauber had indicated that it might represent a main water course with tributaries, but it was the mention of the word 'totem' that came to the fore in Don's mind. He hypothesised many things but settled on it being a variant of the symbol for river. This made sense as the Chinese miners were trying to extract gold from the river and may have considered the river to be an object of worship, a god that would yield up wealth. A totem. Although unsure of the orientation, he painstakingly made a sketch of the symbol in pinyin style from his photographs.

Don's sketch of the character.

It did vaguely resemble the pinyin character 'hé' pronounced 'ho', for 'river' but he remained unconvinced because the horizontal stroke and centre box were not present. The Chinese characters have evolved over the centuries but surely a carving from the 1860s would look something like the modern character.

The modern Chinese pinyin character 'hé' for 'river'.

It is exceedingly difficult to find, using English descriptors, something that is hieroglyphic in nature. Each night he tried googling all the descriptors he could think of but found no match. He spent hours looking through images of Chinese characters and artworks. It did not help that his dial-up modem was slow and began acting up.

On the second last day of the school year when all the marking and reporting was complete, he returned home and went to his shed looking for something to do in the remaining daylight hours. He stopped short, aware that he was being watched. A metre-long eastern water dragon had clambered up to the roof of the shed, as they commonly did, and was observing him intently. He moved towards the reptile and it scuttled away, its claws making incredibly loud scratching sounds on the corrugated roof. *A dragon in the ascendant? Have I chanced upon a Chinese symbol?*

"Why is my shed such a magnet for reptiles?" he shouted to nobody. The frustration over not finding a definite meaning for the symbol was getting him down.

More carelessly than usual he rather forcefully slid open the shed door. There was a quick recoil as he felt soft flesh strike against his cheek and he looked down to see his shirt bloodied by the lacerated body of a heedless gecko. The body of the small reptile twitched on the ground with its head almost detached. He stared at the casualty for a moment. Every happening appeared to be significant to him at this stage.

He could not imagine where the idea came from, but he suddenly saw a shape that intrigued and excited him. He normally would have ensured that the animal was dead and buried it in his compost heap but his imagination was running wild. He rushed to the house, grabbed his camera and photographed the now deceased and bizarrely contorted lizard.

Feeling just a little guilty, he scooped up the corpse with a garden trowel, took it into the house and quickly tossed it into the small compost bin on the kitchen bench. In retrospect he could not understand why he did this. It was not in line with his usual level of respect for hygiene practices, but he was thinking of other things. Perhaps it was a mark of respect to the ill-fated lizard.

Dragons that go up. Geckos that fall down. What is the symbolism! He was perplexed. His brain cells were in overload.

Later that evening Donald felt that he just had to search for images of gecko and water dragon anatomy and then undertake a comparative study. Before that could happen, he enlarged his images of the gecko corpse using image manipulation software. He did not consider that he had the eye of an artist but something about the shape of the body attracted his strong interest. He examined the pictures from different angles and manipulated the contrast, not knowing what he was looking for. The mangled body reminded him of a rampant Chinese dragon.

The word 'dragon' was on his mind. He quickly googled the Chinese symbol for dragon and found an image. It was an ancient Chinese script for 'dragon' pronounced 'lóng' in Mandarin.

The modern Chinese pinyin character 'lóng' for 'dragon'.

Inverting the image he believed he that may have found his symbol. *A headless dragon? Perhaps facing downwards. Perhaps the head on the totem has broken off. But there's no evidence of the stone having been shattered.* He went back to the images of the relief sculpture. *Yes. No. Yes.* He vacillated but decided this had to be a representation of half a dragon. His curiosity was truly in a state of high arousal, having the challenge but somewhat lacking in the interpretive skills. He emailed his theory to Dr Tauber.

Chapter 11

'Green Wattles'. Early December 2005.

Yet another period of uncertainty arose for Donald. There had been no reply from Dr Tauber. The school holidays had arrived. He would not see Linda for six weeks. He would be totally alone at home for nearly two weeks before travelling to his parents' home in Sydney for Christmas celebrations. Angus and Isabel, his younger brother and sister, would be there and he had not seen them for many months. The Christmas shopping at the Redcliffe Plaza was not exciting but he made the annual pilgrimage. All the while his neurons kept firing, pulsing like flames from a dragon's nostrils!

He spent several days tending to jobs about the 'farm' – mowing, weeding, fixing fences, clearing gutterings and so on. He also spent time in his shed tinkering with an old motorcycle he had bought for $200. *It might never go on the road again, but I want to restore a classic.* Despite his attempts at physical activity, the motif on the rock consumed him. Afternoon teatime, 2.30pm, became his signal to head inside to the computer.

It was his conviction that the mysterious symbol showed an uncanny similarity to the lower section of the symbol for 'dragon'. *Am I reading too much into this?* He began to search the Internet once again, this time for information about the importance of dragons in Chinese culture. In his systematic manner, Don listed out all the things dragons symbolize: Greatness, Blessing, Goodness, Power … A symbol of royalty. The list was extensive. He also found that the dragon mythology was thought by many archaeologists to have originated from stories of snakes, crocodiles or big fish. Most experts believed the dragon was probably a type of large freshwater fish that was prevalent in certain seasons.

Don was interested to read that dragons are often associated with water. They were regarded as deities responsible for rain and floods – important to an agriculture-based society. He was also amazed to read that Marco Polo, the Italian merchant who travelled to China at some time between 1270 and 1290 AD, had described living dragons that he had seen in the west of the empire. These were large land-dwelling reptiles described in the Travels of Marco Polo Part 2, Chapter 40:

Leaving the city of Yachi, and traveling ten days in a westerly direction, you reach the province of Karazan, which is also the name of the chief city....Here are seen huge serpents, ten paces in length (about 30 feet), and ten spans (about 8 feet) girt of the body. At the fore part, near the head, they have two short legs, having three claws like those of a tiger, with eyes larger than a fourpenny loaf and very glaring.
The jaws are wide enough to swallow a man, the teeth are large and sharp, and their whole appearance is so formidable, that neither man,

Perhaps Polo had been witness to the last of the extant dinosaurs. Don resolved to discover more of this hidden history in the future. Despite his hours of reading and the fascination he was developing with dragons, a solution to the puzzle of the stone seemed no closer. Christmas was approaching and he would have to prepare for his drive south. There were plants to water, suitcases to pack, Christmas presents to wrap and little time for further study.

The night before he left all the preparations had been completed. The car was packed, the shed was locked up and Don found himself with an idle hour or two. He googled "Chinese Dragon Dance" and watched videos of the rhythmical movements that usher in the Chinese New Year and anticipate happiness, prosperity and fertility. This caused him to reflect upon his own future and how he could now have some promising new goals in his life. Finding numerous images of the dragon dance, he began to quickly flit through, until he came to one that caught his attention. It was an image of young women dancing in what appeared to be a barn. Hanging on the wall behind them was a red sign with a gold symbol that looked remarkably like his. He visited the webpage.

His screen quickly lit up with the website in the Mandarin language. *Wow! I'm onto something here!* He set about trying to translate the text using an online translator that he did not trust to accurately convey the meaning, but he was able to get the gist. His best guess was that the website was called 'The Flow of Chinese Dance'. Oddly, it had a German web address. It looked like a Chinese dance school. There were images of young dancers making synchronised gestures as they imitated their instructor. He scrolled and clicked his way through, observing beautiful images of elegantly dressed young Chinese men and women performing a variety of dances in an old farm-style building. Several of the images showed the same red and gold sign blurred in the background.

To his great surprise, when he clicked on one conspicuous blue link it redirected him to a website that was primarily in the German language interspersed with some Chinese characters. One image had him riveted. The translator was again set to work, this time German to English. The dance was described as the 'dragon slaying dance' and on the wall behind the dancers he could see, in sharp focus, the symbol that had so intrigued him. It now became emblazoned in his mind. Gold on a red background. He translated, printed and combed through the writings for some clue to the symbol's meaning, but none was to be found. The German text appeared to be largely a technical account of the dance movements.

In desperation he looked for a description of the location but again drew a blank. It was almost certainly not in Germany. He could find no contact email anywhere on the website. His exhaustive scouring of the content eventually revealed a name and institution mentioned only once in a footnote to the 100,000 words of German text. Dr. Annika Fluss. This academic was cited as the author of an article on choreography and the publisher was the University of London Press. He immediately googled the name and found a Facebook link. Opening it he was suddenly gazing at an image he would never forget. She was apparently a Professor of Dance at the University of London.

With weariness slowly getting the better of him there was no way he could focus on a search through the staff of the University of London. He had no idea of the institution's structure and didn't know where to start. He also believed that academics probably only shared contact details with their colleagues and some higher degree students. Email addresses of staff were certainly not made public in his high school. Finding the contact was a task that would have to wait until after Christmas.

When the ideas began to flow Don was unstoppable. He bookmarked the page but still unable to leave it, he excitedly composed an email to Dr. Fluss, care of admissions at the University of London, an easy address to find. *It might reach her somehow.* He would use the translator to find out some more next time he had Internet access. Don's parents in Sydney had made a quality decision some years before. They had no wi-fi in their home.

Now it was bedtime. It was almost 3am and he had an eleven hundred kilometre drive ahead of him that day. Further research had to be put on hold for a week or two. He started to think of becoming reacquainted with his family in Sydney. Exhausted, he quickly drifted off to sleep.

Chapter 12

Delmenhorst, Germany. Late December 2005.

It's still pretty dark outside. But Friday is finally here. This is my big day. What time is it? Almost eight hours? I'd better get up. This could be the most important day of my life so far.

There is something very spooky about seeing your father sharing a bedroom with a woman who is not your mother. I guess that's life. Mama and Papa were divorced years ago. Hella seems nice enough. She is, after all, Papa's fiancé. I just hope Papa and Hella will be happy together. I'll always look away when I walk past their door.

Shuffling sleepily down the hallway to the kitchen Annika Fluss looked through the foggy windows to check the weather outside. In the pre-dawn twilight she could see that it was bleak and cold. The road looked wet. There had been no snow overnight. She decided that she would need thermals under her leathers.

Papa was in the kitchen. It was an older style room with a pleasantly warm wood stove, timber benches, racks and open shelves displaying cups and dishes and a blue curtain where one might expect to see cupboard doors. There was no sign of Hella.

"Good morning, Papa."

"Good morning Annika. Did you sleep well?"

"Not really. I was thinking about my interview."

"Annika, you are a brilliant professor. You have done so much in your life and you are so talented.

Now is the time to settle down. You have nothing to worry about. This is your time to shine."

"I know. Thanks Papa. It's just that it will be such a big change for me. Working in a small city like Goslar will be so different from London."

"Yes, but you will be coming back to your home country and you will live closer to your Papa."

They hugged. He was right. At twenty-eight years old she had actually experienced many things. Living in a vibrant city like London. Taking in a different culture. Speaking, writing and thinking in English as well as German. Five years teaching at the University. A lot of travel. Many conferences. Now it was time to be more settled and Germany was her native land.

Hella returned shortly from whatever she was doing. She said 'hallo' but Annika looked away a little as she kissed Papa quite passionately. It was all quite strange, particularly as she had never had a steady boyfriend. She just didn't trust the young guys.

For at least an hour they sat at a large dining table crafted from ancient bog oak and chatted about life in general. She began to warm a little more to Hella, having only met her two days previously. She was obviously mature and intelligent. Though at first Annika thought she was a gold-digger, marrying her father for his money. As they talked more, she could see that they had a genuine love for each other. *That's something I've never experienced with any of the guys I've dated. They only wanted one thing and I was not giving it to them. I'm not like a lot of other girls I know.*

The first rays of sunlight beamed through the kitchen window as they spoke, and the day became noticeably brighter. She slowly picked through her breakfast of bread, ham and cheese. Morning tea seemed to follow immediately. They knew she had to get ready so it was easy to excuse herself and go back to her bedroom. The barre and mirror where she used to practice her ballet were still there. The walls were still decorated with posters of ballerinas and the dresser was still covered with little dolls in tutus. She didn't mind that nothing had changed. It meant that Papa still thought of her as his little girl.

Taking only five minutes she began some of her daily barre exercises. Normally she would do these for half an hour followed by ten minutes in four of her preferred yoga postures, boat, dolphin, bridge and legs-up-the-wall. But today was different, just a minute of each.

The overhead light in the bathroom was exceptionally bright. As she stepped out of her pyjamas and into the shower she looked down and thought how white her skin appeared. *Kind of opalescent. In all my years as a dancer I have never sun-baked in Spain or visited a Sonnenstudio or been sprayed with fake tan. I like me just the way I am. I like my hair long too. Papa calls it my 'beste Eigenschaft'. Mama calls it my 'crowning glory'. It's very dark like my mother's, with just a little hint of gold from my father. I never want to colour it.*

The shower tap was old and fairly loose. She turned it on slowly and at first the water was freezing but within seconds the warmth came through. With her hand under the water, she looked around at the assortment of shampoos and soaps, wondering where they all came from. *Papa and Hella have an ensuite bathroom. Perhaps my brother and sister had been visiting. I will ask at lunch.* With her hair washed and body parts scrubbed with more than the usual attention she turned off the taps and stepped out onto the fluffy mat. *I think I remembered this from my childhood. Papa is definitely not into bathroom decoration or renovation.*

Standing under the heat lamp she towelled herself dry and put on thermal underwear with a dark green tracksuit over. No bra. She wanted to be comfortable for the trip. Papa liked to keep his heating on 'sehr heiß', very hot. She now felt as warm as toast. In fact, a little trickle of sweat ran down between her shoulder blades. That was not so comfortable but at least she felt invigorated and ready for whatever lay ahead.

In the bedroom she took some time to pack her little red suitcase. It was of a size that fitted nicely strapped to the rack on the back of her motorbike. There were not a lot of clothes in her German wardrobe, just sufficient for most occasions. The bulk of her gear was still in London with Mama. *It's there because I may not be successful getting this new job. Then I'll have to go back to London Uni. That's not a bad default position!*

She decided on a red and black theme. It was her favourite. Everybody seemed to rave about her red gypsy-style dress. It had ruffles so it would come out of the case okay without ironing. She packed that for tonight's party. The dress was a bit low cut for winter, but she was wanting to make a good first impression.

Then there was the interview. *Black or red? Businesslike black she thought. Black bra and two pairs of briefs, black of course. Black high heels. Black pantyhose. Two pairs just in case. No. It's all too black. My red calf-length business dress. Yes. Red umbrella in the side holder.*

She laid out the leather pants and coat on the bed. They were all black with silver studs and much too warm to wear around the house. Her helmet and gloves were laid out too. A long black coat went into her biker backpack, which was also in studded black leather. A toilet bag with bathroom essentials and makeup hadn't been emptied since she arrived from London. It needed only to be unzipped a little to pop in her toothbrush. Straight into the suitcase it went without even a second glance. Her work laptop went into the large padded front pocket. *I'm used to being on the move. Now I'm ready for that early lunch. 11,30h in the morning.* Donning her deep blue dressing gown, she sashayed her way out to the dining room. Papa loved the way she danced about the house.

Hella proved to be a very good cook. She prepared a delicious meal of pork meatballs, boiled potatoes and green beans. Although it was quite ordinary food, the white sauce and the spices on the potatoes and beans made them come to life with flavour. And the presentation on the plate was creative. Annika complimented her profusely. *One day I'll ask for some of her secret recipes.*

The three chatted animatedly over the meal. The gravity of the trip was not lost on her father.

"Annika, I will drive you to Bremen Hauptbahnhof."

"No Papa. I want to ride. I don't have much opportunity these days. It's not a long ride. I'll be fine. I already let you talk me out of riding all the way to Goslar."

"Yes, Annika, but this interview is so important to you. Don't risk it."

"Papa, it will be fine. I just need some excitement to get me fired up then some thinking time on the train. I know what I'm doing."

"I know you do. But be safe! Don't risk your future!"

Sensing the air of disagreement between them, Hella intervened. "Would you both like a cup of tea?"

"Yes please," they answered in unison.

One hour later Annika was dressed in full riding leathers, ready for the fifteen-minute dash into Bremen. She wheeled her 500cc BMW Motorad out of the garage. It was one of her fantasies come to fruition. She couldn't possibly ride it in congested London so she kept it at Papa's place. She loved to get out on the autobahn in summer and ride at top speed. On paper it was supposed to be 144 kilometres per hour but she claimed to do a little better than that. *Maybe one day I'll upgrade to a*

K1200S and be able to keep up with the Porsches at 250 kilometres per hour. Papa worries about me every time I ride. Mama doesn't know how fast I ride.

She was heading to the Hauptbahnhof in Bremen to take a two-and-a-half-hour train journey that could well determine the future direction of her life. She could have taken a local train from Delmenhorst but that would have been less fun than riding. That day she didn't ride too fast because of the chill. The sky was now clear and the temperature hovered somewhere near zero. She didn't mind the sting of the cold air on the exposed parts of her neck. *A little bit of pain is exhilarating!*

The bike was parked and locked along with a myriad of other two-wheelers below the overpass. That was the usual parking spot when visiting the city. A quick change out of the riding leathers would be required in the station toilets or preferably a parenting room with a bench. She had done this numerous times before, so there was no stress.

Unstrapping the suitcase, she made her way across the busy bus and tram interchange to the station entrance and quickly found a cubicle in which to lose the leathers and thermals and put on the captivating gypsy dress with black coat over the top. There were quite a few people about browsing the shopping arcade, but the toilets were empty enabling her to quickly transform from biker to elegant dance teacher. Nobody noticed.

With the unneeded gear in the backpack and carefully stowed in a rented locker, she held her head high and marched confidently in the direction of Platform 6. The red dress and flowing black coat attracted the gazes of passers-by. It usually did. Being tall with a well-developed bosom, flat bottom and long flowing hair she always seemed to become the centre of attention. Her skin was very fair and contrasted strongly with her mother's dark hair. *I think this makes my appearance unusual in northern Germany and I can't help but walk with fluid movements because I'm a dancer. People notice me. Sometimes I like that.*

With the usual German precision, the train arrived at the platform on time. Entering the carriage, she looked around for some women to sit near. *I generally feel uncomfortable with men being able to look at me continually.* Fortunately, today there were no men in sight, so she took a seat by the window and left her laptop in the case. There would be no work this afternoon. The short rail journey would be a chance to reflect, a time of quiet amid one of the most turbulent junctures of her relatively short life.

It had been some months since she'd seen her native German countryside but by late December the winter chill had made it look bare and grey. There was no snow about yet. The villages looked friendly and quaint. *I don't mind a little winter drabness. I love the changing seasons. That's something that it has been a little hard to experience working mostly indoors in London.*

She changed trains at Hannover but had to walk through to the next carriage to avoid a group of young men who were eyeing her up and down.

There were only a few stops and the train arrived in Goslar on time at 16,35h. She actually felt quite refreshed but braced herself as she walked out into the frigid mountain air. From the footpath she turned to admire the beautiful Bahnhof architecture with its creamy stone façade, arched windows, grey slate roof and quaint octagonal tower. Quickly she found a taxi. That had become a relatively easy task as most of the drivers were young men. Her suitcase went into the boot and she jumped into the back seat just a little anxious about the next few hours.

Chapter 13

Goslar, Germany. Late December 2005.

It was a very cold evening in the Harz Mountains, two days before Christmas. As the sunlight was fading, the yellow Mercedes taxi pulled over to the kerb on a cobblestone street in an old section of the city of Goslar. The windows were fogged with condensation. As the rear door opened, Annika emerged. The temperature was plummeting by the minute. The sky was clouding over and a few sleety flakes of snow were beginning to flutter down. She was actually starting to enjoy the cold by now. Perhaps that was one reason why she chose to ride her motorcycle earlier. To prepare her for the chill of the mountain climate.

She was wearing her long black coat and black high-heeled shoes as she stepped out and raised her folding red umbrella trimmed with black lace. The driver quickly opened the boot and pulled out her small red suitcase. She immediately seized the handle, pulled it out and trailed the bag behind her. The words 'Danke schön' echoed through the air and the door closed with a heavy 'thunk'. The taxi sped off and she was alone at dusk in a strange city.

More snowflakes were swirling in the air as Doktor Annika Fluss delicately navigated her course down the barely lit, narrow, medieval street. It was a walking street, not open to vehicles. She skipped along on her toes so that her heels would not catch on the cobbles. The clip-clop of her steps and the trundling sound of the suitcase wheels seemed extraordinarily loud. But nobody noticed.

The two-storey half-timbered houses leaning in on each side of her were only dimly lit. Perhaps the residents had left for their Christmas holidays. She had only slight anxiety as she continued down the street. The precinct had a cosy, traditional, even historical feel about it that she really liked. There was one brightly lit building further along. As she approached, she could hear the gradually increasing volume of celebrating voices.

The building was obviously not a residence. It had shopfront windows and inside she could see chairs arranged for a meeting and people milling around tables of food and drink along the walls. Her entrance was, of course, noticed by a number of men who rushed to the door to greet her and offered to hang up her coat and umbrella. One of them carefully placed her suitcase under some kind of hallstand.

She introduced herself to the men. There were four of them. They were all considerably older than her.

"Guten Abend, ich bin Doktor Fluss."

The men smiled, shook hands with her and offered words of welcome. They all knew who she was. She remembered all their names. As a tall bearded man, with the ironic surname Klein, assisted her to remove her coat, the faces of the group lit up with obvious delight. Her long black hair tumbled down over her figure-hugging red gypsy dress. The fairness of her complexion strongly contrasted with her dark hair and she could best be described as stunning. She had long, shapely legs clad in black stockings. In the four-inch heels she looked tall and stylish. All eyes were upon her as she entered the main part of the room.

A rotund man with very close-cropped grey hair and wearing a black suit and red tie made his way quickly to her side. Introducing himself as Herr Doktor Kraus, Chair in the Arts, he informally welcomed her to the Kunstakademie Harz or Arts Academy of the Harz Mountains District. She suppressed a giggle. *Kraus means curly-haired.* The meeting would begin soon. Herr Klein appeared with a drink for her. *A chivalrous gentleman or a creepy ogler?* He was becoming a little annoying with his over-attention. She was glad that he did not stay around for long.

Herr Doktor Kraus asked her about her current position. He probably already knew anyway. He was being polite. Annika explained that she had been working as a Lecturer in Dance at a prestigious Centre for Performing Arts Excellence located within the University of London. She loved that position but was feeling the pull to return to her homeland where she had family and many friends. There was more freedom of expression in the arts in Germany and it would be an ideal place from which to pursue her research interests. Her mother would remain in London, but they would be in frequent contact. She was delighted that this new dance academy was starting from scratch with such admirable objectives. She thought it was a wonderful initiative of the Universität Harz and she was excited at the prospect of being part of the team.

She then asked about the University and the Arts Academy. Doktor Kraus gave a brief overview. He said that the Harz Mountains is a very scenic and historic area and the ideal place to have a concentration of talented students pursuing their artistic dreams. The Tanzschule, Dance School, would not only be training performers but producing talented dancers with a deep knowledge of their craft. She related well to what he was saying. He said little else about the other faculties of the University, but he complimented her at some length on her accomplishments and said that he looked forward to her interview in the morning. There was a sense that he was just making pleasant conversation as men tended to do with her.

She really wanted to know more about the University of which the Academy was a part. But surely there would be opportunity to ask questions at the interview. She hoped there would be a tour. The idea of being the foundation Professor of Dance had great appeal to her. She was ambitious in a humble kind of way.

Tonight was the Christmas function for the academics and an opportunity for faculty members to meet her prior to her formal interview the following day. She felt inwardly excited but showed only calm grace outwardly. Everybody she was introduced to immediately liked her and she had little doubt that the position would be hers.

One of the most significant people to greet her

was Professor Jiang. She was a short, stocky woman of Asian appearance, immaculately dressed in black and gold. She bore a huge, confident smile and made a positive impression immediately. Annika was delighted to meet her. There was a prior association between them. Jiang was an old acquaintance of her mother. In years gone by Annika had written some German descriptions of Chinese choreography for her. It was through that connection that Annika had found out about the upcoming position. Although she had never previously met the woman there was a feeling of mutual trust. That night she would stay at Professor Jiang's home. They spoke only briefly about her mother until Doktor Kraus called the gathering to attention and the older woman said they would be able to catch up again after the formalities were completed.

The twenty or so people moved noisily to chairs. Many were carrying drinks and plates of finger food. Doktor Kraus motioned to Annika to join him behind a table at the front, facing the assembly. That made her heart beat a little faster. There were a lot of men looking at her.

The ceremony began with a welcome. Doktor Kraus thanked his colleagues and staff members for their wonderful efforts throughout the first part of the winter semester and looked forward to a restful break over Christmas and a happy return to work in the New Year. He then turned to Annika, the special guest. He asked her to stand, formally introduced her and then launched into a lengthy discourse about the aims of the Academy.

Annika began to wish she could sit down again. All eyes were on her. Finally, the Chair began to speak about the introduction of the Bachelor and Master of Performing Arts in Dance courses that were to begin in the Summer Semester. Annika was a strong candidate for the position of Foundation Professor of Dance. He then surprised everyone by terminating his speech and inviting questions to her from the floor.

A rather dishevelled man with wiry black hair and a rainbow-coloured bow tie stood immediately and came lurching towards the front brandishing a blunt table knife. In a loud voice he called for blood to be shed. Annika sat down quickly. Everybody laughed uproariously. The man stopped and politely introduced himself as Doktor Neumann, Professor of Drama. At once she understood his antics and smiled as he asked her to dance for them. Shyness was not one of her attributes so she stood and came out from behind the table. There was applause and much laughter.

One of her favourites was a flamenco dance she had learned at a workshop in Barcelona about twelve months previously. The red dress she was wearing was certainly the right colour but just a bit too tight for the movements. She would do her best. Her heels began to tap, her arms rose forcefully and the audience clapped a rhythm. An 'Ole' went up from the group. She delighted them with her expressive movement and amazed them with her ability to create an Hispanic atmosphere without any guitar accompaniment. After the short demonstration she was given a standing ovation, the first she had ever received in Germany. Her performance was a sensation. Neumann may have been displaced as the lead actor in the group but his face beamed with the satisfaction that he had asked the right question.

Several others rose and asked simpler questions such as "where did you grow up?", "how did you get into dance?", and the one that drew most laughter, "are you single or married?" Annika realised that these may well be her future colleagues and that most would likely form meaningful relationships with her so she gave fairly full answers but kept aside a few hidden details that would be revealed later in more personal encounters.

At last Kraus concluded the formal part of the meeting with 'Merry Christmas' and 'Happy Holiday'. Nobody was in a hurry to leave. There were more drinks poured and Annika was swamped by admirers. Noticing the concentration of men about her, Professor Jiang pushed her way through the throng and stood by her as a feminine support.

The Christmas party cum meet-and-greet had been an outstanding success but now fatigue was beginning to set in. Around 20,00h the faculty members had started to leave. Madam Jiang fetched Annika's red suitcase, coat and umbrella and after rugging up against the cold the two ladies stepped out into the street and walked briskly, arm-in-arm through the sleet to a house about three doors down on the opposite side.

Through conversations over the course of the

evening Annika had learned that the whole street consisted of historical, protected buildings that had been acquired by the Academy. Most were from the fifteenth and sixteenth century, built by Cistercian monks and lining the narrow roadway that followed the serpentine course of a clever water management channel. Some refurbished structures were already in use as teaching spaces for drama and music. Many others were in the process of being sympathetically renovated to become offices and classrooms. Just a few were residences for wealthy staff members. The street had come to be known as 'Kunst Allee' and was, in fact, the main campus of the Academy. This accounted for the lack of lighting in the buildings as only dim security lights shone in the empty teaching areas and yet-to-be completed quarters.

Professor Jiang lifted the suitcase to avoid the rougher cobbles and the pair turned quickly into a narrow laneway that was less than one metre wide. They arrived at a heavy wooden door that was promptly unlocked and swung inwards. As the lights were turned on a most beautiful hallway was revealed. Flocked wallpaper of oriental design and the most amazing chandelier. Annika was offered coffee but she preferred to retire to her room, so Professor Jiang led her up the elegant staircase and introduced her to the most splendid guest bedroom she had ever had the privilege of sleeping in. The ceilings were high and the walls were decorated with ornate wallpaper in oriental patterns of red, black and gold. The king-size bed was framed by a metal bedhead that looked like gold rather than brass.

She enquired whether the house had wi-fi and was told the password, 'Drachen6', which she immediately committed to memory. When her host had wished her goodnight, she set her case down gently on a superb black lacquered dressing table and took out her laptop and charger. Getting ready for bed was sheer pleasure as she made use of the marble ensuite bathroom with gold plumbing fittings and investigated the dressing room and walk-in wardrobe. Professor Jiang was obviously very wealthy.

Turning back the covers she climbed into the warmed bed, propped herself up with a pillow and opened her laptop. The password was entered, and she was connected to the world. Her personal emails came rushing through and she scanned the list for anything interesting. Many messages were from friends who wished her good luck with her interview. One email stood out, as it was from an Australian who she did not know. She examined his email address. The writer was apparently an academic in an educational institution. A secretarial assistant she knew well from the University of London School of Performing Arts had forwarded it to her. The message was in English.

Dear Dr. Fluss,
I hope that somebody at the University of London will forward this on to you. You will not know who I am but my name is Donald Kirk and I am a

teacher from Queensland, Australia. My reason for contacting you is that I have found a carved rock sculpture near Gympie and it contains the same Chinese symbol that I have seen on a wall in an image on a German website that gave your name and said you were from the University of London. I have attached images of the rock and of the website page. Can you tell me the meaning of the symbol please? Does it have something to do with Chinese dance? Is it a river or dragon motif? I would really appreciate your help with this. The carved rock is now with Dr. Tauber at the Queensland Museum and he is also trying to ascertain its origin and meaning.

    Best wishes,
Donald I. Kirk
donkirk@ppc.qld.edu.au.

She opened the image attachments and instantly recognised the photograph of the Chinese dance, which had years ago been sent to her along with a video tape of a dance sequence. It came from a German friend of her mother who had worked as a missionary in China. She remembered having written some fairly extensive text describing the choreography but had no idea of the meaning of the symbol in the background. Perhaps she would ask Professor Jiang in the morning. *She is after all Professor of Oriental Arts.*

Now with this puzzle to ponder, sleep would not come so easily. Tomorrow could be a landmark day in her life. Her mind became fired up with questions and anticipation. In her electronic diary she typed:

My focus is once again set upon research into the unknown origins of influences that underlie the creative imagination.

It might have been Christmas, but she found herself firmly entrenched back in academia.

Chapter 14

Annika slept more soundly than she had expected. A gentle knock on her door awakened her before the sun came up. She sprang out of bed, quickly put on her black coat and slipped on her shoes. It was Christmas Eve, an unusual day for a job interview, but the Academy needed to finalise the employment process before everybody went their various ways over the holiday period.

Opening the door she was greatly surprised. The person standing before her was not Professor Jiang but an elderly and diminutive Chinese woman who spoke little German. *Does Professor Jiang have a maid?* The woman motioned to her to follow and led her downstairs to the beautifully appointed kitchen-dining area. Professor Jiang looked up from setting the table and greeted her warmly. She had been up for an hour, was immaculately dressed and had driven to the Backerei to purchase fresh rolls to be served with sausage and cheese. This was no oriental breakfast but a business-like German one. The old woman was introduced, in German with what sounded like a smattering of Mandarin, as Professor Jiang's mother, Madam Long.

Once the three were seated and partaking, the procedure for the 09,00h interview was explained. Annika listened carefully. Every detail was deposited in her retentive memory. There were no pressing questions to be asked so they chatted informally over the meal, mainly about the city and the buildings. The old woman smiled broadly and nodded, obviously not understanding a word that was said.

At Professor Jiang's direction they all stood abruptly just after 08,00h. Annika returned to her room, dressed, applied her makeup and repacked her bag ready to leave. She carried her case downstairs where the ever-attendant Madam Long motioned to her to place it against a wall in the hallway. With her black coat over a now more conservative red dress dotted with minute ballerinas, she waited momentarily with her laptop under her arm, smiling awkwardly at the old woman.

Professor Jiang appeared from the rear of the house just before 08,30h and they walked down to the street and back across to the building where they had partied the previous night. The fog was thick, and some small drifts of light snow lay in nooks and crannies around the buildings. In the eerie morning light it was a very impressive street, quaint but with an air of mystery. *Working here is looking more and more attractive every moment.*

Entering the meeting room, which now appeared to have been rearranged into a dining hall, the two ladies were greeted by Herr Doktor Kraus and three other distinguished looking men. These were members of 'der Aufsichtsrat', the Board of Directors of the Academy. The interview panel was complete so they poured coffee from a rather avant-garde pot, sat near the end of a huge wooden table and began the process. Annika's documentation and references were displayed and discussed for the benefit of two members who had not seen them previously. She was asked questions about her teaching style and previous research projects.

The most difficult questions actually came from her trusted ally Professor Jiang. They concerned her romantic interests, desire to have a family and the possible length of her tenure. Although Annika was single and had no boyfriend, she could not dismiss the idea of marriage and motherhood but was able to state with confidence that Mr Right had not yet come along and that she was in no hurry to find him or to marry. This was a half-truth. Annika was attracted to men but she had never been able to get close to one because their attentions seemed to overwhelm her with apprehension. She was continually conscious of men looking at her and her analytical mind always tried to identify their motives. She simply did not trust them. That was why, at 28 years of age, she remained single.

The interview lasted about one hour. During that time she talked and gestured but was not asked to dance. That pleased but also surprised her. The position not only involved teaching the history and techniques of dance styles from around the world but also overseeing and sometimes instructing practical dance classes. She was delighted to hear that a building to be called 'die Tanzschule' was being renovated and prepared to take classes the following August. The office area upstairs was almost ready for occupation in the New Year. Then there would be a half semester and summer break to prepare the course material for the first incoming class of about fourteen students. The gentle beginning, the specially designed facilities together with small initial class size made her feel warm with anticipation. *Everything can be done just right. I think I can make this the best dance school in Europe.*

She asked about the language in which the classes were to be conducted. To her surprise the answer was not German. One of the board members gave a little background to the Academy. They attracted students from all over the world. In the past, if a class was primarily made up of German speakers then delivery would obviously be best in German. However, if a class consisted of a wide range of languages then English would be preferred. It would be her decision following interviews with her students. She was pleased to be offered that degree of autonomy.

Then there was the question of research interests. She confessed that classical ballet had been her original training but that she was now interested to pursue study of ethnic dance, both folk and ritualistic, exploring the origins and creative stimuli. With her previous evening's accommodation and the unusual email in mind, she proposed that Chinese dance could be an interest. Professor Jiang smiled and nodded. The interview was quite formal and as it progressed the questions became more probing. Annika was finally asked to step into an adjoining room. For that brief time, alone in a strangely beautiful setting, she felt a little nervous. *Have I said the right things? Have I said enough? Do they think I'm too young?*

The meeting was in one accord and within five minutes she was recalled and, there being no other applicants approaching her calibre, she was verbally offered the position. Of course, she had no problem accepting and could not wait to call her mother and message her closest friends. Then there would be the reaction of her father that evening. The paperwork would be sent within days to her address in Delmenhorst. The men rose quickly and shook her hand. In a motherly way Professor Jiang took her by the arm and escorted her to the door. They stood in the cold as the various campus buildings were identified to her. *That was the tour?*

Jiang offered to drive her to the railway station for her trip back to Bremen. Given the temperature and apprehension about unknown taxi drivers, her offer was gratefully accepted. First they would have to call into Professor Jiang's office to pick up a few things. Most of the buildings along 'Kunst Allee' were locked up but as they walked to the office Annika tried to look upon it a kind of campus mini-tour. She certainly began to get a sense that it would be a stimulating learning environment for gifted students.

"Shouldn't we go back for my suitcase?"

"No. It will be at my office just up ahead."

Having seen her home, Annika anticipated that the office could be another oriental delight. They slowly made their way along the beautiful street and came to a red door with black trim and shiny brass fittings. A small plaque said 'Orientalische Kunst'. Inside, the building was lavished with plush furnishings that obviously had come from China. To the right was a small tiered lecture theatre with three rows of red folding seats facing a black, red and gold painted dais backed by a whiteboard and screen. *This Academy has plenty of finance.* They climbed the stairs and opened a glass door into an office that almost blew Annika's mind. The most elaborate oriental antiques were on show in a beautifully appointed setting with wallpaper similar to that seen in last night's guest bedroom. She sat down on a dark red leather couch while Professor Jiang attended to something in another room.

Then she saw it. On the partition behind the reception desk was the same enigmatic symbol from last night's curious email. It was undoubtedly a bespoke piece, beautifully presented with gold calligraphy and covering about one metre square of wall space. Her heart fluttered a little and she opened her laptop to Don Kirk's email.

The Professor returned within minutes accompanied by her mother who smiled and nodded. *Why was the old woman in an academic office?* Annika was a little puzzled but wanted to show them something, so they moved across to a seating area with an exotic carved coffee table. She lifted the screen of her laptop.

"I have been sent this picture of a rock carving…" Professor Jiang and Madam Long both leaned forward to view the image.

They looked at each other in sheer astonishment.

"Where did you find this?" said Professor Jiang after a few moments.

"An Australian professor sent it to me. He found the carving and wants to know the origin and meaning."

Professor Jiang began to speak to her mother in a Chinese dialect that did not sound like Mandarin. The old woman's face lit up. This was obviously something very special. Tears rolled down her deeply wrinkled cheeks and found their way to her chin.

"This is a very rare and secret sign, Doktor Fluss. It is difficult to tell you the whole meaning right now but let me just say that it is a variant of the word 'dragon'. Dragons have always been important in Chinese culture. But it has a much deeper meaning than that because it's like a password to a secret location. It is very special to our family and I have had a version of it specially made for the office wall. It inspires and encourages me to seek truth. I will tell you more at another time. At present we need to get you to the railway station. Your train to Hannover leaves in twenty minutes. My mother would like to come for the ride. She doesn't leave the house very much and the Christmas decorations in the streets delight her. Here, she brought over your suitcase."

This clarified the reason the old woman was waiting in the office. The new insight enthused Annika to find out more. At that moment it was her presumption that she had acquired basically all the knowledge that could be squeezed out. Something in the manner of the Chinese ladies told her they were reluctant to speak further about the symbol. She certainly did not wish to pry into the family secrets of people she had only just met.

They left the office via a back door into a lane where a black Mercedes sedan was parked. Again, it was richly appointed. It drove so quietly and smoothly that no vibration could be felt as it glided over the cobbled laneway and out onto the bitumen road. Their conversation turned to things more mundane.

Questions were asked that probed into some of her family matters. Annika's father was planning to marry his new love and sell his house in Delmenhorst. She had the opportunity to buy it from him at a good price but did not think it was the right time in her life to make such a commitment. It would be a shame to see it leave the family. She had grown up there before moving to London with her mother when she was 15. Her brother and sister were not interested and had their eyes on property elsewhere. It was a dilemma for her. Then she realised that she had not mentioned her mother today. Suddenly she considered how all the talk had been about her and how little she knew about Professor Jiang. She felt it was time to change the subject.

Professor Jiang had an interesting background that she had no desire to describe in detail. She was a highly cultivated woman, educated in Shanghai. She spoke perfect German and very passable English. During the Chinese Cultural Revolution under Mau Zedong she had been hunted down, along with other academics, by the Red Guard and, with her mother, had fled China in 1975. She found political asylum in Germany and learned the language quickly while working for a number of years as a cook in a Hamburg restaurant.

In the eighties her teaching credentials were finally recognised and she began to teach Chinese language in a high school near Hannover. She found great success as a teacher and gained a reputation as a talented organiser of cultural events. She was very frugal and whenever the opportunity arose she purchased exotic eastern furnishings. Then five years ago she had been approached to come to Goslar and teach in the newly established Arts Academy. She was offered a house on campus to rent and an office and classroom. She had really enjoyed decorating them to give an Eastern ambience.

How extraordinary she's a Chinese dissident who made a success of her life here in Germany. I could be inspired by this woman. There were brief goodbyes or more accurately 'see-you-soons' at the Bahnhof entrance since there was no parking available. She suddenly found herself alone.

The train trip and her short motorbike ride home were taken up with all kinds of thoughts about the wonderful position she had been offered, the course content, the research specialisation and how and whether to reply to the email from Australia.

Arriving at Delmenhorst, her father and his fiancé were at home and excitedly listened to her news.

The question of buying the family home seemed to have been resolved. As she was moving to Goslar, the house would go on the market. That saddened her but life must go on. Her siblings would arrive in the morning for a family Christmas. She would fly to London next week to celebrate with her mother. The conversation over a meal was bright and enjoyable but after a life-changing day she retired early to her room, deciding there might be time to reply to the Australian email tomorrow, Christmas Day.

Chapter 15

Mona Vale, New South Wales. Christmas Day.

It was going to be a hot, muggy day on Sydney's northern beaches. Don struggled out of bed for the traditional family Christmas Day gift-giving ceremony in his parents' living room. This would be followed by a worship service in a local Anglican church, as there was no nearby Presbyterian Church. His drive down from Queensland had been pleasurable, tiring but incident free so he had spent Christmas Eve recovering and chatting with his family. He felt relaxed but a little awkward to be once again under the roof of his mother and father.

The early morning ritual around the Christmas tree was a lot of fun. Don received three significant gifts. The first was a calligraphy pen set from his parents. That set his mind spinning. The second was a shirt with oriental symbols from his sister Isabel. She had been on holiday in Thailand and had bought it for him there. The third came from his brother Angus. It was a small, electronic usb microscope with a magnification of six hundred times. He could hardly wait to try it out. His family members had been very astute in their selection for him. He felt blessed to have such a wonderful family. Their love for him seemed almost overwhelming. After a very quick breakfast he needed to find a quiet spot.

Don sat on the bed and opened his laptop. There was a wi-fi hotspot nearby. It was unsecured and the signal was weak, but he persisted. He intended to search for images made with usb microscopes but was distracted by some incoming emails. Most were Christmas greetings accompanied by advertising from businesses. The one that he chose to open was from Dr Tauber. It showed a distinct change from the brusque tone of their meeting some weeks before.

Dear Dr. Kirk,
Apologies for taking so long to get back to you. I have some interesting news. The "rock etching" you so kindly placed in our collection has been carefully examined using SEM technology that we outsource to the university. That's what took the time. I was surprised that there is a level of intricate detail that is barely visible to the naked eye. We believe it to be a kind of cartouche although it lacks any decorative scrollwork border. It may be the name of an important person. How it came to be in the bush near Gympie we have really no idea. But you may be interested to know that this is a rare piece and our experts have dated it at around six hundred years old. We intend to do more investigation.
I will be off on leave until 14 January. I will send you some SEM images when I return. I also have the email address of Dr Fluss that you sent me so, I'm sure with your consent, I will also send the images to her for comment.
Best wishes for the holiday season,
Arne Tauber

As he showered and dressed for the nine o'clock church service, Don could not get six hundred years out of his head. He wanted to get back to his computer but the priority was family time today so that would have to wait.

The church service was short but powerful. The small stone church building was packed. The singing of the carols was loud and stirring. The Kirk family were in varying degrees committed Christians, although Don believed himself to be a little backslidden. They walked home together in high spirits, looking forward to an unseasonal hot lunch. Don felt just a little alone as his younger siblings seemed to prefer each other's company. He found himself talking more to his father, who seemed to take a personal interest in his activities. Gordon Kirk was an active and fit man who always found something to talk about. He was a keen golfer and frequently shared his story of the time when his drive hit an overhanging bough, bounced off a rock and ended up inches from the cup on a par four hole. His eagle putt had become legendary. He had been president of the local Golf Club for several years and tended to spend his Saturdays there.

Don's mother Rhiannon was also a golfer but preferred to tell of her exploits in the kitchen. Although not employed by the Golf Club, she figured largely in the catering, especially for larger functions. Her specialty was cake decoration for which she was widely applauded and in constant demand.

Isabel and Angus were both single and considerably younger than Donald. He was thirty and they were 24 and 26. Angus was an economist with a large investment company in the city. He worked at modelling future trends so that the company could give timely advise to their many wealthy clients. Although he liked his job and the harbour views his office provided, he had a passion for boats and wanted one day to be out of the office and sailing as a career. Isabel was a little too avant-garde for her parents' liking. She was an emerging fashion designer who lived a rather bohemian lifestyle and shared a flat in inner-city Glebe. Gordon and Rhiannon worried about her health, safety and virtue. She was a happy-go-lucky girl with long blond locks and an alluring smile. Don found it almost impossible to get close to her.

The family dining table had been decorated with holly and ivy accessories. There was a silver candelabra in the centre and it was only ever brought out and polished for this occasion. Rhiannon insisted on being alone in the kitchen to prepare the meal. Gordon was permitted to enter to carry plates to the table. The others sat chatting and awaiting this year's festive fare. Gordon emerged with a roast to be carved at table.

"Oh, it's roast pork this year. Yummy. My favourite," said Isabel, trying to add some excitement to the occasion.

Donald was surprised. He thought she would be a vegan or something. *She probably is vegetarian and she's just trying to make Mum feel good. Nice thought anyway!*

"It's a big roast." Although Angus still lived at home, he had not seen one that large on the table previously.

"Yes, it's the biggest they had at the meat market." Gordon was almost boasting about his find.

"You mean you didn't get this from the local supermarket?"

"Ha, no. I went down to the supplier we use for the club restaurant. It's called … wait for it … 'What's at Steak'. Pretty good name hey?" There was general laughter. Don looked for the reaction on Isabel's face. He thought he saw a slight roll of the eyes.

"Now, how many slices each?"

"Dad, they're not slices, they're slabs. Just one for me thanks," squawked Isabel. Don was now convinced she was not an habitual meat eater but he wouldn't question her about it.

The slabs of meat were allocated and passed around. Boiled vegetables also did the rounds. *Isabel's plate has decidedly more plant than animal. But I don't care. I love my meat.*

"Can I have another slice please Dad? And some more crackling please. This pig didn't die in vain." Don was trying to make his point. Isabel whacked him very hard on the arm. *I was right about her!* He laughed, but he would check for a bruise later.

When Gordon finally stood and took away the remaining meat, they knew he was about to return with dessert. This year it was hot Christmas Pudding containing silver threepences and covered with creamy, thick custard. It was just what they all anticipated but there had to be some sort of ritualistic unveiling.

"Ta-dah. Here it is. Mum's pièce de resistance. Beautifully decorated, of course." He motioned to the garland of herbage that surrounded the pudding. *Isabel seems more content with that. But I'll bet she makes some comment.*

"Has it got metal in it this year? I nearly broke a tooth last time."

"Yes it has, so chew gently. But it's a family tradition. Don't you care for tradition, Love?" Rhiannon looked at her in expectation of a humble reply. She didn't receive one.

"You know Mum, I'm not a traditional type of person. It doesn't make sense to me to put coins in a pudding and then warn everybody. How is that a tradition?"

"Issy, by tradition we mean something that goes back centuries. In the middle ages they used to put things in puddings, stones, wishbones, peas, all sorts of things. Finding one was supposed to be good luck." It seemed Gordon had looked this up recently.

"Dad, this isn't the middle ages. And we're Christians. We don't believe in luck."

Gordon and Rhiannon looked at each other in amazement. Isabel had just professed to having a faith. Angus was aware of what was happening, so he felt the urge to say something.

"I think you're right Issy. We believe that God directs our paths so there's no luck involved. But look at it this way, in this family we have never said oh, you found a threepence, you'll have good luck. We just laugh when we find one. It's fun and it's just an old custom that Mum and Dad grew up with and they've carried it on to us. I think we should respect that."

Everybody at the table nodded quietly in agreement, even Isabel. That was the last it was mentioned.

"It's a nice day. Let's all go and play some beach cricket this afternoon." Gordon lightened the mood.

For a time the ancient cartouche was not in the forefront of Donald's mind but as lunch ended he wished he could get away to his computer. *I have to go and play cricket? It's just like the end of school. But I do respect my family. They come first. I'll go.*

"I bags first bat," he said, trying to make the most of the situation.

The three walked together down to the beach, recalling past Christmases. Their parents followed later in the car, having cleaned up after lunch. He wanted to share the news of his archaeological find but thought an emerging fashion designer and a graduate economist might not be interested.

They swam in the warm ocean and played beach cricket until well into the scorching afternoon. Children and teenagers from other families joined in their game and at times there were at least twenty fieldsmen. This was followed by an ice cream from the corner shop and then Gordon drove the family home for a nap and some light finger food for tea. It was seven at night before Don opened his computer again. He was stunned as he looked at his first email.

Hallo Doktor Kirk,
*My name is Doktor Annika Fluss. I was surprised
to read your email concerning the Chinese
symbol. I have showed the photographs to two
Chinese colleagues and they have indicated that it
has both a river and a dragon connotation. It has
very deep meaning for them but I have not yet had
the opportunity to establish what that might be. At
present I am in the process of moving to a new
position in Germany. I should be settled into my
new office by the middle of January. I will look
forward to more interesting news about the item. I
will keep you informed if I should find anything
more. Please use the email address
2fluss8@googlemail.com until I have established
my new connection.*
Bis später! Fluss

Now Don had a veritable network of things to
think about. *Six hundred years old. Cartouche.
Chinese experts. Deep meaning. A German
academic working in England who writes a mixture
of two languages. Fluss relocating, perhaps losing
contact with the Chinese colleagues. She gave me
her personal email address?* His head was spinning
faster and faster. He reopened the Facebook link he
had found for Annika Fluss. The banner showed a
line of dancers but his eyes fell straight onto the
profile picture. It was an over-the-shoulder shot of
the most beautiful woman that Donald had ever

seen. She had fair skin with long, jet black hair flowing down one side of her face. She looked simply stunning in her frilled red dress. He wished he could see more of her face.

To his amazement she had accepted his friend request. There were many new posts on her timeline, in English and German, mostly sending Christmas wishes and congratulations on the new position. She had not 'liked' the posts and possibly had not read them at this time so he looked through her images. Almost all were of young women dancing and he became a little confused as to whether she was actually in any of the pictures. From her email address he guessed that she might be 28 years old.

He was becoming more interested in her for reasons that could not be considered academic. The thought of having to wait three weeks for Tauber and Fluss to be back at work annoyed him greatly. He did not want to antagonise either of them so he decided to wait, return home to 'Green Wattles' and have fun with his new microscope and calligraphy set while wearing his Thai shirt.

He also decided not to tell his family very much about the cartouche. Just that it was something interesting from the gold rush that he had found and it was now in the Queensland Museum. An archaeologist and German academic had an interest in its origin. His family members asked no probing questions about it. There was not a word said that would indicate his growing infatuation with the mysterious European dance lecturer. He felt somewhat tortured having to play games and go out to coffee or the beach with his younger siblings and their friends for another week but he was mature enough to realise just how precious this family bonding time would be. *The way life has many twists, we may never again have this much time to spend together.*

Don headed north after lunch on New Year's Day. It really had been an enjoyable family break but also a period of the most tangled thoughts he had ever experienced. He likened his brain to an old-fashioned switchboard of crisscrossing wires and flashing lights. So many conversations going on at once. The late start brought on fatigue so it was an easy decision to break his journey. He pulled into a motel in Coffs Harbour. They had wi-fi. His curiosity was insatiable so when he could wait no longer, he sent a hopeful email to Annika Fluss.

Dear Dr. Fluss,
Merry Christmas and Happy New Year.
I was delighted to receive your email on Christmas Day. I have not had a very good internet connection while visiting my family so I apologise for the delay in replying.
You may be interested to hear that Dr Tauber has had the artefact examined and it is thought to be a Chinese Cartouche from the 1400s. That was a surprise to me. Would you please share that with your Chinese colleagues?
Dr Tauber will send you a copy of the scanning electron microscope images when he returns from his holidays. They will show the design in greater

Friendly. Professional. He re-read the message over and over, finally but hesitantly pressing 'send'. *What will she think of me? Will she look at my crummy Facebook page? I'd better do some work on it.*

The remaining weeks of the school holidays were spent at home with the geckos and dragons, photographing his gold slivers and semi-precious gemstones plus other assorted curiosities with his usb microscope. The results were astounding. He had found a new hobby. Some of his better images graced his updated Facebook page. He even found time to get out his wood router and make a new sign for his gate – 'Green Wattles'. *I'll leave off 'Farm'.* It was painted olive green with yellow lettering and also graced his revitalised fb page.

He also made a brief excursion to the site of the find near Gympie, spent a few hours and took some photographs of the environment. The weather was fine this time. There were no more carved stones to be found on the surface and he left without visiting John and Pat. There would be a better time to show them the images when he possessed more information about the cartouche.

On 15th January he went into his staffroom at school to begin preparation of his courses for the new year. He sat at his computer and, before opening his work files, idly googled 'Chinese 1400s'. He was alone in the room when a strange image popped out before him. It was an Amazon advertisement for a book called '1421: The Year China Discovered the World' by Gavin Menzies. He read a fairly comprehensive synopsis and it mentioned Gympie. The reviews were scathing but he felt compelled and immediately ordered the book. He had difficulty concentrating on his work from that point on.

That evening, in the solitude of 'Green Wattles', two emails arrived that would turn his world upside down.

Chapter 16

Goslar, Germany. January 2006.

The first day of work at the Academy in Goslar was a new awakening for Doktor Annika Fluss. She had found an interesting apartment to share with a single female dentist. It was only 500 metres from her workplace. A lovely morning stroll if the weather was good. It had a wide ground floor hallway that easily accommodated her motorbike. It was such a nice-looking machine in shiny red, black and silver that it was seen by her flatmate and visitors as an artistic statement rather than an impediment to freedom of movement.

The Academy was decidedly a boutique educational establishment with highly specialised, intimate teaching spaces. The well-organised builders and shopfitters had worked tirelessly to have her office ready for use on 10 January. She had begun to settle in, but her telephone and data cabling was not connected until a Deutsche Telekom technician arrived on 14 January.

The first floor School of Dance administrative area was made up of a reception desk with computer and copier, an informal meeting area, a kitchenette, a small bathroom and a substantial office room with whiteboard, two huge desks and a complete bookcase wall. The lower floor consisted of a 45 square metre expanse of sprung wooden flooring with tiered seating at one end and a dais and lectern at the other. It would take longer to finish. One whole side wall was to be mirrored and have a ballet barre installed. A huge motorized screen designed to mask the mirrors during lectures was already in place. Significant progress was made every single day. She was delighted to be able to sit at her new desk with a view over the beautiful streetscape. It was easy to ignore the noise of the tradesmen below and they never bothered her by coming upstairs.

It had been agreed that the new Dance School would share one of the Music School's two secretarial assistants for the first year. That made sense, as Doktor Fluss would be doing preparations and teaching only a small summer semester intake. The arrangements were to be reviewed before the winter semester. Hundreds of metres of communications cabling had been installed and everything was connected and working well by mid-afternoon on the 14th as expected. With that hurdle overcome she booted up her new all-in-one large screen computer flanked by two equally large monitors. The rest of the afternoon was spent customising it to her needs and taste. When she had set up a partition in her mail program to send professional and personal messages to different folders, she felt a sense of accomplishment and excitement. There was a smile on her face as the first mails came rushing in. She scanned down the list in her professional folder first. They were mostly welcome messages from her new colleagues making contact and inviting her to drop by for a chat.

Her perusal was interrupted by the arrival of Professor Jiang, her first office visitor. She came bearing two most delicious slices of cake and two cappuccino coffees in paper cups. This colleague was obviously a thoughtful woman who had realised that the kitchen facilities would not be in operation just yet. Doktor Fluss had come to like her very much. The older woman was rapidly becoming a mentor to her and frequently offered to help in any way she could. There was indeed a developing personal friendship. This was revealed when Professor Jiang invited Professor Fluss to call her by her given name Lihua. She proudly announced that it meant 'beautiful and elegant'. She also demanded that it never be shortened to 'Li', which means plum. Not a shape she wanted to be! Doktor Fluss responded similarly with "please call me Annika but never 'Annie', she was a little orphan."

"I'd be honoured if you would come to a little dinner I'm hosting tomorrow evening. Just a few friends. Will you be free to come, Annika?"

Despite the now permissible use of first names there remained a note of formality between them.

"Oh, yes I'd love to." *Anything to make for good staff relationships.*

"That's wonderful. It will be at the Butterhanne Restaurant at 19,00h. Do you know it?"

"Yes, it's only a couple of kilometres from my apartment. How should I dress?" She was thinking of Lihua's expensive tastes.

"Not too formal. Just casual party dress. I have invited somebody you will love to meet. A little secret for the moment."

"Oh. I do like secrets. Okay. I will see you there

at 19,00h."

Annika was happy to accept because she thought there might be Chinese guests and she had become interested in their culture. She was not tempted to ask who they were. *Secrets are secrets. Revealing them suddenly is more exciting than sleeping on them.* She wondered why this colleague was making such a fuss over her. Then she reflected on how little the woman had revealed about her own life. She was planning to call her Lihua but, for some bewildering reason, she could only think of her as Madam Jiang and her mother as Madam Long. The first name would take considerable adjustment.

When Lihua had departed she opened her personal Googlemail folder and found two new emails that caught her attention. They were from Kirk and Tauber. She eagerly opened the first one and read with interest the message from Don. A little bit of new information regarding the age of the cartouche. Then she opened the second message.

Dear Professor Fluss,
My name is Dr. Arne Tauber. I hold the position of Curator of Archaeology at the Queensland Museum in Brisbane, Australia. Mr Donald Kirk gave me your email address. Mr Kirk has found and donated to the museum a Chinese cartouche that we believe dates back to the Ming Dynasty. It once may have been gilded. I understand that you may have some knowledge of the meaning or significance of this artefact. I have attached several images taken by our museum

photographer and a very detailed image made by scanning electron microscope.
If you are able to share with us information about the item could you please contact me as soon as possible?
Kindest Regards,
Dr. Arne Tauber
Acting Curator of Archaeology
Email atauber@qm.qld.gov.au

Annika quickly opened the image files and on her large screens they looked amazing. She decided to try her new printer and out they came, A4 size in full colour. Having no expertise in rock carvings and only a smidgeon in archaeology, she determined to show them to Madam Jiang, Lihua, at the next available opportunity. *That probably will not be at a dinner with friends.*

Next she returned to Don's email. Stunning good looks had made her very vulnerable and very wary. She still had questions. *Is he Australian or Scottish? He is apparently a man committed to his family. He doesn't know me but offers congratulations. He'd like to hear more about my position. I don't think he's stalking me, but I'm still not sure.* She googled his name and found nothing that she could use to identify him.

What about Tauber? There was plenty of information about him. Australian born. Married with three children. Parents from Gebsattel, Germany. She did not know the town but could see no reason why he would be stalking her. She decided to reply to Tauber when she actually had some information. She would not reply to Kirk unless she knew more about him. *His first email was unsolicited, and he found me by combing the internet. That's highly suspicious!*

For the remainder of the day she uploaded teaching materials and useful files from her laptop to the Academy server and to the hard drive of her desk computer. She tried to immerse herself in her work but thoughts of her new position, Australian emails and a dinner with a secret guest unsettled her. She walked home around 16,30h, donned her leathers and took her motorbike for a quick spin. *I must keep the engine lubricated and warm up the tyres. Then I'll give her the polish she deserves.*

The following day was also mainly spent at her desk apart from a one-hour meeting with Meike Gottschall, her new part-time secretarial assistant. Her duties were clarified and she was briefed on the course content so that she could field phone enquiries. Meike appeared to be a very joyful girl with short, honey-coloured hair who looked younger than her twenty years. She had a particular talent in playing cello and viola and was a member of a number of ensembles in the district. Annika found her to be inexperienced in office procedures but enthusiastic. She could work with that. The girl had a grace of movement about her that was very pleasing to a dance specialist.

Meike's first task would be to scan a folder of papers and upload them to the server, nothing too difficult. She took the folder with confidence and began working. They established a regular meeting time on Tuesday mornings. Meike was to work in the Dance Office Tuesdays and Thursdays. Their professional relationship had started out well.

That evening the snow was quite deep around the buildings. The roads had been gritted and were clear but slippery. It was several kilometres from her apartment to the restaurant and Annika did not want to ride her motorbike in the dark under such treacherous conditions. In her fashionable party gear with heels walking would be slightly difficult. She phoned Lihua. Hesitantly she folded the images and placed them in her handbag – just in case. Within twenty minutes the Mercedes drew up gently and noiselessly like a stately limousine to her front door. Annika found herself too tongue-tied to call Madam Jiang by her first name, fearing she might mispronounce it. She determined as much as possible to avoid calling her by name for the evening.

The dinner turned out to be quite a surprise. There were only two other guests, Uwe Holzmann, a building contractor from Hannover and his wife Senta. She was a former teacher and currently worked as her husband's business manager. Both were greying, probably in their late forties or early fifties. It was only minutes into the conversation when Annika was able to work out that Senta was born in 1966 when she let slip mention of a landmark birthday coming up later in the year. *She'll be fifty. Mama was fifty in January last year.*

The greatest revelation of the very pleasant and

jovial dinner was that Senta actually knew Annika's mother and had, for a short time, been at school with her in Bremen, but one grade apart. The ages tallied. She thought that Senta may have even bourn a resemblance to her mother.

Madam Jiang had befriended the couple during her teaching years. Today they had come over to stay with her while they looked at a prospective building job. They were obviously good friends. *How does Madam Jiang know so much about me that she would invite me to meet a childhood friend of my mother?*

The five of them travelled afterwards to Madam Jiang's luxurious home for coffee. Madam Long had the place warm. She obviously knew the Holzmanns well and even said things to them in Chinese, although they only nodded in reply. She enjoyed serving them coffee with cakes and lebkuchen while they continued their conversation, mainly about building and decorating. There was a hush. Annika pulled out her images of the stone and began to describe how she had come by them. They passed the sheets around and there was a kind of stunned silence. Tears welled up in the eyes of the other women. *Senta was moved by these images?* Composing herself, Madam Jiang flattened out the SEM image and began to speak, choking occasionally on her words.

"As you know Annika, this symbol has deep meaning for our family. Some of that meaning is very secret and I can't share it all with you." She switched languages and repeated herself in a

Chinese dialect. Madam Long began to sob. Annika went to apologise, but Madam Jiang went on.

"There is a tributary of the Yangtze River called Hanshui. It is shaped like a dancing dragon." She had Annika's undivided attention now. "In one place there have been landslides on the steep banks. Most of them happened a long time ago. Thousands of years. The slate rock exposed there is soft enough for carving. It is too soft for roof tiles. There is a tradition of slate carving in the area. In this picture you can see the fine detail of the design although this one has been worn down over time. So it is both a river and a dragon but it means so much to us because my mother and I were born there. It is like our family crest. A family that is now scattered by the ideology of madmen…" She stopped to draw breath but her mother, wiping away her tears, began to speak in Chinese and pointed to features on the image. Madam Jiang translated.

"My mother says that the dragon represents power. The force of the river through the gorges also represents power. But many times China has lost direction. The head of the dragon has been cut off."

"How old is the carving?" asked Annika politely, trying to substantiate Donald's claim. To her surprise Senta offered an answer.

"If this is a tradition of the region, then it would have been carried on over millennia."

Finding this less than useful, Annika pointed to the gold flecks on the image and asked another question.

"Why was this carving covered with gold?" She

had the impression that Madam Jiang knew but was not willing to say. There was a brief exchange in Chinese before a reply came.

"Many years ago, these images were proudly displayed in homes. It was like placing the family shield above the mantelpiece. But now there are few of these around. And the more recent ones are painted, not clad with gold. So this is indeed an old one." The group were enthralled and finally Madam Jiang released some information she had been withholding, after so many years, perhaps still for fear of being reported to the Chinese authorities.

"I have never told anyone in Germany about this so please don't repeat any of it." She hesitated, thinking about the wisdom of giving out this information. "The community that lives in that area is secret and, some would say, subversive. They serve a Master other than the state. Even today they live in fear of being arrested. We are the fortunate ones who were able to get out. They do have a legitimate front organisation. It is a school of traditional Chinese dance. Chairman Mao encouraged that sort of thing in the Cultural Revolution. They do have dance instructors and competitions but it is primarily a centre where the whole community gathers in a big barn about one kilometre from the river. It is quite inaccessible by car. Those people are our family. We miss them and will never see them again. We can't return to China." She sobbed, said a few words in Chinese and another tear ran down mother's cheek.

The whole group sat stunned. Madam Jiang

addressed Annika in a very matronly tone.

"Now that you know some of our family secrets, please call me Lihua." This was a very formal reiteration of a previous conversation, obviously for the benefit of the Holzmanns.

Annika nodded vigorously. "I will not tell your secret." In reality her thoughts were whizzing around the traditional Chinese dance school in a barn. That was where the internet image had originated. *I think I may have found my new research interest.*

The goodbyes were more intimate than expected. The Holzmanns hugged her and kissed her on the cheek. Lihua also embraced her, then Madam Long. This was unlike German protocol. *This is more like London! Maybe this is Chinese custom?* She decided to walk the freezing half kilometre to her home, heels and all. Before going to bed she relaxed into her stretching and yoga poses. That done, she hopped into bed and sent a very guarded email to Tauber, a recognised and trusted academic, but not to Kirk, the unknown quantity.

Chapter 17

Goslar, Germany. Late January 2006.

Late January to early February brought with it a flurry of activity for Professor Annika Fluss. The snows had been fairly heavy and she was finding the heating in her office just a little too enervating, but she ploughed on regardless. One of the most interesting aspects for her was the interviews and telephone conversations with prospective students, and their parents in most cases. She was meeting some very talented young people who were seeking a career in dance but in many diverse fields from ballet through jazz and tap to hip hop.

Although the course content had not yet been finalised nor approved by the Academic Board, she took time to explain that the coverage of the lecture and tutorial components would be very broad indeed, looking at the origins, history and cultural aspects of many dance traditions. It was difficult for an eighteen-year-old who wanted to dance Krump-style on television to grasp the importance of being educated in the whole dance genre. But Professor Fluss was very persuasive. She made sure they understood that dancing can be a short career, although there are dancers over forty years old. Ballroom dancing was an obvious exception. They must plan to have other options such as teaching, choreography or directing, as they get older. The course would give them a good basis for these occupations. Her logic was flawless and her manner engaging. She had been told to expect fourteen or fifteen students in August but now she had double that number of prospects.

One nineteen-year-old student particularly caught her interest. She was from Thailand and had found herself in Europe when her father relocated to Germany for work. She spoke good English but little German. This helped Annika decide conclusively that the course content should definitely be delivered in English, the emergent international language. For the practical tuition she would be bringing in expert teachers and they would communicate in various lingoes. The Thai girl was a very talented dancer, instructed at one of the biggest dance schools in Chiang Mai. She was a graceful young woman and wanted to pursue a career in oriental dance. At her interview she handed Professor Fluss a brochure from her former dance school. It was written in Thai but later that day Annika found the same document on the Thai website and used Google translate to read some of the material.

She found that every March the institution hosted an international symposium on Asian dance. *Only a month away.* She immediately had Meike make some calls, filled out an application form and within days she had approval to travel to Chiang Mai for the conference. The Academic Board had a sub-committee that dealt with research and in-service training matters. Professor Jiang was chair of that committee and had no problem convincing the others to spend four thousand Euros in-servicing their new and very promising dance lecturer.

Over the week since the Jiang family revelations concerning the cartouche, Annika had been in email contact with Dr Tauber in Brisbane. She wanted to know more about the fascinating story behind the symbol being found so far from China. She had raised the subject with Lihua and had a little more insight but something was being withheld from her. She made a list of what she could reveal and adhered rigidly to it.

- A family crest from the Hubei Province in China
- Family history dating back over 1000 years.
- Gilding was used only on special community carvings and primarily during the Ming dynasty period
- The family lived in an isolated community on the Hanshui River
- It is a symbol of power - a dragon and a surging river
- An ancient landslip had been the source of soft slate stone for carving
- The intricate techniques had been developed as a means of putting hidden characters into the carving
- Today the community runs a traditional Chinese dance school with boarding facilities

- The sources were a woman of sixty and her mother of eighty who were both born and raised in the area but did not want their names associated with the object

With the possible exception of the ages of the women in the final point, she had secured Lihua's permission to tell the museum these things. There was a nagging hint that Lihua did not think the museum was the place for the artefact. They both hoped Tauber would take up the investigation into how it came to be in Australia. Kirk was a wildcard. Annika knew very little about him but he had found the object. Maybe he was an Indigo Jones style adventurer who would be an excellent research assistant in the field. She now wanted to make contact with him.

It had been an aside in one of her emails to Tauber when she mentioned she was going to Thailand. She was surprised and delighted that he wrote back inviting her to fly to Brisbane for a few days to see the artefact and the work of the museum. Meike made the calls and organised the flights. She had special international-style business cards printed. She also requisitioned some lightweight film and sound equipment that could be taken into the field for research. Despite her tender years, the new secretary had turned out to be an excellent personal assistant who thought everything through and executed every request with speed and accuracy. Annika found her original fears about the girl's inexperience were groundless. Meike also made

excellent coffee and was a whizz in the tiny
kitchenette.

Chapter 18

Redcliffe, Queensland. Late January 2006.

Weeks had passed since Donald Kirk had had any communication with Tauber or Fluss. He had expected to hear something of the reactions to the SEM images. His new school year had begun in earnest. He attended whole staff meetings, a team-building day and department meetings about new curriculum guidelines that had to be met. It was then all hands to the computers to update and, in some cases, completely rewrite work programs. There had been little change to the mathematics syllabuses so that pleased him.

Then he was asked to take on a senior physics class. He had taught physics before. It meant many, many hours of work. He liked fiddling with mechanical and electrical gadgets so the practical work would be much more enjoyable than the paperwork. He had this head filled with thoughts of practical lessons, extended experimental investigations and response to stimulus assignments. His weekend was spent course writing and there was little time to think of the cartouche.

Then came the Year 8 camp. He had to go away to a secluded ranch with almost two hundred young teenagers for four nights. No sleep. Monday. Tuesday. Wednesday. Thursday. For him it was like imprisonment. Day visitors could go home for the night but he had to stay awake until all hours, quietening talkative boys and ensuring that they did not stray towards the girls' dormitories. It was more mind-numbing than exam supervision. He couldn't count bricks in the dark but at least he was exercising by walking around. *I have to put a positive spin on this. Commitment is one of the qualities that I must pass on to my students.*

In the long midnight watches his mind eventually turned to that exciting discovery that he kind of remembered. It seemed so distant now. He had new challenges, the most pressing being how to keep young adolescent boys asleep in bed.

During his holidays he had played endlessly with his usb microscope. He built a stand to raise and lower it then he tried different lighting, different backgrounds, inserting lenses and taking images and videos of flowers and mineral crystals. Having seen the SEM image of the rock carving, he was never satisfied with the clarity of his own images. He wanted to do a course in electron microscopy but he already had a doctorate in mathematics education although he never used the title Doctor. *Could I change to a new field of work? Making discoveries about very small things would be fun. No. The challenge of teaching practical physics will be my new goal.*

There was no Internet or mobile phone access at the campsite. This was a good thing for the students as they would have to engage in real social interaction. But Don felt cut off from the world. He could make a local phone call on the black antique telephone handset in the camp office. That was only for emergencies and there was nobody he wanted to phone anyway. When all was quiet around one in the morning, he climbed a nearby rise and to his delight he had a mobile phone signal. He checked his email. The usual. Then he found one from Dr Tauber, which he opened with great delight. It took ages to open. When it did the message was short and somewhat enigmatic, like a telegram used to be when you had to pay by the word count.

Dear Mr Kirk,
Unable to reach you by phone. I have a wealth of new info. Fluss is going to meet with me. Please call asap.
Dr A. Tauber

Standing on a hill, his face lit only by his screen, nobody saw his amazement. He returned to the common room to find two weary colleagues having a hot chocolate before turning in. An English teacher and a physical education teacher. Both middle-aged women. *Will I share my secret with them? Now's not the time.* Their bunks beckoned. He didn't really take in the bit about 'wealth of info' but Fluss coming certainly struck a chord. *Coming where? To the Museum? Perhaps Tauber has a meeting with her at some overseas conference.*

On Friday afternoon, Don and his colleagues handed over their charges to the hoard of waiting parents. He watched the family reunions. These people really loved their kids. Several came to thank him for taking care of them. He went to the staff common room for an informal debrief. It took all of five minutes. The principal thanked the four teachers and asked whether there had been any serious issues he should know about. There were none. Everybody wanted to go home. Don could not wait to call Tauber but Friday afternoon at four o'clock was probably not the best time. He went to his desk and dashed off a quick email in the same style as the one he had received.

Dear Dr Tauber,
Thanks for the message. Sorry I've been out of phone contact in the field. Will call you Monday.
Regards,
Don Kirk

Within one minute his mobile phone echoed through the otherwise empty staffroom.

"Hello. Don Kirk speaking"

"Oh, Mr Kirk, I'm so glad I caught you. Your artefact has turned out to be very interesting indeed. Dr Fluss from Germany has been able to identify for us the meaning of the symbol and the area it came from."

Donald sat up in his chair and listened intently to the story of rivers and dragons, the family crests and the dance school in a barn, a contemporary remnant of an older empire. How it came to Australia remained a mystery but the Chinese miners in the 1860s most likely bought it with them as a prosperity symbol.

"How did you come by this information?"

"Well Dr Fluss, the one whose webpage you found, has colleagues who come from that region of China and they told her the story. I spoke to her on the phone last week. But this is what has excited me, Mr Kirk, her new university is sending her to a conference in Thailand next week. The topic is Dai culture. She's a dance specialist researching oriental cultures. Anyway, here's the exciting bit. She had booked her flights through Singapore and, at our invitation, was able to get an additional flight to Brisbane and she can spend two nights here. Apparently she has moved heaven and earth to get the visa. She wants to see the artefact and to meet you. So could we set up a meeting for the week after next, Tuesday March the seventh? She's arriving Monday the sixth at night, leaving Wednesday the eighth at night. How are you placed?"

Almost reeling with the overwhelming pace at which things were moving, Don stuttered, "well, well … er … I have a teaching program but I could probably be at your office by four thirty on the Tuesday. I can't really take any time off so early in the semester."

"I quite understand. I've been in that position myself. Four-thirty on Tuesday the seventh then. We'll have dinner afterwards. This is a great contact for us as we need some help with Asian cultural stuff. I'll slip you a reminder of the place and time by email. See you then." Click.

Don was now a lather of sweat. *Fluss wants to meet me? Why didn't she email me? Tauber sees her only as a good contact? How can a German dance specialist tell us about a Chinese family crest that might be six hundred years old? Oh, the dance school in the barn, of course.*

He turned to his computer and opened the original page that had started all this. 'The Flow of Chinese Dance'. *A kind of departmental blog maybe.* He began to get it. *'Fluss' is German for a stream or river. The page name was a play on words. Smart girl!* He then viewed her Facebook page, never sure which images revealed her. There were no tags. The same profile picture showed only part of a fair-skinned face, red dress and long, black, bouncy hair. He felt more nervous than he could ever recall, even more than he had at the thought of having his wisdom teeth extracted ten years before.

Chapter 19

Chiang Mai, Thailand. Mid-March 2006.

The International Symposium proved to be a real eye-opener for Annika. It was not her first visit to Asia but it was her first real immersion into Asian culture. She was able to gain a much deeper understanding of the importance of dance as a dramatic art form. The topic for the five-day event was Dai dance traditions going into the twenty-first century. Dai people come from Laos, Burma, Vietnam and Thailand. There is also an ethnic minority comprising about 1.2 million people living in China. The sessions were in a mix of English and Thai, but she was surrounded by many other tongues including Mandarin and Hindi. The experience was delightful and strengthened her resolve to research the beautiful artistry.

The best sessions were the afternoon visits to other dance schools. The fun and grace of children performing a village fan or ribbon dance contrasted strongly with the ritualistic and formal high art she had seen in the presentations. *I wouldn't call it low art. Ethnic maybe. I'm definitely going to research village dances. They're the future. They're evolving. They do have elements of the older styles but I see many modern influences. I'll take lots of footage.* She always asked permission and was allowed to freely record almost sixteen hours of demonstration dancing over the length of her stay. This was excellent audiovisual material for her course and her proposed research interest. Hopefully she did not have too much camera shake from the thundering of the bare feet transferring to her flimsy tripod.

She expected to stand out as one of the few Europeans present but her long dark hair and penchant for red clothing made her blend in relatively seamlessly. It was her height that set her apart, so she remained seated as much as she could.

Always a practical thinker, she looked to how she might conduct her research in the future. *Field research into ethnic dance. Rural dancing in villages, fields and barns. Remote places. I'll need my future research assistant to be strong and able to carry all this gear into the field. The person would also have to be very good at video and sound recording.* She was thinking big. *Television specials. Classic recordings for future generations. Treks to remote mountain communities. Totems and spirituality expressed in dance. The possibilities are endless. I need Indigo Jones. I wonder whether Dr Kirk might be interested. I'm not sure.*

Following the conference she had three days' break in Singapore where she sought out traditional Chinese shops and eating places. At one market the chilli in the food was so hot she had to go searching for ice cream and a serviette to sooth her burning mouth. It was all part of a delightful learning curve.

On her third day she tracked down a restaurant with Dai cuisine. *A perfect end to my stay.* As a solo diner, the waitress seated her at a round table with a rowdy group of middle-aged American businessmen and women. She joined in the hilarity and the group found her to be a very welcome addition. To her amazement , between courses, eight waitresses came marching down the food service aisle and began to dance. They joyfully wheeled around and around the tables. The diminutive girls each grabbed a man and pulled him up to dance. They were so strong that they could fling the overweight western men like flags in the wind. After a minute the men sat down exhausted. *Well, there's an urban adaptation of traditional dance. Pity I didn't have the video camera. Oh well, I caught a bit of it on my phone. And tomorrow I'm off to exotic Australia. A place I've never visited before. What a great conference! Wonderfully immersive and a great excuse for a good time!*

Qantas. What a funny name for an airline! From the air Australia looked like a dry, uninhabited wasteland that she traversed for five hours before reaching Brisbane. *Why would the Chinese come here? Surely there's not much to trade here. It must have been gold that drew them.* Of course she had yet to see the more fertile and well-watered eastern coast.

At the Brisbane International Terminal she was met by Dr Tauber and his wife Jenny, an Australian woman with a weird accent that was totally unfamiliar to her. Tauber himself had an Australian twang but it was less pronounced. The Taubers talked about their family life and their children. She knew this man was not stalking her. The trio dined at a little restaurant at the terminal and they drove

her to her hotel in Talbot Street in the city. She
would spend the next day and a half at the museum.
Mr Kirk was coming at four-thirty to meet with
them. He would ask Mr Kirk to look after her from
there for the evening and take her back to the airport
the following evening. She was a bit uncertain about
that arrangement but trusted her host. Tauber was
concise as he laid out his plan. His German heritage
was apparent. Annika was actually delighted to be
visiting Queensland. The hot, humid evening air was
exhilarating for her as it had been in Singapore.
Chiang Mai, however, had been unexpectedly cool.

The next morning she was picked up from her
hotel by Helen Peters, a gushing extrovert with two-
tone browned and blonded hair, who introduced
herself as the Museum Director. The short drive to
the Museum at Southbank was loud and raucous.
Annika wondered whether all Australian women had
a rough-and-ready side to their character. She liked
the straightforwardness of these people. They did
not seem to have secrets to hide like others she
knew.

The morning was spent meeting with Dr Tauber,
caressing the artefact with gloved hands and viewing
all the SEM images. She was shown the printed
information card that would accompany the
specimen on display. She took some selfies to show
Lihua and Madam Long on her return. In the
workroom she saw, amid much loud joviality, that
restorations and preservations were being performed
with great skill and accuracy. *These happy people
obviously love their work.*

The lunch at the museum cafeteria was a bit of a disappointment foodwise, but an interesting time of conversation with Dr Tanya Pierce who worked in the area of ethnic cultures of the Pacific region. Pierce was keen to be informed of Dr Fluss' Asian research. They both agreed to keep in communication and exchanged business cards.

In the afternoon Tauber, Pierce and Peters had coffee with her and the discussion was of past experiences and new directions for the museum. Fluss raised the thought of returning the cartouche to its original custodians but was quickly told, in the nicest possible way, of its extreme importance in the short history of Queensland. She smiled and said no more. The topic changed to future interactions. At three-thirty they disbanded and Tauber took Fluss to show her a special exhibit of a recovered treasure ship. She liked their work very much and it gave her the idea to begin the development of a small museum at the Academy. *More big dreams!*

Chapter 20

Brisbane. Mid-March 2006.

Donald Kirk drove out of his school before the final bell that Tuesday. Usually he worked until late but today he beat Peter out the gate by a good five minutes. He parked his Peugeot in the underground carpark at twenty-five past four and hurried to the museum entrance. Presenting the email from Dr Tauber at reception, he was ushered through a side door to a private lift. The clerk gave sufficient instructions to get him to the meeting room next door to the curator's office. Room 121.

Although he had been in these offices once before, he was approaching from a different direction and everything in the corridor was unfamiliar. He eventually came across the room. It was empty save for a cardboard storage box and some white gloves on a large table. He found a chair and sat in the corridor. After five minutes Dr Tauber came along apologising for his lateness. They entered the meeting room, sat at the conference table and exchanged pleasantries.

"Dr Fluss will be along soon. Call of nature," he said in a voice more jovial than his usual abrupt manner.

Donald's heart fluttered wildly as he waited. Then she came through the doorway. A tall vision in a red short-sleeve, figure-hugging top and businesslike black skirt to just below the knee. Her eyes gave just the slightest hint of the orient. He felt a stirring in his body as he rose to shake her hand. There was a faint whiff of exotic perfume. She smiled and with a lovely gentle but perceptible German accent said, "Doktor Kirk, I am Doktor Fluss, it is a delight to finally meet you."

"Yes … well … it's a … um … a really great pleasure to meet you too." The words seemed to fall out of his mouth like sheep droppings, smoothly pronounced but tumbling intermittently. He was also not using his Dr title at work, so it felt very strange to be addressed in that way.

"Tell me how you found this treasure."

She motioned for him to sit next to her. What followed was particularly unnerving. He tried to look away as she crossed her long legs. Her toes peeped out through her glossy black shoes and were just inches from his leg. Tingles were coursing through his bachelor body.

Dr Tauber stood and donned a white glove. He lifted the artefact from its box. Donald could not believe his eyes. The conservators had properly cleaned the stone. The gold glittered and was more extensive than he had first observed. The symbol stood out in greater relief and each line was actually an intricate series of finer lines, somewhat reminiscent of a Celtic knot. He dared not mention that he had once taken to it with a scrubbing brush!

Dr Fluss carefully watched Dr Kirk's face as he narrated the fortuitous slip into the ditch that resulted in him picking up the stone. He held back no details and he seemed to be a very humble version of the adventurous type she had imagined. Tauber added some supporting information about the Gympie gold rush.

Dr Fluss then repeated the approved information she had from Lihua and Madam Long. She must have let some extra detail drop because Dr Tauber asked her about an essential disparity between the Cultural Revolution authorised dance school and the remote and secretive nature of the community. Dr Fluss was not evasive but just said that the informants had not been forthcoming with that information. She expected there were family values, perhaps even saving face involved.

The conversation then turned to the interpretation of the symbol. Dr Tauber raised the matter of dragons, rivers, power and gold for wealth. Could the intricate lines be some kind of map like the Australian Aboriginal dreaming art? Neither Dr Fluss nor Dr Kirk could answer that. Annika knew a little more than she was permitted to share but she hid it well and promised to dig a little deeper and keep them posted. It was almost seven o'clock and all the other employees were long gone when Dr Tauber dropped a bombshell.

"We'll meet at eight I've made a booking at the new Mongol Restaurant in Anne Street. Mr, oh I'm sorry, Dr Kirk, could you take your car over there so that you can drop Dr Fluss back to her hotel? I'll have to leave you a bit early because one of my kids is sick and Jenny needs me at home. Then, is there any chance you could pick her up at the museum tomorrow afternoon around three and drive her out to the airport and see her off?"

Donald was mortified but agreed without protest. *How can I refuse?* He would need the afternoon off school, a difficult one as he coached an interschool sporting team. Dr Fluss had watched his reactions and felt he could be trusted so she smiled and graciously accepted the arrangement.

Everything went according to the plan. Donald found a street park near the Mongol restaurant. As he entered he saw Dr Fluss and Dr Tauber waiting for him on a sofa near the counter. A short immaculately dressed man with Mongol features escorted them to a table by the window with views of the city lights. It was a well-appointed establishment. He admired the beautiful yurt-shaped pendant lights, gorgeous table centres featuring dolls dressed in blue and white and the extravagant flock wallpaper with gold soyombo symbols. The prices on the menu were very high. *I'm glad the Museum is picking up the tab.*

They ordered three mains to share and talked happily. Dr Tauber laid out his plan for the next morning. Dr Pierce would show Dr Fluss videos of Polynesian and Aboriginal dance and they would look at Pacific island and Australasian artefacts. Dr Kirk would pick up Dr Fluss at three and drive her to Brisbane airport. All was agreed.

The food arrived promptly and it was excellent. Not too spicy for the Australian palate. Donald had never before heard of red and white food or of Buuz or Khorkhog. The others seemed more familiar with the cuisine.

When the shared main courses were complete Dr Tauber excused himself from coffee. Suddenly Donald and Dr Fluss were alone at the table. They ordered coffee and a much more personal conversation began.

"Dr Kirk, what is your job?"

"Oh, please call me Don. I teach mathematics and physics."

"Wonderful. Would you like to call me Annika?"

"Oh. Yes please," the words slipped out.

"So you are a professor of mathematics? What is your University called?"

"Oh, I teach in a high school." It sounded so lame that he added his qualifications. "I completed my doctorate at the age of twenty-three. I was accelerated as a Dean's scholar. But with university cutbacks I took the practical route and stepped into a teaching job straight away. This is my eighth year of teaching."

Annika was very perceptive. She liked his forthright honesty and could see that he was nervous. She calculated his age. Her next question nearly floored him.

"So, you are thirty-one years of age. Do you have a wife and children or a girlfriend?"

He twitched and quivered. *Where is this leading?*

"Well, no I don't actually. I've had a couple of girlfriends from time to time. Nothing too serious. Just holding hands. I did kiss one once. But I'm certainly not married. I live alone on my little rural property. I've got lots of interests and I make things in my workshop."

Annika loved his innocent shyness. "What kind of things do you make?"

"Oh, mechanical and electronic gadgets mainly. My latest is a kind of small lab for my digital microscope. Would you like to see some pictures?"

He pulled out his phone. She moved her chair closer to him. Their shoulders touched. He melted inside but tried to maintain his hopefully professional demeanour. He had never before been so close to such a glamorous woman. She, on the other hand, had never been so close to such a kind and gentle man, except her father, of course.

Annika flicked through his images of geckoes, crystals and flowers examining each one with an unexpected degree of interest. She tried to go back and inadvertently flicked to an image of her own Facebook page. Donald looked up sheepish and falteringly explained that this was the part of his research that led to him finding her. She thought of cyber stalking but looked at him and dismissed the idea. He was unlike any man she had ever met.

They stood to leave. Don was relieved to find Dr Tauber had already settled the bill. Walking out onto Anne Street, Don asked where she was staying. He knew the hotel was one block away on Talbot Street so without any forethought he asked if she would like to walk, he would be her security in the city at night. She agreed and took his arm.

This might have been a German tradition, but it made an Australian boy feel very uneasy. They smiled and laughed as they sauntered along and he bid her goodnight in the hotel foyer. She reached out and shook his hand and said she would see him at the Museum tomorrow at three.

Don was on a high as he drove home to 'Green Wattles'. Then he thought about missing sports afternoon. It was an away game. It was out of character for him to lie but it might come to that.

Chapter 21

'Green Wattles', March 2006.

Donald tossed and turned all night. He was conflicted over how to get the afternoon off. At seven in the morning he phoned the school on the sick or absent teachers' special number. He expected the Deputy but this time the principal, Len White, an aging bureaucratic type, answered the phone. Don gulped. He decided to tell the whole truth.

Len listened incredulously. His mind ticking over with all sorts of publicity ideas. *One of my teachers has found a rare historical object. There was an after-hours meeting at the Museum. My teacher hasn't slept and has to go back to the museum today. Of course, he can take the day. I'll need a picture for the next quarterly newsletter and for the local newspaper.* Eventually Len interrupted Don's lengthy excuse.

"Listen Don. I can tell this is something really important to you. It's a contribution to our culture as well. You go for it. Take the whole day. I'll get cover for your morning classes. Can you email me some work?"

"Yes, straight away."

"Good, well you take the whole day off then. It's been quite a while since I've been away with a rugby side, so I'd like to take them over to Sandgate myself. Make sure you get some pictures to show the staff back here at school. Go well, mate."

That was not the reception Don had expected but he felt relieved to have been honest. Now that he had the day off, could he sit in on the dance videos and cultural exhibits inspections? He emailed Dr Tauber to ask permission.

The reply came back a minute later. *Tauber is remarkably efficient!*

> *Dr Kirk,*
> *No problem at all. Come to my office at nine.*
> *Dr Fluss will be pleased.*
> *Dr Tauber*

In order to be there at nine Don had to skip breakfast, dress quickly and jump in his car. Tauber did not have a concept of how long it takes to drive from Burpengary to Southbank in peak hour traffic, but Don didn't want to make that an issue. He knew that now he was embroiled in something he could never have dreamed of. Although he rarely read fiction, for him, the truth of his life had become stranger than any fiction. And this was just a beginning.

Once again he parked his car in the Museum carpark just a couple of minutes before his appointed time. The museum was not yet open to the public but the clerk recognised him and nodded for him to proceed through the 'staff only' door. Hot and flustered he arrived at Tauber's Office cum Workroom, Room 119, just as the clock on the wall changed from 8:59 to 9:00.

Peering around the door he observed that the

room was messy as usual. With nobody in sight, he now had the confidence to sit inside and wait. Dr Tauber never appeared but after ten minutes Annika and Dr Pierce came down the corridor chatting excitedly. Annika had just been told Donald would join them for the day. She was wearing a black and white top and a narrow, knee-length red skirt over black stockings. He rose and they all shook hands.

"Dr Kirk. Sorry. Don. I'm so pleased you're able to join us today." Annika gave him a genuinely beautiful smile.

"Yes. This is quite a surprise but you are very welcome to join us. We'll be behind the scenes a fair bit and it might be a bit squashy," added Tanya.

"No, that's quite alright. I'm honoured to be here. In fact it's quite a miracle that I'm here at all."

"Can you tell us what happened?" Annika inquired with genuine interest.

Don went on the relate the morning's events. The phone call. The unexpected reaction of his principal. Being given the whole day off. Gulping down breakfast. The city peak-hour drive that was calmer than expected. Feeling strange about coming in through the staff entrance. How he didn't want his fifteen minutes of fame through the local newspaper or at a staff meeting.

Annika watched him closely as he spoke. His slightly posh Australian accent had her laughing on the inside.

"That is a really funny story. I love hearing your stories. You must tell me more."

"Oh, yeah, I have plenty more."

"Well I move that we begin the day's proceedings," joked Tanya in a loud voice.

"Seconded," shouted Don.

"All in favour?"

Tanya and Don shot up their hands. Annika's hand went up slowly, but she was not sure why. *This is not a formal meeting. It must be the Australian sense of humour. Oh. That's it. I don't get it but it sure is funny.* After a second or two she let out a little giggle which Don found quite playful. They all laughed and moved off down the corridor.

The morning was spent in a kind of storeroom. It was crowded with numbered storage boxes, some on shelving, but most in piles on the floor. A television monitor on a desk at one end was used and the three of them squeezed around it on less than comfortable folding chairs. Tanya sat in the middle and gave commentary. Mainly native Australian and Pacific Islands dances and ceremonies. Don found it a touch boring after the first hour but Annika was obviously captivated. She asked about copies of the videos for her courses. Tanya would look into the copyright and see what she could do.

Don made the occasional comment on improving camera angles and things of a technical nature, just to stay involved. Annika was completely delighted to have met a man who would take an interest in her work. She was unaccustomed to her strange feelings, but she knew something was happening when their hands innocently brushed as they skirted around the piles of boxes to leave the room for morning tea.

The midmorning session looking at artefacts was

much more interesting for Don. He went to the car for his SLR camera and lagged a little behind the women as he took lots of close-up pictures. He asked a staff member to take a group shot. Later he thought he should get a group shot with the cartouche. Hearing the idea, Tanya reached for her phone and within ten minutes they were in Dr Tauber's office, wearing white gloves and displaying the stone. Helen Peters appeared with a photographer also. Don asked for a copy of the photo and was promised one.

There was work to be done and a public to entertain and educate. They all stood and said farewells. The museum staff exited one by one. Finally, Tanya decided to return to her office and asked Don to take over hosting duties. It was only lunchtime. Not knowing the Brisbane restaurant scene, he offered to take Annika to lunch at the airport. They would have a few hours to chat. She seemed happy with that.

This is when a degree of trepidation set in for both of them. A few awkward words concerning luggage were exchanged. From the corner of Room 121 Annika grabbed her large red suitcase covered with various tags and stickers and they headed for the carpark.

The Peugeot was parked out on its own. When Don indicated where they were headed, she let out a subdued shriek of delight. *A well-polished classic European car, even if it is French. This man is amazing.* She loved fine, polished machinery too. She listened to another of Don's funny stories as the suitcase went into the carefully partitioned boot. There followed a brief inspection of the vehicle. The bonnet was lifted. The seats were stroked. Eventually she slipped elegantly into the passenger seat as Don looked away and pretended to adjust his exterior mirror. Awkward. To break the tension she began to tell him about her motorcycle. His eyes lit up almost in unison with the engine turning over. The old Pug lunged forward towards the exit.

The drive to the airport was smooth. The conversations started to become a bit more relaxed and personal. Where they lived. Their families. She liked the sound of family gatherings on the northern beaches of Sydney, a city she had yet to visit. He felt more compassionate towards her. Her family was split and her father was remarrying and selling the family home. *That would be traumatic.* Both began to feel a little more relaxed in each other's presence. She commented on his smooth driving style. He gave credit to the car. Then she began to confide.

"I'm nearly twenty-nine and I have never had a boyfriend. I have plenty of acquaintances of course but I have never been able to form a close bond. If I was married I would buy my parents' house. It's our family home. I'd like to keep it in the family but I just can't do it. My brother and sister are not interested either. It's the same with the cartouche. I'd like to see it go back to its home in China. It would be so special to the community there. Maybe we could work out a deal to get it back to them."

As she spoke, Don had been glancing at her stockinged knees as the red skirt had ridden up a little. She was aware of his glance but somehow she liked the attention and made no attempt to pull the skirt down. He stopped looking when she mentioned returning the artefact to China.

"I hadn't thought about that. It would be a bit like Britain returning the Elgin marbles to the Parthenon. Wouldn't it?"

"That will never happen," she said. "Not without a war."

Donald smirked. *She mentioned the war!* Then, just like the British Museum, he came out with a justification for displaying a heritage piece in a new context. He wondered where those thoughts came from, but he had read something. Annika was very impressed that he was so well informed.

"Tell me about your dissertation," she said.

"Er. Well. I did a longitudinal study, over only three years mind you, of a group of non-English speaking migrants who had come to Australia and their post arrival progress in mathematics as opposed to English language. It involved videos of interviews, using an interpreter, developing and administering tests and surveys. It was only a pilot study of thirty-five students, but I wrote the thesis and a little book on it. The Maths Education Department at the University still use it as a supplementary text in their courses. I've been asked to come in a couple of times to give guest lectures on my study. I really enjoyed that more than I do teaching classroom maths. But this year I'll be teaching physics as well. I'm looking forward to that because I'll be doing mechanical and electrical experiments with the students. They'll love the practical approach."

They had parked in the Brisbane International Terminal carpark while Don was still talking. She discerned that he was essentially an academic. *A true researcher. Interested in discovering new things.* He opened the boot and lifted out her case. In the sunlight she saw that his storage compartments were so well constructed and organised. He had built in bespoke storage for tools and other devices. She thought she may have spotted a partly dismantled boom microphone or tripod.

Don carried the case for her, saying he did not like the trundling noise. It wore out the bearings in the wheels. She was quickly becoming more and more impressed. *Is this the kind of assistant I will need for my dance research. maybe in China? He would be great in the field and a well-educated and valuable native English-speaking proof-reader for my papers. But that would be a very professional relationship. Do I want that? Maybe not. He's such a lovely man. I want to see him some more.* She gave him no inkling of what she was thinking.

In his appealingly awkward manner Don led her to the check-in counter. He deposited the red suitcase onto the scales with little effort. *It weighs 22.5 kilograms. He's strong.* Being now unburdened, he offered to take her carry-on bag, a maroon leather satchel containing her laptop and other necessaries. When she willingly handed it over he knew for certain that there was trust growing between them. Perhaps even a little romantic spark.

She had sensed this the previous evening and was now more willing to pursue it. Her smile and the gentle brush of her hand were intended to communicate her growing interest. He still felt a bit klutzy around her. He's adorable, she thought.

Following the check-in procedure they headed up the escalator to the departures level. Security. He had to place his phone, wallet, belt and keys in the x-ray tray. She, on the other hand, had to unpack her computer, peripherals, make-up, and a bunch of other paraphernalia. Then the metal detector beeped her. She was required to remove her shoes and a metal pendant. Turning to him, she asked him to unclasp the pendant as she bent down to remove her shoes. There was that stirring in his loins again. He smiled and placed her items in another tray while she went through for the second time.

Moments later he was walking out of the detector himself. It was like meeting her again. Something had changed by the mere fact of assisting her to remove personal items. He held her bag as she repacked it. He even leaned over several trays to grab her shoes. Then she helped him thread his belt back through the keepers. They laughed at the goofiness of the situation. It was one she had often been in but had never before shared with a young man. As he looked into her eyes, her face lit up with the most radiant smile he had ever seen. No words of thanks were required.

With all their accessories back in place it was close to 4.00pm. Time to eat a late lunch or an early dinner.

"I just hope we can find somewhere decent here," he said as they ambled along looking around.

"What do you mean by decent?" she asked, forcing him to come up with some sort of scholarly definition.

"Well. Good food – not takeaway junk. Um. A pleasant table where we can sit and talk…er…Maybe some wine?"

She already had spotted a little restaurant with no customers, small round tables for two and a bar. In fact she had eaten there with the Taubers two days previously. Taking his arm she turned him slightly and pointed.

"I like that one over there." He nodded and was in no way offended that she had taken the initiative. At this point in time he needed some direction.

He was pleased with the choice because it enabled him to lavish on her the sumptuous meal he had wished for. It was a little restaurant in the corner of the food court that everybody else obviously thought was too expensive or they just didn't have time for a proper sit-down meal.

The two (they could not be called a couple) sat opposite each other at a small corner table. Knees brushed from time to time. They talked and laughed about the long flight to Frankfurt via Singapore and the cramped aircraft seating a bit similar to what they were currently experiencing. Knees seemed to brush more readily as they laughed. Don revealed that he had never been out of Australia. His sister had been to Thailand for a holiday once. Their knees touched a little more solidly under the table. There was that feeling again. This time both of them felt a tingling. *Wow, that was not static electricity.*

The cook took a long time to prepare their meal of lamb shanks with vegetables. They did not mind waiting. The first course was delicious. Annika took up Don's suggestion of pavlova for dessert. As they talked and picked at their 'pavs' the conversation turned to Annika's research aspirations. Don was all ears. The idea of visiting exotic locations and learning new things aligned so perfectly with his own aspirations.

The meal over, they stood and looked at each other wondering how to spend the next half hour.

"A farewell drink?" Annika once again took the initiative.

There were stools tucked under the bar. He gently lifted one out for her and watched as she sat. *Her legs are beautiful.* He had a mojito, she a white wine. The staff wondered why they were still there. Most customers had a plane to catch. The talk about research took a different tack. Capturing ethic dances on video. That had his attention. He suggested the type of equipment she may require. She was impressed but kept it well hidden.

Eventually the bill was paid and it was time for Annika to go to the departure gate. Arriving there they discovered that it was crowded. Without saying a word they turned and walked over to some empty seating near the next gate. There was a bench seat on which to say their final farewells. Don went to shake hands. She laughed and leaned forward to give him just the lightest touch of her cheek on his. *Another*

European thing? Stunned, he took her hand to shake it but just held it while they thanked each other profusely and agreed to keep in touch. She gave him her business card. He didn't have one to offer but said he would email his contact details. The final call came over the speakers. They both felt a little sad to part so soon. There was a backwards glance and smile as she walked off shouldering her satchel. She was a seasoned traveller who could sleep on a long-haul flight.

Donald went home wondering what had just happened. *Will I ever see her again?* He determined to make up a business card that he could send to her.

Chapter 22

'Green Willows'. Late March 2006.

Feeling exhilarated and at the same time exhausted from restless sleep, Don climbed out of bed at six the next morning and went straight to his computer. The business card mock-up from last night was there on the screen. He checked it for accuracy and went into his email program to send it to Annika. To his great surprise there were two new emails waiting for him. The most recent was from Annika. She had emailed him while waiting to board her flight at Brisbane International the previous night.

> *Hallo Don,*
> *I just want to thank you for your hospitality and your wonderful company during my stay in Brisbane. I am on the plane waiting to take off for Singapore, then on to Frankfurt. The cartouche is very special. I think we will uncover more about it. Please keep in touch with me.*
> *Best wishes,*
> *Annika*
> *PS. Here is a photograph of me dancing in costume. It was taken last year in Barcelona. I hope you like it.*

Annika had mentioned that she would start writing messages of thanks to everyone she had met on her trip while she waited in her departure lounges. *She wrote to me on the plane. Was I the first one she wrote to? I guess I must have been.* This time Don received more than he expected. He uploaded the image and watched it slowly tumble into place down his screen. It was Annika in a full red Spanish flamenco dress with black shoes, her black hair tied up with red ribbon, her teeth bearing a red rose and her hands raised with castanets. It was a truly beautiful image.

Immediately he printed the photograph in full colour on glossy photographic paper. It would be framed and placed proudly on his lounge room display unit. For the rest of the day he would be reflecting on how she had thought about him. He rechecked the time stamp on the email and figured that he really must have been her first 'thank you' message. It was sent less than ten minutes after they said goodbye. *She wants to maintain contact. Have I now got a long-distance girlfriend? I haven't got a recent photo of myself to send her. Should I even do such a thing?*

The second email had been sent earlier than Annika's. It was from the Museum photographer who had remembered that Don wanted the group photo as soon as possible. He downloaded the attachment. There they all were. He thought he detected that Annika's eyes were looking at him and not directly at the photographer. This was the only formal picture he had so he wasted no time in forwarding it to his principal with just a short note of explanation. That task was out of the way. He showered, partook of a bite to eat and headed off to work.

The 8.00am daily staff briefing started five minutes late. Principal Len had a laptop and projector and put up the image Don had sent him. He said a few words of congratulations to a staff member who was a quiet achiever. Then, to his great embarrassment, Don was called upon to speak.

He stood rather hesitantly but was not lacking confidence in front of his colleagues so he described the cartouche, identified the people in the image, the curators, the German Professor and the Museum Administrator then said precisely two sentences about it having historical significance in Queensland. This was followed by subdued applause, a ripple of surprised remarks and a few mumbles from those who had covered his Tuesday morning classes.

Then came the announcement that the rugby team had been victorious. Again he stood up as coach and nodded his appreciation of the restrained clapping. Australians are not always supportive of achievers. Don did not want to be considered a tall poppy so he lowered his head. He was saved further embarrassment as the bell rang for home class. The teachers raced out the doors. *Amazing how urgently they need to leave a meeting!* There were plenty of quick congratulations and a few slaps on the shoulder.

There was also, "I had to take your bloody year nine maths class so you'd better cover my drama class next week when I'm out for the day." Don's least favourite cover lesson was drama. The brief was always the same. 'The students break up into groups and rehearse their lines.' Invariably they would disappear and he would have no idea what they were doing. He would be spending most of his time just searching for them behind racks of costumes or in bushes outside the drama room door. That put a slightly sour edge on his awkward start to the working day.

That day eventually turned out to be one of the worst in his short teaching career. He had not had time to prepare his lessons. He only glanced at his work programs to find where he was up to. The planning was done in the smallest room in the school, the doorway as he entered the classroom. The period two lesson was with his year nine maths group of lower ability. From the outset of the term the girls in the class had taken a dislike to him. This morning they chose to execute their wicked scheme. Several of them toppled simultaneously from their chairs during class. He ran over to help them up and see they were not hurt. When they laughed he reprimanded them. There was a well-known saying around the schools that 'year 9 are animals'. Don could well believe it. Fortunately, the other classes that day were better. They were mostly senior groups with more maturity and better application to their work. He had begun to find his physics class more difficult with two very bright, engaged boys and three others struggling with the concepts. *Senior physics is always a bit hard for students at first. They'll get it after a while.*

Don was preparing lessons at his desk around four thirty when Len phoned and asked him to come over to the office. He thought it would be about the museum business. But when he arrived, he was informed that a parent had phoned in to say that Don had molested her daughter in the year 9 maths class. Len had no option but to stand him down from teaching duties until the matter had been investigated. It was the worst experience in his eight years on the job. He was asked to leave immediately and return to the office at ten o'clock next morning. Then the extra workload. Would he please email in work for his classes for the next two days before eight in the morning? It was the most unhappy ending to a day that should have been a triumph.

He went home deflated and told nobody what had happened. That evening he moped around the house doing little odd jobs and wondering how his career had come to this. *A great day at the museum. Followed immediately by a bummer of a day at school. How unpredictable life can be. A real rollercoaster ride. Tomorrow is going to be another dark one for me.*

Arriving at Len's office on time, Don was greeted by Marion Higgs, the Girls' Supervisor, who escorted him into the principal's office. Len introduced Mrs Jones and her defiant-looking daughter Jessica. Both sides put their stories forward. The principal asked Jessica what Mr Kirk had done.

"We fell off our chairs. Then he looked up our dresses. Then he grabbed me."

"Where do you expect a teacher to look if you fall over, away from you?" asked Len.

"No," she pouted.

"And if you fall, do you expect him to help you up?"

"'S'pose so." Jessica turned away.

"Which parts of you did he touch?"

"My arms."

"Just helped you up by the arms?"

"Yeah, but I didn't want to be touched by him. He didn't ask me. He just grabbed me." The pouting continued. Len turned to the mother.

"Well, Mrs Jones, I think we have a misunderstanding here. This teacher has taken the correct course of action to help her but unfortunately Jessica has misinterpreted his actions. I'm sorry this has occurred and I'm sure Mr Kirk will try to make his intentions clearer next time."

"There had better not be a next time. I want Jess out of his class," said the protective parent.

"We'll be happy to look at that for you, but for now can we let the matter drop? It's important that we agree that no further accusations will be made and that the school has adequately dealt with your complaint. Mr Kirk will be given some guidance to help him deal with these situations if they should occur in future."

"Yeah. Guess so. But I want her out of that class."

After a brief but generally convivial chat about other aspects of school life, the parent and child left.

Don was counselled by the Principal and Girl's Supervisor. That was done according to regulations but the conversation was friendly and he was reinstated immediately to recommence next morning. Despite his exoneration Don felt devastated. He had been riding along on a wave of success and the wind had been taken out of his sails. For the first time in his life he began to feel very uneasy about being a teacher.

Len sensed that he was feeling down. In an effort to buoy up his spirits he shared a little piece of more positive news. His physics class of five boys had now been reduced to two. Three had decided on easier study options. Len went to pains to assure him that the boys had indicated it was definitely not Mr Kirk's teaching that had made them change subjects. Physics was just too hard. That class would certainly not be economically viable for the school but for Don it might become his special interval of daily calm, doing experiments with two motivated and bright boys who liked having him as their teacher.

He made his way home and again did some chores to take his mind off the trauma of his morning. After an easy lunch of cheese on white bread, he opened his email and found this:

Hallo Donny,
Hope you don't mind me calling you that. I listened to some Irish music on the flight. James Galway was playing Danny Boy on the flute. It was beautiful. Donny Boy was going around in my head. I'm here in Singapore waiting for my next flight to Frankfurt. The flowers in the airport are beautiful. I would

*just like to thank you again for your help and
encouragement. How did you like the
photograph I sent you? Please keep in touch.
With Love,
Annika*

*Donny? Donny Boy? With love? Is she still
thinking about me?* In his turbulent mind he felt as if
he was experiencing the most ginormous
rollercoaster ride life had to offer. This gorgeous
German professor had spent eight hours on a plane
thinking about him and her first action on arrival
was to not so subtly tell him so.

He decided to send her a gift. Something uniquely
Australian. As he looked around the house, he found
a flat steel gecko wall ornament beautifully painted
in an aboriginal dot design. He had planned to hang
it upside down with the lizard walking down the
wall but he just had not gotten around to doing it. *It
would look great in Annika's Dance Academy.*
Although it was brand new, he meticulously cleaned
and polished it and decided to make a card. Then he
remembered he had no photo of himself so he
hastily set up his SLR on a tripod in the garden with
gum trees in the background. *She was in costume.
Maybe I should be too. Australian clothes?* He
donned his Akubra hat, Steve-Irwin-style khaki shirt
and shorts and sat waiting for the timer to release the
shutter. He did this at least ten times, contorting into
successively more Indiana-Jones-like poses as the
session progressed. One of the images was notably
better than the others, a cloud had come

momentarily across the sun and his face showed less of the harsh contrast of the Australian light. He made and printed a greeting card with that image. His wording was carefully considered. She had to know that he liked her calling him Donny.

> *To My Dear Annika,*
> *I was so pleased to meet you in Brisbane.*
> *Thank you for the beautiful photograph you*
> *sent me. I hope you will like the Australian*
> *Indigenous design on this tin gecko. I thought*
> *it would be so appropriate on the wall of your*
> *Dance School, walking down your wall with*
> *such wonderful poise and balance, just like a*
> *dancer.*
> *With my deepest regards,*
> *Donny*

He quickly bundled everything up in bubble wrap and drove to the post office where he picked out a postage bag, copied the details of her Goslar address, signed the customs form and sent the item by international express post. It cost nearly seventy dollars to send an item for which he had paid only thirty. Normally that would have concerned him but now the wind was picking up again in his sails and he knew it would be worth the expense.

Chapter 23

Frankfurt, Germany. Late March 2006.

Waiting on the Fernbahnhof platform at Frankfurt Airport for her train to Bremen, Annika opened her email.

> *Hi Annika,*
> *Just a little note to let you know that I thought your photograph was beautiful. I have framed it and it stands proudly in my home. I am honoured and delighted to have met you. There is a parcel for you on the way to your Goslar Academy by express post. Look out for it over the next week. I hope you will like it. I have attached a copy of the group photo from the museum, just in case you haven't seen it.*
> *Best regards,*
> *Donny Boy*

My picture is framed and on display in his house? He must really like me. Donny Boy? He liked that too. Does he want me to call him Donny Boy? He's too much a man!

She went to stay overnight with her father in Delmenhorst. They talked long into the night about her trip. He could see there was a new glint in her eye when she mentioned Donny. Next day he drove her back to Goslar and had a brief inspection of her apartment and workplace. It took a great deal of restraint to keep from telling him about her deepening involvement with Chinese dissidents and secret communities. *Fortunately, this is a short visit.* He left after an early dinner to drive back to be with his Hella.

Next morning the hard work commenced. Annika began spending fourteen-hour days in the office, documenting her trip, cataloguing her videos, writing course outlines, lecture notes, handouts and filling in paperwork to have her course approved by the Academic Board. She took little breaks to do some of her ballet exercises while trying out the new barre that had been installed in her absence.

Meike proved to be an invaluable aide but her English was somewhat limited and there was a lot of editing to be done to her typing. After work Annika spent time with Lihua and Madam Long, telling them about the trip and gleaning a little more insight into their story. She presented them with a framed photograph of the group in the museum with the cartouche. The frame was red and gold. They were ecstatic to receive it.

A week had passed when Meike came into the office with a postal article. Annika opened it eagerly and held the gecko against the wall. They both liked the grace and ethnicity of it. Meike was taken with the exotic notion of the distant land downunder. It was a perfect piece of décor for their bland administrative suite. Annika read the card and quickly put it aside so that Meike would not see the photograph of Donny Boy in his jungle gear. They decided to put the new acquisition on the wall behind the reception desk, facing downwards as suggested. Meike called the handyman and it was hanging there within the hour. When Annika was alone in her office she looked again at the photograph of her Indigo Jones and composed an email to be sent from her private Googlemail account.

My Dear Donny Boy,
Thank you so much for the very thoughtful piece of Australian artwork. It is the first object we have mounted on the wall of our School office and it steps proudly down the wall behind my personal assistant Meike's desk at reception. Everybody will see it there. You are correct, it is very appropriate for a school that teaches about international dance. We love it very much. Thank you. I have attached a photograph of Meike with the lizard.
I gave my Chinese colleagues a framed copy of the group photograph from the museum. They were wild with excitement over that. I would really like to try to have the cartouche returned to China. Do you think we could do that? Probably not but it is worth trying again.
I have been very busy back in the office, but I will email you again soon. I hope your classes are going very well.
I liked the photograph you put on the card. Would you send me a digital copy? Please write to me again soon.
Mit Liebe,
Annika

She went back to her paperwork. There were now twenty-three confirmed enrolments in her course commencing in August. She would be busy for weeks finding specialist dance teachers and interviewing them. Arrangements would have to be made to use a larger hall in Goslar as her wooden floor would only be adequate for demonstrations, not for full tuition. There would be more student interviews and finally a meeting with the Academic Board to discuss her course and research aspirations.

The weeks passed quickly. Annika and Donny Boy exchanged short messages every other day. He was astounded when she signed off with 'Ich liebe Dich', on many of them. He knew little German but he did know that expression and it melted his heart. He also saw pictures of Meike and he liked what he saw. Two beautiful women in the same office.

Annika was a dynamo. The Academic Board approved her course and wanted to support her research into Chinese Dance. There were many Chinese people living and working in Germany and this would be a drawcard for the Academy. Meike, with rather reluctant consent from the Professor of Music, was given a third day of work in the School of Dance. Together the women organised television and radio interviews to present to the public the new course and facilities and the stories of some of their talented students about to commence. Enquiries at the Academy were increasing and the Board of Directors was delighted at the lift in their public profile.

Shortly after the first classes had begun in August, Professor Jiang came up with a total surprise. The Research Sub-committee had approved in principle a research trip to Hubei Province in

China for the winter holiday break from June to August the following year, 2007. The budget was open and they wanted to possibly make a television documentary of the event. Annika was, of course, totally astounded and delighted. She would need to find a research assistant for that period with the technical skills to record quality footage and help her with the logistics of visiting an isolated community. She knew just the man. There was also a need for a Chinese-German-English interpreter. She knew just the woman. But would they be able to accompany her on this adventure? They both worked fulltime and may not be able to get away. Also Professor Jiang was a dissident and may not be able to re-enter China. The two livewire professors went to work on the idea.

Late one evening in September, Donny Boy's mobile phone rang. That was unusual as he had no close contacts who called at night.

"Hello, Don Kirk speaking," he answered without looking at the number.

"Hallo Donny. This is Annika. How are you?"

"Annika. I'm so glad to hear your voice again. I've missed you. I'm going well. A few hiccups at work but I'm getting through. You've been busy by the sounds of things. What are you up to?"

Her voice became more serious. "Donny, I have something to ask you."

He sat to attention now. *What's coming?*

"I have received provisional approval for a research trip to China next year from June to August. It is to study dance. And we'll be spending at least a week in the community where the Cartouche originated. I need a research assistant to help me with the recording and equipment. Would you be interested in coming with me?”

Donny Boy did not even have a passport. He gulped.

“Yes, of course I’d be interested. I would have to make some arrangements here of course but this may be just the change I am looking for in my life. When do you need to know by?”

“Oh, Donny Boy that’s wonderful. Just take your time. No hurry. It’s not until June next year. You’ll be needed for three months. You’ll be paid well. I’ll have Meike send you through more details of the offer. She will be helping us with the planning. Oh, that will be so good. I won’t keep you. I’ll send you emails as soon as I know more.”

“Wow, what a surprise. I don’t know what to say. What a wonderful surprise! I’m already looking forward to it. Just let me organise things here.”

“Of course. I’m sure you can work it out.”

They said goodbye and each thought each detected a faint kiss sound from the other. Donny Boy could not sleep that night. But it seemed not to matter.

The next morning he went straight to Principal Len, gave him the full story and asked about Long Service Leave for June to August next year. He was not eligible. He had not been in the system for ten years. Leave without pay? That would be too difficult for the school and detrimental to the continuity of teaching for the students. His only real option was to resign, forego his long service leave and take some cash in lieu. He went away to consider his options. Resigning from one's career path is a very big step into the great unknown. Nevertheless, he was already mentally planning his trip.

That evening Don composed a long email to Dr Tauber expressing his excitement at this new opportunity. He raised the issue of returning the artefact and then suggested what was to be a very agreeable alternative. He proposed scanning the cartouche, 3D printing it in polymer and having the restorers gild it and mount it for presentation as a gift to the Chinese community. He also asked whether there was any possibility of some equipment support as he needed to make a high-quality recording suitable for a television documentary.

When Dr Tauber received the message he was more exuberant than usual. This documentary could be a great piece of publicity for the Museum as well. He began to imagine a television special and an interactive museum display on the Gympie gold rush. The 3D printing idea was also well received. It was an emerging technology the Museum would like to have for creating replicas and here was a perfect reason for purchasing now. He could also offer Dr Kirk the use of some high-fidelity sound recording gear but not a TV camera.

This news came back to Don within a day and the pieces were starting to fit together. Of course, he kept his heartthrob fully informed. His passport took a few weeks to come through. He sent it on to the Chinese Embassy in Canberra for a short-term study visa for three months from June to August the following year. This was where the fun started. They refused. The region he proposed to visit was apparently restricted and off limits to Westerners. That was a blow to have to reveal to Annika and it threw him into a state of confusion.

Chapter 24

Annika printed out Don's email and rang Oriental Arts for an appointment. Between classes she walked over to Lihua's office and sat down with her. They had not bargained on visa refusals. So, they discussed at length the implications for their research trip. Perhaps they would just avoid going to the secret community. The thought of that upset them greatly. Maybe study visas for work in larger cities would be easier to obtain? After half an hour and with no further ideas they tried to relax over coffee. Lihua had not been her usual optimistic self. She obviously felt this burden very heavily. She took her first sip and suddenly her face lit up.

"I know. I will write a supporting document to the Chinese Embassy in Australia."

"How will that make a difference?"

"Well, if I can convince them to give Doktor Kirk a visa, then I can use that as a leverage to get our visas."

"Really?"

"Oh yes. The officials at these embassies are young. They don't know much about the Mao era. If I write a very good argument, they will give the visa. China wants to make friends with other countries and Australia is one of their important trade partners. I will write to them this weekend."

Chapter 25

'Green Wattles' Queensland. Mid-September 2006.

On Saturday morning Don Kirk opened the sliding door to his beloved shed. There were no geckos sleeping in the tracks and there was no scratching of water dragons sunning themselves on the roof so he walked in confidently. A little streak of brownish-grey and a slight movement drew his attention. Two mature geckoes, the largest he had seen, in a loving embrace tumbled from the rafters to the floor. The fall did not interrupt their coitus and he watched them writhing in obvious bliss for several seconds before they looked at him and ran away. While he did not feel any kind of arousal in seeing this, his curiosity was fired. He thought about how people with a passion of any kind can possibly become so hypnotised by it that they lose sight of life going on around them. He thought of Albert Einstein ignoring his wife to work on equations all night and he reflected on his own condition.

As he set up his microscope to photograph the pads on the foot of a dead gecko, a pivotal thought came to him. *Fixated on a passion. Perhaps that's my problem. Is that the wall that prevents me from socialising? Is that a bad thing? Are things changing as beautiful Annika is now interested in me? Is she my best friend? Really? Do we think alike? Am I actually more German than Scottish? Could my captivation with Annika be blinding me to the issues I'd face if I resigned from school?* The questions came flooding in. *This is perhaps the plight of the introvert mind. Insoluble questions by the truckload.*

There is a small country church in Burpengary, just up the road from Don's 'farm'. In good weather Don would attend a service there every second Sunday at 3.00pm. The preachers came from a number of evangelical churches and the small congregation of about twenty were almost all people older than himself. This was his only deference to his Christian family heritage. He did not know the people well and he generally left during the final hymn before he would have to spill out his life to strangers over tea and a dry biscuit.

On the third Sunday in September he actually knew the preacher and waited behind to speak with him. His name was Col Chalmers and he was a layman who lived across the road from the church and maintained the grounds. A grey-haired man with the face of an old farmer and an astute ability to discern, Col could see that Don needed to talk so he invited him to walk across to his home. That was difficult to refuse.

Within minutes he found himself sitting in the lounge room of the Chalmers' house. The décor was simple and dated. There was a slightly musty smell although everything looked to be well cared for. Col and his wife Mary prepared coffee and scones in the separate kitchen. Don looked around at the lounge room walls. Almost blending into the floral wallpaper there were two framed religious prints that particularly grabbed his attention. *I've seen these before. In Sunday School?* The first was the famous Holman Hunt picture of Jesus standing at the door knocking. He was amused as he thought about the that. *Is Jesus waiting to see if any geckoes fall when the door opens? No. He already knows where they are!* The second print was one of Peter stepping out of a boat onto the Sea of Galilee to walk on water. *That's a bit how I feel at the moment!*

When the coffee was served, Mary left the two boys to talk. Don mentioned the pictures he had noticed. Then Col began to preach another sermon.

"Yes, Don. It says in the Book of Revelation that Jesus stands at the door of our hearts and knocks. If we open the door he will come in and sup with us. You'll notice there's no handle on the outside of that door. We have to open it ourselves from the inside. Here, have a scone."

Although Don had heard this teaching many times before in sermons, this time it was more personal for him. The shed door experiences made it more real in his mind. *Perhaps there is something missing in my life. Certainly, my avoidance of people must mean there is a gap. But also, there might be a lack of faith, whatever that is.*

He said the other picture made him think because, like Peter, he was about to take a big step out into the great unknown. He spent the next twenty minutes, almost uninterrupted, telling his newfound confidante about his situation. He talked about Annika but tried to conceal his growing passion for her. Eventually it came out that he was in love. Col listened intently and did not want to interrupt. He knew Don was a bit of a loner and had not had long conversations with the other people in the congregation, ever.

"I hope I'm doing the right thing. You know, resigning from teaching. And I'm worried about the visa not coming through," Don said in summary.

"Mate. Everything you just told me shows me that you are doing the right thing. I'm especially impressed that you wanted to tell somebody about your thoughts and feelings. Aussie blokes don't do that enough. I think that you've just got a narrow perspective on the world. A bit like looking down a microscope."

Don was immediately engaged and considerably amazed. He hadn't mentioned his microscope. *Perhaps this man has some special power?*

Col went on to say, "and it's like going through the door. When you go from your house to the yard, your perspective is immediately changed. You know what's in both but it's totally different being in them. Then you go into your man cave and it's different again."

Don sat involuntarily to attention! He had not talked about his shed. So he began to tell Col about the geckoes and water dragons.

"Well mate. God's creation teaches us lessons all the time. I love being out in the paddock. I have a few acres, you know, and I see something different out there every day. When I see something special, I say to myself there's a sermon in that! We're alike.

We see meaning and signs all around us. You've picked up that your season in life is changing. You want to resign from teaching and do something entirely different. This girl Ann something. She sounds wonderful. Get to know her. You said you want to do a TV production course. Just go and do it. Then work a bit in Germany and in China and you'll see things differently. You'll know where you're going after that. That's the way God shows us His plans for our lives, I'm pretty sure of that. It's taking a step out in faith. You know, faith is a now thing, not something in the future. You have to take the step now. Rent your place out. I'll keep an eye on it and mow it for you if you like. Anyway, when you get back we'll want to see your TV show and have you speak at our men's group in Caboolture. You're a very inspirational person and I think you could help other blokes to start to share more."

Me? Inspirational? I've never heard that one before. I like this guy.

"I can't thank you and Mary enough. The talk was great. The scones were beautiful? Were they Lady Flo Bjelke-Petersen's recipe?"

"Yes mate. How did you know that?"

"Oh, I read a bit. The Bjelke-Petersens were politicians but they also stepped out of the boat so to speak. They made a real impression whether you agreed or disagreed with them. Even an impression in the kitchens and cafes of Australia."

"Ha. Yes. You never really know what influence you have. You'd be aware of that as a schoolteacher. Those kids will remember you for the rest of their lives."

Don was again sitting to attention. He knew Jessica Jones and his two year 12 physics students would remember him for totally different reasons. He still wondered about resigning from teaching and raised the topic again.

"You can always go back into teaching with your new perspectives. Your qualifications won't change and you'll have more experience. But listen, I can see the cogs turning in your head. You know, Christianity is not a set of principles or doctrines. It's a simple faith. You mustn't overthink things. Just step out and do it. It's like that with most things in life, isn't it? You just gotta have a go. Hey, you've got a bible haven't you?"

"Yes, I have a few of those."

"Well, promise me you'll go home and read Hebrews Chapter 11. Then you'll understand those pictures up there."

"Sure, okay."

Col smiled, reached across to touch his shoulder and led him in a short prayer asking for confirmation about his future.

Don drove the short distance home with a new outlook. He walked in his front door and saw the house in a different way. Sitting up in bed with a New King James translation he read Hebrews 11. *Faith. Not the things you hope for. It's the evidence of things not seen. What does that mean? I think it's your life taking a sort of step into the unknown. You can't plan for it. You just do it. Like Col said, it's a now thing. I'm still not sure.*

Sometime after 11.00pm he was puttering around in cyberspace when he decided to put his laptop to sleep. One last check of the emails. He sat bolt upright. A golden image of the cartouche symbol appeared with a short message.

> *With Greetings Herr Doktor Donald Kirk*
> *My name is Professor Jiang Lihua. I am head*
> *of Oriental Arts Harz Academy. I am a work*
> *colleague of Professor Annika Fluss. We*
> *discussed the visa problem. I wrote a note in*
> *Chinese. It is attached. You should print it*
> *and send a new application for a study visa to*
> *the Chinese Embassy. If you send this note as*
> *a supporting document they will give you the*
> *visa. I am sure of this.*
> *Friendly Good Thoughts*
> *Jiang*

He assumed that this message came from one of Annika's Chinese informants. As he opened the attachment a high-resolution image of a page of hand-drawn Chinese characters rolled onto the screen. He could make out no meaning from it. *Surely it has to be worth another try.* He printed the page, downloaded a fresh visa application form and set to work.

It was well after midnight as he sealed the documents and his passport into an envelope ready for express post that day.

This unexpected message had given him a new optimism. He fell asleep thinking that perhaps Col

Chalmers' prayer for him had been answered.

Chapter 26

Goslar, Germany. Early October 2006.

A new door plaque in keeping with the period building read 'Tanzschule – School of Dance' over a slightly smaller font announcing: 'Professor Anika Fluss.' German workers are generally very meticulous, but on this occasion the signage contractor had neglected to see that there was a variant spelling of the Christian name involved here.

"Meike, could you please telephone the sign company and have them fix this up?"

"I have already. Somebody is coming around this morning."

"You are so efficient. Your blood's worth bottling."

"You want to take my blood?"

"Ha, ha. No. Of course not. It's an English expression I learned. It means you are invaluable to us."

"Oh. Thank you. I love working here. Would you like coffee?"

"Yes please. And could you arrange for somebody to come and fix my microphone downstairs. I'm not satisfied with the sound. It's a little crackly. In fact, get the people who installed it to come and replace it."

Since commencing her lecture course Annika had begun to establish herself more as a no-nonsense, professional academic and less as the friendly village dance teacher. Meike liked her direct style and quickly launched into dealing with the various contacts in the same efficient way. Within minutes she had the electrician organised to replace the faulty microphone. This was accomplished with a swift but totally enchanting affability that no service provider could argue with. The plaque was removed and came back next day corrected and artistically enhanced. The young installer was very willing to demonstrate his work to Meike. Despite her young age, she was getting a reputation in the city as a schönes Mädchen through her very frequent and pleasant community interactions. The microphone was a more difficult achievement. But she handled it with ease.

"There is nothing wrong with this microphone," the electrician said with frustration in his eyes.

"Well Professor Fluss does not like the crackling sound."

"A little bit of feedback is normal with these."

"Well it is not good enough for the Harz Academy. If you want more work from us then you must replace it with a better one. Would you like me to get the professor to come down?"

"No. No. I have a more expensive one. I could fit that, but there will be a cost. I have a brochure."

"Come upstairs and have a coffee with me. We can get Professor Fluss to authorize it."

"I would like to but I have a busy schedule today. I will fit the new one. No extra charge, just for you."

"Oh. Thank you. Professor Fluss will be so pleased."

Annika came walking down the stairs at that time. She had heard everything and gave a smile of approval. The man went to work. She motioned to Meike to join her outside the building.

"You are doing a great job. Has my name been changed on the sign?"

"Yes. It looks better than before."

After admiring and approving the new plaque, Annika took a telephone call in her office.

"Fluss."

"Annika, it's Lihua here. Something sad has happened."

Annika feared for Madam Long's life.

Lihua continued, "Herr Behrmann, one of our very first steering committee members of our Academy has died in Hannover. He was an old man. Eighty-five years. He was the one who invited me to come to Goslar. He is a very special friend and through him I was reunited with Senta."

Annika did not see the reason for her use of the word 'reunited' but since this was a sensitive conversation, she allowed Lihua to continue.

"My mother and I visited him last week in the hospital. We heard he was very ill. I would have liked you to meet him but, of course, it's too late for that now. But I'd like you to come to the funeral with us next Monday. You will learn a lot about the Academy when his eulogy is given. It will be a little part of the history of the Academy that you can be a part of. Will you come? It's at the Evangelishes Kirkencentrum at Kronberg. The service is at thirteen hundred hours. I'll pick you up at nine hundred so we can have a light lunch before it gets under way."

Annika thought that funerals could be sad and upsetting but she wanted very much to be a part of the Academy so she agreed to go. After only a short time working together she had the utmost confidence that Meike would do an admirable job in the office for the day. She thanked Lihua and went back to her planning documents. Course modifications were required to incorporate more content on the Pacific Islands and Australia so that she could use the DVDs kindly sent to her as a gift from Curator Tanya Pierce in Brisbane.

The day of the funeral came around quickly. It was a sunnier day than there had been for many weeks. The autobahn was relatively clear of traffic and the 95-kilometre trip took only an hour. Lihua and Annika sat in the front chatting about the Academy in general. Small talk really. Madam Long sat in the back listening without comprehension.

On arrival in the suburbs of Hannover it was morning teatime. Lihua made a call and Senta came to meet with them at a café. The four women began chatting. Well, three actually. Madam Long received only smidgeons translated by her daughter. It did not take very long before Annika realised that this was a pre-arranged meeting. She listened carefully as Senta did most of the talking and initially she could not understand why it seemed to be directed at her.

"Annika, let me tell you a little about Herr Behrmann. He used to teach mechanical engineering in a university in Shanghai. His wife Jia Jaiying was also a tutor there. She came from a little place near Wuhan in Hubei Province. Herr Behrmann was a German citizen who had a good command of Mandarin. He was a truly brilliant man. They fell in love and married back in the early nineteen-fifties."

Annika was starting to become a little restless with all this detail. She did not know the man and she would hear all this again in the eulogy. But she could not interrupt. Senta noticed her unease and went straight to the point.

"Annika, prepare yourself for a shock. Herr Behrmann is actually your biological grandfather. I am his daughter and Heide, your mother, is my sister. We are his two biological daughters. In 1975 he had to suddenly leave China with us two girls when his wife, Jai Jaiying, was imprisoned as a dissident. We were only eleven and nine-years-old at the time. We don't know what happened to our mother or whether she is still alive. When we came to Germany our father feared for his life and had to go into hiding so he decided to place us in long term foster care. We were fostered by two different families, one in Bremen and one in Hannover. Your mother became known as Heide Fischer and I became Senta Wagner."

"Then the Fischers are my foster grandparents? I always thought Mama didn't look very much like them. She has dark hair and eyes and they both have fair complexions. My mother married my father, Gerhardt Fluss, in 1976 when she was twenty-two. Then I came along in 1977," said Annika, trying to put the pieces together.

"That's right. The foster families were not told very much about our real parents so over time they were consigned to the backs of our minds as we went through school here in Germany," said Senta regretfully.

"Did Herr Behrmann visit you? Did he want to take you back to live with him?"

"He did see us at a sort of secret meeting in a park on at least three occasions but he was very protective and did not want any Chinese spies to find us. Then he went to stay with friends in Erfurt which was in East Germany. I don't know how he crossed the border but he was not able to return to the West until after 1989 when the wall came down. By that time we had both moved away from our foster families and he decided we would be better off without him complicating our lives. So he worked in Goslar for some years and later retired back to Hannover. All the time he wanted to reunite the family but he was constantly wary of being watched. Now that he has passed away all these secrets can be shared within the family, but we still need to be careful about who else we tell."

"And so you are actually my aunt?" probed Annika with tears in her eyes. Senta nodded vigorously towards her.

At this point the ladies were all in tears and Senta was hugging her niece as the coffee and sandwiches arrived. Sensing the emotion of the group, the waitress hastily withdrew with a quick "bon appetit" appropriate for the somewhat French style of the café.

Annika could barely contain her emotions. Yet she wanted Senta to tell her more. She felt a rising resentment that all these things had been kept from her for so long but that was accompanied by an incredible desire to delve deeper into the story of her family. The funeral had taken on a new perspective and she now realised that the other ladies had orchestrated her invitation as part of the family reunion that Senta had mentioned before. But there was much more to it.

"Heide and I did see each other on a few occasions. They were planned meetings, usually in Hannover, but we never visited each other at home or anything like that until we were in our late twenties. We seemed more like cousins than sisters."

"So you were not very close?"

"No. Not really. I did go to her wedding but I stayed in the background. I went as an old school friend she had invited. I only ever saw pictures of you and your brother and sister. I was very upset when she left to go to England with you all, because I wanted to see you grow up. But she is part Chinese, as we all are, and saving face is very important. When she had a marriage breakdown after a few years, she simply had to leave your father in Germany. That is why she won't be here today, but she sent flowers and will be watching the funeral on a live feed so you can say hallo to her."

"Does my father know any of this?"

"No, he was never told. Heide is very good at keeping silent and he just accepted that her parents were the Fischers."

She then went on to explain that Professor Jiang also worked at the same university in Shanghai and knew the Behrmanns well.

"Lihua's husband and her father were both arrested as dissidents in 1975. Lihua was able to escape to Hong Kong with her mother. Herr Behrmann sponsored them to come to Germany to seek asylum and finally found them positions in Hamburg. Last week he had visits from myself and Lihua and his final wish was for us to continue to reunite the family. He and Lihua worked together to bring you to Goslar. He wanted you here, Annika."

"My grandfather's funeral? And I never met him?"

"Well, to be honest you did meet him once when you were a little girl. We all met at the *Tiergarten* in Hannover in the early 1980s. Do you remember the animals in the zoo?"

"Yes. I was about six, I suppose."

"The man you met was Herr Behrmann."

"Uncle Friedrich?"

"Yes. And I was introduced to you as Aunty Greta."

"It's coming back to me now." Tears welled up in her eyes.

"When your father remarries there is a plan to bring Heide back here too, but she's not ready to come yet. I hope you can understand all this, it's a lot to take in. You're a strong person and we know this is sudden, but you had to know before the funeral."

Annika was stunned. She was not often lost for

words but right now she was dumbfounded. So many questions were racing through her head. *Why wasn't I told earlier? Is my grandmother still alive? Uncle Friedrich was my grandfather? I'm one quarter Chinese? Is that why I am so motivated to do this research?* She had opportunity to ask only a few more details as they ate their sandwiches and travelled over to the church. Then it hit her. *They have new identities. I don't know the real names of any of these women, including my mother.* But she was finding out her own true identity, bit by bit. *I must phone Donny after the funeral.*

"Do my brother and sister know about this?"

"Yes, they are with Heide. She is explaining it to them. They will be watching from England. The family is being reunited there too. You must travel to see her as soon as you can. It's only a short flight."

"I know it is. I'm happy to do that. What about my father? Should we tell him something?"

"He actually does not know very much about this, but he will find out more in time. It is twenty years since they separated. Heide didn't want us to invite him as it might upset his wedding plans to know so much more about her. He was deemed to be a slight risk to her anonymity, so she never shared a lot with him. You can all share it with him after his wedding if you wish," explained Senta.

They were joined at the funeral by Uwe Holzmann, Senta's husband. The couple had no children and Uwe knew the story. Their dinner in Goslar had been set up so that they could meet

Annika. This was, of necessity, a very discreet and almost secretive family but, on the other hand, they were beautiful, sensitive people who planned to gently bring about one of the most amazing family reunions ever. Herr Behrmann's sudden death had simply accelerated the process.

The church was elegantly dressed in the most amazing floral display in red and white. The congregation was overflowing into the foyer and the hymns were bright and very loudly sung. Herr Behrmann was a much loved and devout Christian man. His funeral was a happy celebration of a life well lived. Annika would never see life in the same way again. She wept through the eulogy knowing that many aspects of his life were not mentioned. She regretted that she was never able to speak with him as an adult. There were, however, even greater revelations awaiting her.

Shortly after the service a phone call to her mother and siblings was brief and tearful. They promised to get together soon. When they were waiting to leave for the graveside service and interment, Annika turned to Lihua and Senta and confessed something.

"The man I met in Australia, the one who found the family crest, I think I'm in love with him."

She pulled out his card from her handbag. They looked with wonder at his photograph. This was indeed a day of many revelations.

She excused herself, walked over to a tree in the churchyard and phoned Donny.

Chapter 27

'Green Wattles', Queensland. Early October 2006.

It was the second week of the school holidays. On Monday morning Don looked again at the Chinese visa in his passport. It was very ornate featuring an archway, the sun and the great wall. It reminded him a little of the sinewy curves on the cartouche. He had never seen a visa before. Obtaining it must have been a miracle. How did Professor Jiang do it? But there it was. A three-month study visa for 1 June to 1 September 2007. *I need to tell Col Chalmers.*

Donald did something totally out of character. It was truly spur of the moment. He phoned the Chalmers and invited Col and Mary for a barbecue tea at his place that afternoon. He had spoken to them briefly the day before at church but now he wanted to talk and he needed a friend.

The Chalmers readily accepted.

This sent him into a spin. *Will I go food shopping? No. I have enough in the house. I had better clean and tidy the barbecue area.* He pulled out frozen steaks, rounded up all the vegetables he could and started to come up with a meal plan. Barbecued beef, bananas and onion with boiled peas and carrots. Colourful but not exciting. It was all he had on hand. *Why didn't I plant a vegetable garden? I won't need much for lunch. Just a cheese sandwich.*

Then he set to work cleaning every inch of the gas

barbecue and outdoor furniture.

Once the food was organised he dressed in farmer-style clothing and sat at his computer. He studied the map of China and looked at tourist websites. His imagination went wild. It was a wonder he even remembered to eat his cheese sandwich. Then with several more hours to kill be went out to the shed and decided to dismantle, clean, shine and reassemble his motorbike headlight. It would remind him of Annika. At 2.45pm he made a cup of tea and tried to relax. His mind wandered to the church service he had attended the previous afternoon.

The elderly guest preacher was Presbyterian. That pleased him because his family was Presbyterian. The sermon had been a little boring. He had nodded off once or twice but quickly took notice when he heard China mentioned. The old man had been a missionary in China in the early 1960s. He gave an example of faith among the Chinese Christians. He claimed there could be as many as fifty million of them meeting in secret because of the fear of being sent to camps for indoctrination. Yet they still met regularly in homes. He went on the say something that struck a chord with Don. He recalled it almost word for word.

"There are also Christian communities in isolated places. These people have been persecuted for centuries. Long ago they had faith to give up everything and go up into the mountains. A bit like Abraham leaving Ur to go up to Canaan. We have it so easy in Australia. It's hard for us to know what faith is."

I'll try to speak with him after the service.

Some of the congregation had stayed for a cup to tea but being Spring, the majority wanted to get back to their farms. The preacher had also wanted to get away for some family celebration. Don simply asked whether he might give him a call. Of course. The phone number had been jotted down on the back of a pew slip. He had then dashed home himself to study more about China.

An ambulance with lights and siren passed his gate and stirred him from his daydream. *Pfew! Hope it wasn't headed towards anyone I know.*

When Col and Mary arrived shortly after four o'clock, he was ready. He gave them a quick tour of his homestead and shed then sat them down at the outdoor table and fixed glasses of fizzy orange drink with mint floaties. He chatted about his school while he cooked the barbecue and asked Mary if she would attend to the peas and carrots inside. She jumped at the opportunity.

"Col, I have my visa for China."

"I knew you'd get it. I just had a feeling, not a word of knowledge mind you, that you were meant to go there. So that's great that it came through."

"Want to see it?"

"Oh. Yeah. If you like."

He pulled the passport from his jeans pocket and opened it proudly. Col commented on how detailed the visa background looked. They decided that was to prevent forgery.

"And it's amazing that old Rev Calderwood was a

missionary in China."

"Yeah. He has a lot of stories."

"I've got his number. I'm going to give him a call."

"Good. You should do that. You really are becoming committed to this China deal, aren't you?"

"I guess I am. But I'm still churning up inside about resigning from my school in three months' time."

"Hey, that's natural. But listen, you didn't think you'd get the visa. But you did. You know what that's called?"

"No, what?"

"The evidence of things not seen." They both laughed at this quote from the book of Hebrews, but Don took the words seriously. He had stepped out a little and there was the evidence.

Mary came out of the house with buttered bread slices and plates of boiled carrots and peas. The steaks sizzled, the onions caramelised and the cooked bananas erupted through their skins. A symphony of flavours and colour. They sat down to a meal far beyond what Don had imagined. Mary had a way of arranging things on a plate that made the food look and probably taste so good. The soft drink with mint was a perfect accompaniment.

Mary now joined their conversation and Don found her to have a kind of profound wisdom that he really appreciated. It made him aware that women have different thinking processes and hence bring a different perspective to life.

"Well, Don, my husband tells me you're giving up your teaching job."

"I haven't put in my resignation yet but I'm close to doing it. The school won't give me leave, even leave without pay."

"Yeah. It's hard to make a break from something you've done for a long time. You know I was once a newspaper reporter. When I first met Colin I was writing editorials for quite a few regional papers. Then one day my boss called me in and fired me. After eight years. He was nice enough about it. Just not selling enough papers. The staff had to be cut to keep the company's head above water."

"How did you take it?"

"I was upset but it didn't depress me. I did other things to put it out of my mind. I began to do a lot of work, like renovation, on my father's yacht. I described the change to be like opening up a hatch and coming out of the cabin onto the deck. Taking the next step in my life."

"So what did you do?"

"First I met Colin. He was a boatbuilder over at Scarborough harbour. I saw quite a bit of him while I was doing the work on Dad's boat. There was a job going at his work. Like a general hand. So I started building boats too. That was a change from writing news articles."

"Wow. I love boats. My brother Angus is into them too. We grew up on Pittwater. I love building things too."

"We can see that," said Col.

"But we didn't keep doing it. The market

changed. Not many people wanted bespoke boats.”

“So what did you do then?”

“We Got married. Colin set himself up in business doing repairs. We thought we’d have children but none came along. We both wanted to do something with boats. After a few years we bought a nice catamaran and started taking fishing charters and day trips around Moreton Bay and over to the islands. We sold that boat when Don retired. Now we just have a little half-cabin that we moor down near the fishing fleet.”

“So, Don, the message from all this is to be excited about what’s coming next.” Col looked at him to see if he comprehended.

“Yes, you never know.” Don looked thoughtful.

After the meal he showed them some photographs. They then looked at his lounge room shelves and he began giving the story behind each little memento. When Col picked up the photograph of Annika the tone of the conversation changed.

They sat down as he told them in more detail of his meetings with her. The Chalmers were obviously delighted for him and continued to encourage him to get to know her. He could not deny that he was in love with her. Then his true problem emerged.

“Yes, I do like her a lot. But is it a good thing to give up my secure job here, fly around the world and work for six months with Annika? What if we just end it then. I come home to no job and I’ll probably never see her again. I don’t want her as a work colleague.”

Mary’s wisdom poured forth. “Don you are in

what I call the 'love paradox'. This woman makes you feel happier than you've ever felt before. But if you lose her or don't get along at work you know you'll feel worse that you ever have before."

"So what should I do?"

Col now took over. "Mate, we've discovered that love is like the human heartbeat. If you don't have it, you're not alive. Earlier you said something seemed to be missing in your life. It's not the Australian dream of home, family and kids that's missing. It's what the New Testament calls 'eros'. Love for a husband or wife. You need to go after that. This is a lovely lady and she wants you to be with her. She's missing the same thing as you. You can give each other a wonderful gift of love."

"That might sound a bit soppy, Don. But it's true. We found it back in the boatyard. You can find it in the mountains of Germany or China." Mary smiled and looked for a response.

Instead he felt a little too exposed. Only a slight hum came from him in return. He looked at her. *How does she know all this about me?*

Perceptive as usual, Col put him at ease. "Mary hears everything we talk about. That's not a bad thing. We haven't been talking about you behind your back. We just want to help you. You're going into the third most exciting venture of your life. It's a major career turnaround. We want to encourage you."

"What are the numbers one and two?"

Mary now contributed. "Marriage. Children."

Donald nodded. The conversation then took on a

less intense tone as they had coffee and the Chalmers related stories of their fishing charter adventures.

Don could now see that they were of one mind with different perspectives. *My view is too narrow. Perhaps I need Annika to share life with me. We have to do things together. Not boatbuilding. Maybe making a documentary. I am doing the right thing.*

Following a little prayer, Don promised to come to church more regularly. He found the words to express his sincere appreciation. As they stepped out past the rock garden to leave, he bent down and picked up a large pebble.

"You know this all started because I found a rock."

"That's a pretty good sign that it's divine intervention.

Bye. See you Sunday."

They were gone. He could do little more than clean up and go to bed. *Divine intervention. God made me find the cartouche? This is weird!*

Chapter 28

The mobile phone charging by his bedside erupted in the silence of the night. He woke up startled and after a few rings he looked at the number. Annika!

"Hello. Annika, it's Don. Sorry it's the early hours of the morning and I was asleep. How are you?"

"Oh Donny," sobbed Annika, "I've just been to a funeral in Hannover for one of our Academy founders. It was the happiest funeral I've ever been to. I found out some really devastating but exciting things about my family and myself. I just had to call and tell you. I'm sorry I woke you."

Don was listening to a different Annika. She was crying her eyes out. Her words gushed out amid the sobs and the emotion was almost tangible. He thought he recognised the words 'evangelical' and 'Kirk', which caught his attention. Although he failed to pick up every detail of what she said he recognised that some family events had suddenly given her a different perspective on life. He sat to attention and listened almost without interruption for twenty minutes. *Escape from the Red Guard. Dissidents. Splitting families. Reuniting families.* It seemed his mind was expanding faster than the speed of light. *Talk about a different perspective. What do you say to a girl who has just lost her grandfather and found out who her mother really is?*

He came up with: "Oh, Annika. I'm so sorry to

hear about your grandfather.”

I'm not a counsellor but she's called me because she needs somebody to talk to. She respects me. She actually trusts me! I had better step out of the introvert boat right now.

“Life has a way of throwing up things we don't expect. For you and me both. We often have to take a step out of the boat and explore unchartered waters. Sorry I just mixed my metaphors.”

She laughed a little. There was less tension. He had said what she needed to hear.

“Hey. My visa for China came in the post this morning.”

“Oh, that is wonderful news. And thank you so much Donny. You are a very special man. And speaking of unchartered waters, I have something else I need to tell you…”

“Yes. I'm listening.”

“No sorry. Later. I have to go.” She whispered this as other voices could be heard coming closer. She gave him no chance to respond.

Before the line went dead he heard a very soft 'Ich liebe dich'. He hoped that it was for him. That uncertainty would be with him for days.

Chapter 29

Goslar, Germany. Mid-October 2006.

The approval of Donald's work visa for China set in motion a chain of events at the Harz Academy. The initial refusal of his visa had dealt a severe blow to the research plans. But the tenacious Professor Jiang had been able to intervene. She had managed, through carefully worded argument, to persuade the bureaucrats in the embassy in Canberra. Now it was time to work on those in Berlin.

She had not told the Chinese Embassy in Canberra that she was a German citizen, but she did ask for a written confirmatory reply in Mandarin. When she was in possession of that supporting document, she set about writing a compelling case for the study visas for herself and her colleagues.

Annika's visa would probably not be a problem. The expedition would also require a guide and translator. Lihua was obviously going to be that person. She knew the area and had contacts there. She was aware of certain regions being closed to foreigners. She had no intention of making application to visit such regions. In her submission she stressed the importance of sharing culture, particularly with expatriate Chinese people throughout the world. There were assurances that her presence would ensure that Chinese interests were protected by not allowing filming or recording of sensitive information, places or people.

Miraculously, by the beginning of November Professor Fluss' visa had been approved. There followed an anxious few days. The Embassy staff were obviously needing time to process the application. The Chinese faces on the German passports would have aroused their interest. Perhaps they had been studying the hand-written manuscript for any clues relating to security issues.

Unbeknown to all but Professor Jiang, an accompanying application had also been submitted for Madam Long to obtain a visa to travel with the group as a research assistant. Meike had also wanted to apply but she knew that her role was to keep the School of Dance office open and to help with all the formalities, enquiries, enrolments, reports and general odd jobs that related to the post. Three days per week would hardly be enough.

On 2 November Annika emailed Don from her professional address to let him know that her visa had been approved. She asked him to send his official acceptance of the six-month position as research assistant. Within the hour she received back a brief, formal email. It had to be acceptable to the Academy administrators. Donald provided exactly what she required.

Dear Professor Fluss,

I have decided to accept your kind offer of the position of Research Assistant for the period 1

May to 31 October 2007. I am happy to accept the stipend of € 5000 per month. I understand that travel, food and accommodation will all be provided. I look forward to this great opportunity.

Yours faithfully,
Dr Donald I. Kirk

Moments later another email appeared in her personal folder.

Dearest Annika,
I have sent you my acceptance of the offer. It was going to be hard to make the final decision to change my path in life so completely. When you asked for a formal letter, I decided not to think about it, just to step out and do it. So, I am all yours. I think we can work together really well.
Now that it is a firm appointment I have to apply for a German work visa. That should not be a problem. Could you send me some documentation to support my application please?
I will now send my resignation to my principal. I will finish up in early December. I decided to enrol in a short course in film and television production before I come over to you in April.
I will be so happy to see YOU again. I can't wait until April.

With lots of love,
Donny Boy

The message had quite an impact on Annika. She had an ultimate realisation that he was giving up his teaching career to be with her. And it wasn't purely for academic or vocational reasons. She tried to think what he meant by 'I am all yours'. Then there was 'so happy to see YOU again' and 'lots of love'. *He is not trying to hide his intentions. I love his honesty. He is the most wonderful man I have ever met. Should I write back? Should I tell him how I feel? I'll think about it.* There was a real conflict in her mind. She was very professional and wanted a good working relationship, but she also longed for the romantic relationship. *Will this work?*

Stepping out into the reception area she stared momentarily at the dancing gecko with Meike working diligently below it.

"Meike, I have just received Dr Kirk's formal acceptance of the Research Assistant offer. I forwarded it to you. Could you contact Dr Kirk for a copy of his Chinese and German visas? When you have them please send them through to Elke in personnel."

"Certainly. Are you feeling alright? You seem a bit pale?"

"Yes I'm okay. I'm just a bit emotional about Donny coming to work with us."

"Are you in love with him?"

"I think so. But I'm not sure. We only saw each other for two days. But we have been writing to each other for months. You know, everyday chit-chat, photos, even a few phone calls. But they are difficult because of the time difference and we both work. I'm worried about a romantic relationship with a work colleague."

"You shouldn't be worried. From what I've observed he is very reserved and compliant and he will not compromise your professionalism. This will be a good way to get to know him without being too close. You know, lovers often meet in the workplace."

A twenty-year-old is telling me this? She has an old head on young shoulders. Lovers? Now I won't get that thought out of my mind. How can we not be too close? Back to work!

The first semester of the Bachelor of Performing Arts in Dance was proceeding really well. Annika was doing four hours of lectures per week and two hours of tutorials. She also instructed a small ballet group in her lecture room cum 'boutique studio'. The bulk of her week was spent in the office, liaising with dance instructors, preparing course material and completing official paperwork. Her daily correspondence with Donny and the occasional wild weekend motorbike ride through the mountains became her primary means of recreation. A short visit with her mother in London had to be placed on the back burner.

The research project planning progressed slowly but the surprising news of Annika's family associations gave a whole new dimension to the trip to Hubei Province.

She could see a grand plan unfolding but a dinner with Lihua and Madam Long revealed it to be an incredibly daring plan indeed. The first surprise was that Chinese visas for Professor Jiang and her mother had finally come through. There would be three ladies travelling there on special research visas. The second surprise took Annika's breath away. Lihua and her mother planned to return home under cover to find their husbands, and reconnect with the very special and isolated community in which they had been raised.

"But your visa does not permit you to go to that area."

"As I told you before, we serve a different master, not the State."

"Yes, but you could get caught and thrown in prison."

"We have to take that chance. The families have to be reunited."

Annika could not say any more. The whole idea of dissidents returning home covertly had her both frightened and thrilled at the same time. It was something akin to riding her motorbike at high speed but the feelings remained much longer. In an effort to prepare herself for the venture she began exercising more. Apart from her regular dance and yoga she took up jogging and resistance band training. Espionage movies she had watched came flashing into her mind. The need for strength, flexibility and cunning had begun to dominate her thinking.

The expedition was still seven months away but

there were many errands to be run in order for it to be successful. Annika believed herself to be in a very special position. The older ladies were returning home to find their husbands and it was not known whether they would ever return to Germany. They could all be arrested. Annika, being part of the Behrmann side of the family would definitely be uncovering her roots, researching a rich and unique culture, bringing home ancestry information for relatives and siblings while possibly growing closer to the man of her dreams. One of her secret desires was to locate her grandmother Jai Jaiying if she was still living. With all these and so many other thoughts crashing through her analytical brain, she had ahead of her many months more preparing while completing two semesters of teaching and assessment. Given the secret agendas underlying the trip, her task seemed overwhelming. *I can't tell Donny anything about the family reunion yet. That is going to be so hard! He must not know what he is walking into.*

It was fortuitous that her personal assistant, Meike, also worked in the School of Music. Annika's peaceful but energetic pleas for more administrative assistance were finally heard. She did not want to work alone for two days each week so she developed a proposal that Meike continue to work in both schools but be permitted to spend her time working primarily from the Dance School office. She would check in at Music in person for instructions each morning. As her work was mostly computer based and the two schools were about one hundred and fifty metres apart this could be a workable system for the months ahead. The Professor of Music was not enamoured with the idea but agreed to a trial.

The varied and heavy workload would have been impossible for most twenty-year-olds but Meike, inspired by the challenge, rose to the task with incredible zeal. As the weeks went by her work actually bound the two related schools closely together and brought about a degree of cross-curricular collaboration.

An unused and high-quality audio system was relocated from the Music School to the dance classroom and musicians with various instruments were rostered, as part of their course, to provide accompaniment for some dance demonstrations. Musicians were rehearsing with Meike in the dance school lecture room at times and she was able to coach them in the dance music.

Annika had begun her first formal lecture classes in early August. In her first semester she taught units of choreography, origins of dance, Latin Dance and Modern Dance. Her students attended four hours of lectures and two of tutorials with her each week. These took place four mornings a week, then in the afternoons they had practical instruction from part time dance teachers in a number of Goslar locations. The only student she had difficulty catering for was the Thai girl. Professor Jiang and Madam Long suggested she attend the School of Oriental Arts where the two ladies would instruct her. After all, they came from a community that was centred around a school of classical Chinese dance. It was a learning curve for them but the arrangement worked extraordinarily well. The graceful young Thai dancer featured in local concerts and as time went by she was in demand for local events and television shows.

The all-female class of students adored their dance lecturer and they were always eagerly waiting to begin when Professor Fluss walked to the dais at 08.30h. All her students were enrolled in Bachelor of Performing Arts (Dance) and she appreciated being able to complete the semester without having to give a lot of attention to developing the Masters course. Towards the end of the first semester, two refurbished television cameras were donated by a local TV station. These were invaluable aids and were robust and suitable for the fieldwork in China.

Everything was running like clockwork. But for how long?

Chapter 30

Online chats became routine, so Don was continually made aware of any developments. He was experiencing a growing sense of excitement tinged with an anxiety that he couldn't quite pinpoint. Perhaps it was the family's reaction. His parents in Sydney had not received his news of resignation well at first but as he told his mother about Annika she warmed to the idea. His father was adamant that giving up a secure fulltime job for a six months overseas romp was not in his best interests. His principal Len White also lectured him several times along similar lines. In reality he was discovering that when stepping out in faith you will often encounter opposition. Some of his anxiety was soothed by Col Chalmers' advice. The words kept echoing in his head.

"That's to be expected. If you only ever do things that please other people then you're not stepping out of the boat. In fact you aren't even in control. They are. The important part is that you, inside yourself, believe in what you're doing. It's something you just can't escape from. And you'll be prepared to push through no matter what. I think you have that conviction in you Don."

When a teacher is leaving a school at the end of the year, the students are generally aware of the fact and the discipline in the classroom becomes a little more difficult. This was the case for Don, especially with his Year 9 lower ability maths class. However, it was also a developmental experience for him. He found that his anger level rose slightly as the students became more difficult and this voice and body language began to change. He felt more in control. By December the students had begun enjoying his classes more and they were working better than ever before. He felt he must have discovered the secret to good teaching. It was simply not accepting bad behaviour and being in control at all times. He could look forward to leaving the school on a happy note.

Jessica Jones was no longer in the troublesome class. She even came and apologised to him. Her friends told him that she wanted to return to his class. Most likely the motivation was to be back with her friends. On the second last day of term he had some positive interaction with her group in the playground. They said he was a good teacher. That was one of the most profound encouragements to him in all of his school experience.

The Christmas holiday break of six weeks was mostly spent in and around his property. Research led him to purchase fifty tubestock *Acacia dietrichiana,* a pretty wattle that is native to dryer areas of south east Queensland. With the help of his friend Col they were planted around the boundary line of his property. Now he could justify the name on the gate.

He took a special interest in gathering tools, small pieces of equipment and electrical parts that he thought might be useful in China for repairs and maintenance.

Again, he spent a wonderful week with his family in Sydney. They were now more supportive. His father loved the photograph of Annika. The Christmas presents he received were mostly thoughtful and very useful travel goods. That confirmed for him that he had the family's support.

Late January brought yet another change. Don commenced a short television production course that involved commuting to Brisbane four days per week. It was a disappointment initially. The other students were all older teenagers with little application to study and hard work. This actually turned out to be a blessing in disguise as the teacher, named Sam, took Don under his wing and taught him much about sound and video production while the younger students messed about giggling as they moved lights, set camera angles and dressed up in the studio costumes.

Within a few weeks Sam had become Don's other friend. They were of similar age. It pleased him greatly to have found a kindred spirit but also astounded him as he looked back over his past hermit-like existence. They spent two weekends together on location making a commissioned television documentary about a local beach community. That project developed into Don's assignment and, as might be expected, he passed with distinction. From that undertaking he received a small amount of money and an enormous amount of practical field experience. The vibe of the community members interviewed really sealed for him the essentially social nature of people. Sam was excited and supportive of the forthcoming research expedition, but he did express his sadness at being separated from his friend so soon. They would keep in touch.

By the end of March all his arrangements were in place. Don 's brother Angus asked if he might live in 'Green Wattles' for six weeks in July/August as he had the opportunity to do a Sydney-Brisbane exchange within his investment firm. He had a new girlfriend called Gloria and she wanted to come too. No hanky-panky, he promised, just some nice days at the beach on Bribie Island. Don trusted him and accepted the offer provided he started the Peugeot engine at least once a week to circulate the lubricant. Don's parents also offered to housesit, and perhaps chaperone, for a short time.

Fortuitously, Col Chalmers also had a cousin who was prepared to house-sit 'Green Wattles' in May and June. The two cousins would keep the place in good condition and, of course, give the old Peugeot an occasional outing.

* * *

His packing was complete. Two large suitcases weighing a total of 37 Kilograms. Not bad for a six-month jaunt. His brother Angus drove up for a couple of days to say goodbye on behalf of the family, and to check out the new digs. When he was returning to Sydney it was a simple matter to drop

Don at Brisbane Airport, his point of departure for Frankfurt and places beyond and unknown.

Journeying to a foreign country for the first time is an astonishing experience. The eight-hour flight from Brisbane to Singapore was not unlike others he had taken within Australia. After all, about five hours of the trip involves flying over Australia. It's a very large tract of land. Changi Airport is, however, a unique experience. Out came the SLR and he spent several hours walking around the huge terminal, riding the moving walkways and photographing the orchids that were in bloom all over. He felt a new sense of adventure rising within him as he waited at the departure gate for his flight to Frankfurt.

Connecting to the airport Wi-Fi he checked his email as he waited. There was only one new message in his inbox, and it was concerning.

> *Dearest Donny,*
>
> *I hope you are enjoying your flights to Germany. I am so looking forward to seeing you again.*
>
> *I just thought I would let you know that we are a little worried because yesterday two Chinese men visited Professor Jiang at her office. They said they were seeking information about her courses. She suspects that from their questions they were possibly from the embassy or maybe even undercover intelligence officers checking up on her. They didn't ask to see her mother so that is good. We still have hopes that our research trip can*

proceed. Don't worry too much. See you in two days.
Mit liebe,
Annika

Chapter 31

Frankfurt, Germany. Late March 2006.

Twelve hours is a long time to sit in one place and sleeping on a long-haul flight is very difficult, especially for a fledgling traveller. His arrival at Frankfurt, Germany was less than electrifying. Standing in the aisle waiting to alight. Traversing what looked to be kilometres of carpeted passageways. Customs and Immigration queues. Waiting to catch a glimpse of his two black cases that looked remarkably like all the others appearing on the baggage carousel. These are some of the delights that await a tired traveller who hasn't slept for twenty-four hours.

With all the formalities completed, he had to wait for a train at the Flughafen station, changing at Frankfurt Hauptbahnhof and Goettingen for his four-hour trip to Goslar. The train arrived precisely on time and the journey actually proved to be more relaxing than the flight. There was room to move and the tapestry of fields and villages whizzing past was enchanting to fresh eyes.

The transfers to connecting trains proved a little more difficult. He found himself smiling at a couple of immaculately uniformed railway personnel, both attractive females, who had only a very basic knowledge of the English language. They were very willing to help a young man in distress and he was directed to the correct platforms. *Missing a connection would be so difficult for me. I just have to push to get some help. Hey, that's a new me!*

His last train arrived at Goslar railway station around midday. As he stepped from the train he was enthralled by the beautiful old-world architecture, something he rarely saw in a country as young as Australia. He had the feeling of actually arriving as he stepped down from the train.

A most attractive young woman appeared beside him as he walked into the concourse. She spoke in English with a German accent.

"Dr Kirk?"

"Yes, that's me!"

"Hallo, I am Meike Gottschall, Professor Fluss' assistant. I recognised you from a photo. Have you had good trip to Germany?" They shook hands. Don had seen a photograph but would not have recognized her. She looked much more beautiful in real life.

"Well I am certainly glad to be here."

"Come this way, I have a taxi waiting for us. We will go to the Academy for lunch."

The taxi driver somehow managed to pack the heavy cases into the boot and Don and Meike climbed into the back seat. He looked across at her, his heart beating faster than normal, and saw just how beautiful she really was. Her blond hair cascaded down over her shoulders and her blue eyes staring unashamedly into his face. He did not know what to say.

"Professor Fluss is looking forward to meeting you again. She has been working very hard to make her dance course a success. I have enjoyed working with her. My English is improving. I also play viola and sometimes cello when she teaches choreography. That is my favourite part of the job. The students love to have live music."

Meike was not short of words and her English was indeed very passable. He was regaled with anecdotes from the classes for almost the entire taxi ride. She was obviously loving her work. He asked only the shortest of direct questions such as "Oh, you are a musician?"

Stopping at the end of a cobbled street, Meike and Don emerged from the cab into a seemingly alien world. They walked down a narrow, meandering alley lined with immaculately restored, if slightly warped, medieval buildings. The structures were two or three storeys high and some had stone walls at street level. Meike insisted on pulling one of his suitcases along. As she strode out a little in front of him he admired her elegant figure and graceful movement.

Groups of young people were standing around in the street but they did not appear to be the residents. The whole scene was just a little surreal. They arrived at a building labelled 'Tanzschule – School of Dance'. Professor Annika Fluss.'

As Meike reached to open the door, Annika almost bounded out into the street. She reached for Don's hand then threw her arms around him in a welcoming embrace. Their cheeks touched tenderly.

"Donny, I am so pleased to see you. How was your trip?"

"It was extremely interesting but very tiring."

She nodded and took his arm just as she had in Brisbane.

"Come. Let's go inside."

As the three moved into the building he could smell perfume and fresh flowers mixed with the odour of some kind of cleaning agent. At the top of the stairs he saw the gecko displayed on the wall behind reception.

"I love where you've hung the gecko."

"Everybody asks about it," said Meike. "You will have to give us a little more information so that we can tell our visitors."

"Yes, I'll do that."

They sat down at a coffee table in an intimate seating area to one side. Meike brought a tray of delicious cheese, sausage, bread, salad and fruit. Don thought how much fresher and more vibrant it looked than anything he had been offered over the past two days. Both women wanted to talk with him. They sat leaning slightly towards him as if hanging on his every word. Never could he have imagined the stirrings that were going on in his body. Two gorgeous women just wanted to be with him. How his life had changed.

The lunch was indeed very appertising. Meike took away the plates and seeing the glint in their eyes she adjourned to the kitchenette for some intensive washing up and eavesdropping. The conversation between Annika and Don continued. She reached over and took his hand.

"As I mentioned in our emails, Donny, I've

organised a bedroom and an office for you while you are here with us in Goslar."

This was information Don had been waiting to hear. *Important and practical.*

"That's great. Where are they located?"

"The office is downstairs. You can see it in a little while."

"Fantastic. And where's the accommodation? I'm sure it will be very nice."

"Yes. Well. Actually, I share a house with a friend who is a dentist. It is only about half a kilometre from here. There is an extra bedroom. It is quite large. We have agreed that you should use it. How do you feel about that?"

Naturally Don was shocked but in a nice kind of way.

"Yes, I'd like that very much. I hope your friend is okay with that arrangement."

"Oh, yes, it was her suggestion. She wants to meet you too." More shock. "I have a tutorial to run at fifteen hundred hours so if it's okay with you, Meike will take you down to the house and help you to settle in. My housemate Anke will not be home until late."

So it was that after a relaxing yet stimulating lunch meeting, Don again followed Meike's sinuous movements along the streets until they arrived at another half-timbered building. They entered and, skirting around a motorcycle in the hallway, went up an immaculate timber staircase to a backroom that contained only a single bed, cupboard, desk and wooden chair. It was spartan but very clean. Meike threw the heavy case up onto the desk and partly unzipped it ready for Don to unpack. He felt less than comfortable being in a bedroom with such an attractive young woman. She handed him an old-style Nokia phone and showed him the important numbers she had saved for him. Reaching out she shook hands with him and said she would go back to work, if he needed anything, just call. Annika would join him in about two hours' time.

After she left he quickly put his clothes into the cupboard and collapsed onto the bed, which was a little harder than he was accustomed to. The next thing he knew was a faint whiff of perfume and a hand gently stroking his hair.

"You must be very tired," whispered Annika. "Come, and I'll show you around the house, then we'll go out for some dinner. There's a pizza restaurant just down the street. The owner is an Iraqi refugee. He makes the best pizza you will ever taste. I thought that would make a good light meal for us and I don't have to cook."

This was the first indication he had that there was anything she didn't like doing. Or maybe she was just too busy. That would be a topic for conversation later.

They had a quick tour of the house and the motorbike. She then left him in his room to change and half an hour later she appeared at his door, elegantly dressed in red with black accessories. She took his arm as they stepped out into the street. Despite his jetlag he felt very proud to be walking out with such a beautiful woman. If being in a strange land was a new experience, this surpassed it by a long way.

As Annika had predicted, the pizza was excellent and the friendly Iraqi sat down at the table with them and told them in a mixture of German and English of his escape from Iraq and the joy of finding political asylum in such a lovely country. He also introduced his wife and two daughters. There was an atmosphere of friendliness that was quite strange but delighted the quiet Australian. Annika kept touching him on the arm as they talked.

After dinner they enjoyed the twilight stroll back to the house, where Annika surprised him yet again.

"Would you like to come for a spin around the city on my motorcycle?"

Having a liking for all things mechanical, Don readily agreed. With helmets on, they manhandled the bike out through the door and he sat behind her ready for the thrill. It came with a rush. With her long hair streaming out under her helmet and into his face, she accelerated down the left-hand side of the road in busy traffic. When you drive on the right-hand side of the road in your country, the change to the other side can be alarming at first. Everything seems wrong. But he had confidence in Annika and found that she was highly adept and most definitely full of life. At the next intersection she brought the bike to a halt and glanced around. Taking the cue, he let go of the handgrips behind him and clinched his arms around her waist. This was the closest they had ever been. Her perfume filled his nostrils.

Annika had withheld the information that this was the first time she had ever had a pillion passenger. He didn't need to know that. He was now enjoying his adventure more than he could ever have imagined.

Suffering sensory overload, the pair arrived back at the house at the same time as Anke. She rode up on a pushbike. Don was impressed by how straight she sat in the saddle. She had long, mousy-coloured hair and wore black slacks overlain by a white, clinical blouse embroidered with a molar motif. She seemed to lean back a little as she shook Don's hand and welcomed him to their house. He noticed that she was looking closely at his face. Perhaps she was sizing him up for some dental implants.

As they entered, positioned the bikes and retired to a sofa, Anke artfully disappeared into her room whilst Annika sat close to him, her knees touching his.

"Do you have it in your room? I'd like to see it."

Donald knew immediately what she was talking about.

Chapter 32

Goslar. Late March 2006.

In the morning Don was somewhat unprepared when Annika knocked on his door and opened it. He had not previously seen her without makeup, and she was wearing pink shorty pyjamas that revealed significantly more of her body than he had glimpsed previously. Keenly aware of his shyness she remained by the door and invited him to breakfast when she would outline the day she had planned for him. He would need to bring the parcel.

Breakfast was a new experience for an Australian boy used to his muesli clusters with fruit and milk followed by toast and marmalade and a cup of tea. As he sat at the small kitchen table with Annika and Anke he saw steaming hot bread rolls and an extensive range of cheeses and meats he had never before encountered. Keen to fit in with the culture, he asked the names of the foods. Anke stood and obliged.

"Wir haben Schenken, Speck, Geflügelleberwurst, Salami, Butterkäse, Harzer, Brötchen, Marmelade und Schokoladenaufstrich."

Well, I understood two of those words salami and marmalade. You might need to repeat the others a dozen times."

The two girls laughed uproariously. Don joined in. *I'm laughing at myself. That's new. No. I'm laughing along with others. Hey, that's new too.* What he did not suspect was that these clever young women were giving him a little test to assess his willingness to adapt to a different culture and diet. His passing grade was awarded as Annika leaned over and pecked him on the cheek. Something stirred within and he began to slide a little under the table. The girls kept on laughing. *I think they may have noticed something.*

Breakfast proceeded with considerably more laughter than usual in that kitchen. Annika affectionately leaned closer and whispered the English name for each titbit. He found the chocolate spread to be a little bizarre but on a warm bread roll with a morsel of Harz cheese it tasted delicious.

A number of coats of different sizes hung by the front door. Annika lifted down the largest of these and handed it to him. A look of surprise came across his face.

"We have these for guests. It may be Spring but it will be cold outside. Maybe two degrees. We are in the mountains and the central heating in here is good. It will be a shock for you going outside. You live in the tropics."

"Subtropics."

They both laughed as she helped him on with the coat. She picked up a briefcase, he tucked the parcel under his arm and they were off.

Their first port of call was to be the School of Oriental Arts, where he would be introduced to Professor Jiang. He felt the icy wind against his face as they meandered arm in arm along past the medieval buildings, stopping at a bright red door. Annika opened it without knocking.

Entering the building was, for him, another sensory overload. The black, red and gold theme. The smell of exotic fragrances. The opulence of his surroundings. All of these things made his jaw literally drop. The coats were left at the door and Annika took his arm yet again and led him up a carpeted staircase to a gleaming office. And there it was. The symbol emblazoned in gold on the wall. This was the place!

Professor Jiang appeared moments later. She was a short, rather stout woman with a beaming smile who welcomed him with a handshake that bore witness to her brute strength. She knew about the parcel he held and as they sat down she asked him not to unwrap it yet. She walked over to a reception desk and made a phone call in some Chinese dialect. Within a few minutes, an elderly and diminutive Chinese woman, Madam Long, appeared at the top of the stairs bowing to Don in an overtly submissive manner. He bowed to her as she was introduced.

"This is my mother, Madam Long. She will accompany us on our trip to China. She knows the area very well."

He suppressed his astonishment as she motioned to him to commence the unwrapping.

The unveiling of the 3D printed copy of the cartouche then took place. The two Chinese women picked it up and held it against their cheeks. They did not seem to mind that it was only one quarter of the weight of the original. Tears flooded forth. Annika and Don both found their eyes reddening, as they became a little choked up with the emotion of the moment. The museum technicians had done a marvellous job of colouring the plastic and gilding it to look very authentic. It was clear that this symbol was far more to these women than just an archaeological find. It represented who they were.

"I am glad you enjoy the gift. It obviously means a lot to you."

"Thank you. Thank you so much. You are such a kind man. We will take this to China with us. Our family will want to see it."

Don asked no questions. He told them about how he found the stone, pausing frequently for translation to occur. The Chinese ladies were enthralled. He discovered Annika's hand on his leg for support. Everything was a surprise.

There followed a morning tea he could only think of as 'decadent' and then on to the next phase of the day. An office for Don. So, with coats on and arms entwined there was another stroll down the enchanting street to the School of Dance. He was aware of a small group of young girls looking in their direction and sniggering. Annika just smiled.

"Some of my students early for class."

"Oh. You have a class today?"

"Yes, in half an hour. It is a one-hour lecture. You can come too."

"I'd love to." He knew he would feel out of place. But that was not unusual for him.

The downstairs of the 'Tanzschule' consisted mainly of an entrance hall, staircase and large open-plan lecture room. Don drew in the smells of newly lacquered timber and acrylic paint. Through a door at the rear there was a long and somewhat dark room that Annika called the 'Arbeitszimmer'. It looked like it had not been part of the recent renovation. The room had centuries old brick walls and a well-worn stone floor with only one little window high up and it was so dirty that very little light came into the room.

"Donny, do you think you could do something with this to make it your office and workshop?" Her words were so smooth and tantalising. How could he say no?

Nevertheless, he took a moment, looked around and then nodded sincerely. Annika handed him a tape measure then pecked his cheek, excused herself and disappeared upstairs to get ready for her presentation.

He walked around the room lit only by a single light globe. *I wonder when I will kiss her.* His moving shadow made it difficult to see into the corners. *I'll need some fluoro lighting. That will be my first project. Then shelving here. Workbench along this wall. Drill press and tools on a bench here. Storage of longer things underneath. I'll keep the electrical stuff down the other end. Maybe in a cupboard over there. This could be a damp room. I'll pace it out. No, wait, I'll use this tape measure. I think there's paper over there.*

Planning the optimal setup, he was really in his element. At ten o'clock his dreaming came to an abrupt end as the front door was flung open and about twenty young ladies carrying folders and pens hung their coats or placed carefully them into a pile.

More hooks needed. Professor Fluss came to the dias and began to address the class in slow, deliberate English. They quietened and opened their notes. As they did so she looked over to Don and motioned for him to sit in a front row lecture seat with writing table. He was just sliding in when, seemingly from nowhere, a hand touched him on the shoulder. Meike smiled and slithered in beside him.

"She is a very good teacher," she whispered. "See how her students pay her attention."

He nodded as he thought about the stark contrast with his Year 9 maths group. The lecture was about ceremonial and ritualistic dance. There were some snippets of video showing Native Americans. To his absolute surprise Annika at one point stepped down onto the wooden floor and demonstrated several moves involving formal steps and hand gestures. Then she spoke about and demonstrated a whirling dervish. *Truly international.* He was enthralled.

The lecture concluded with a question time. It became apparent just how dedicated these students were. They wanted to try some of the movements themselves. A dozen of them spilled out onto the wooden floor. Annika stood amongst them. To his great horror she motioned for Don and Meike to join them.

Don really had no choice. Meike grabbed his hand and virtually dragged him out of his seat. Once he was installed among the dancers Annika announced a Basque dance, ran over to the stereo and some Spanish sounding music blared out from the speakers. Slowly and gracefully she demonstrated a number of steps and everybody copied and joined in. Don had a smile on his face. The girls were totally amused by his awkwardness but they loved him joining in and he received a lot of smiles.

Ten minutes later there was collective laughter and as if on cue everybody began to leave. Meike headed upstairs to the office leaving Don and Annika alone. A greater embarrassment was about to come. The students were watching through the streetfront windows.

She put her hand on his shoulder and led him in a kind of tango. No music. She was easy to follow. It was slow and sensuous. It lasted about a minute then they laughed and headed upstairs for morning tea. Don began to reflect on his embarrassing morning. *It was fun. It was different. I stepped out of my comfort zone. Most of all I joined in with other people. What have I got to be worried about? Nothing Really.*

Annika sat close to him and outlined the remainder of the day. At exactly twelve o'clock she handed him over to Meike and disappeared downstairs for a tutorial. He could hear the students returning.

Meike sat down with him at the coffee table and produced a blank pad. Her youthful beauty did not go unnoticed but now she was strictly business.

Together they sketched up plans for the downstairs workroom. A list of materials and essential tools was prepared and when Don assured her it was complete, she flew into action. She invited him behind the reception desk to learn and observe

German efficiency. Websites were accessed. Images appeared on the screens. Don pointed to his choices. She made phone calls, placed orders and organised deliveries. He understood little of what was being said but he certainly knew what she was doing. *Meike is amazing. Annika is amazing. Have I always been so laid back? They get things done. Wow.*

For a half hour Don sat at Annika's desk and with ruler and pencil produced more accurate plans. Meike furiously worked the phone and computer. At precisely 13,00h she suddenly stopped and headed to the kitchenette to prepare lunch. The microwave jingled and the smell of bread and cheese wafted through the office.

"Doktor Kirk! We eat over here at the table at thirteen thirty hours. Herr Doktor Kraus will join us today. The Head Professor! He is talking with Professor Fluss now."

"Okay, I'm just about finished with the plans."

"Bring them over to lunch in ten minutes. You can show Doktor Kraus."

New experiences kept rolling out. *Just as I expected but not so soon. I only got here yesterday.*

Lunch turned out to be a fun affair. Doktor Kraus greeted him heartily and presented him with a welcome pack of information, stickers, a coffee mug and other bits and pieces. There was great mirth as Don lifted the items out one-by-one and examined them. Annika offered explanations. Meike kept the plates and glasses topped up.

"Lunch is not like this every day. Tomorrow we have only peanuts," Meike chuckled. It was amazing to see how well the academic staff and office staff could mix together. They appeared to be equals with different roles but all integral to the functioning of the Academy.

* * *

Over the next eight weeks, leading up to the departure for China, Don built benches and shelves in the workroom. He met electricians and other tradesmen and his German began to progress. When the room was suitably equipped, he began to investigate and test the cameras and sound equipment that would be used in the research. He enjoyed listening to Annika's lectures and tutorials often accompanied by Meike's viola. Later on he began filming classes for practice.

A succession of evening dinners introduced him to other staff members. He and Annika were quite frequently invited to dine with Lihua and Madam Long. At these times the family story was gradually leaked to him and he began to see the significance of their quest. There was never any mention of finding the husbands. Don was so overcome by the whole experience that he had no inkling of the scheme that was being withheld from him.

In the evenings at home there were some very flirtatious times but no kissing on the lips. They touched less than before and there developed a tacit understanding between them. They were housemates and work colleagues. He became used to Annika and Anke in pyjamas at breakfast. The house ran in an extremely orderly manner. Everybody had appointed times and adhered to them strictly. Each knew their role. Don was allocated garbage and laundry duties. The underwear was a little confronting. He figured that these were not the lowlier tasks but rather the jobs that needed to be done by the housemate with the freest schedule. That was okay, but in an effort to somehow prove his masculinity he volunteered for motor bike and bicycle maintenance. That required little more than a bit of cleaning and polishing in the odd spare moment.

When the semester ended, his work pattern changed markedly. He found himself more often using the computer on the second desk in Annika's office. It was all business and no romance. Meike would attend him with coffee and biscuits on a regular basis. Even when he worked with equipment downstairs, one of the women would be likely to come in to ask him something. It seemed that both ladies wanted to be close to him yet they maintained a strict, professional demeanour that he initially admired. He began to feel more comfortable around them, knowing that nothing untoward was going to happen. His feelings towards Annika soured a little over time as he became more aware of an abruptness that irked him somewhat.

Two weeks before the trip the research group began a series of team meetings. These were attended by other academics who gave input on the research methods. A television cameraman from the station that had donated the cameras also joined in. He offered to take Don out on location and into his studios for some intensive training in documentary production. At last he had some male company and the two men really enjoyed their time working together. Professor Jiang was obviously regarded as the leader of the expedition and she, rather forcefully, explained travel arrangements and cultural issues. Don liked her direct manner and got along well with her.

One day he was asked to film, in Jiang's building, a kind of documentary to be shown to the folks in China. That is when she started to tell him about dragons. Throughout his years of study and from subsequent reading he had always believed that dragons were mythical creatures. No animal can breathe out fire. The scientific consensus was that dinosaurs became extinct before the emergence of man so the legends of dragons could not be based on the interaction of the two species. Professor Jiang, however, placed some doubts in his mind.

She told him the story of her ancestor Hé Lóng Zhǎnshǒu who had lived in the region they were about to visit. He was famed for having killed a large and ferocious dragon by severing its head. The dragon had taken a number of villagers and it was a threat to the community. She had some evidence that he lived around the twelfth century, which would place him at least twenty, possibly thirty generations before the present. Nevertheless, there were records of a continuous lineage going back to him.

The tradition of slate carving meant that the patriarch of each generation had a cartouche fashioned to record their name for generations to come. In the case of Hé Lóng Zhǎnshǒu, the symbol was the lower half of the dragon. The finer lines within the carving showed the snaking watercourses that defined the shape of the river gorges in his time. That was why Don's finding was so significant to this community – it was a record of their heritage. Don could not escape thinking of the parallel with the story of St George and the dragon – perhaps there could be something in it. *Could there still be dragons living in that area?* The adventurous spirit was soaring within him. The possibilities for discoveries during this trip were increasing by the minute.

He filmed Professor Jiang in her office and classroom, speaking to camera about her work and her surroundings. She asked Madam Long to be in some of the shots.

While Don was filming the two ladies holding the cartouche he asked, "Did he kill the last dragon?"

"No. The dragons are still there."

Don was puzzled by her answer.

"What do you mean?" he said.

"Our tradition is that he killed a large, dangerous dragon. It is also symbolic. You see, about one millennium ago there were visitors from the west who came to our river gorge community. They were Christian. And they left copies of the New Testament in Latin with the villagers. The language was a problem but over the years and with the help of other visitors, some parts were translated into Chinese. Then around the time of Hé Lóng Zhǎnshǒu a picture, a woodcut I believe, was given to the community by a traveller. It showed war in heaven and the Archangel Michael fighting against the dragon Satan. Immediately the people saw Hé Lóng Zhǎnshǒu as an archangel sent from heaven. So you see a community in China that holds these beliefs will always be regarded as rebellious. But they have managed to carry on their traditions and my mother and I were born into that community. So you can see what this means to us."

Don was astounded and could only nod. When he was back at his desk he looked up the bible story and found:

> *And there was war in heaven: Michael and his angels fought against the dragon; and the dragon fought and his angels and prevailed not; neither was their place found any more in heaven (Revelation. 12:7)*

Annika, he found, had already been informed of this tradition. She had made notes on the folklore behind the traditional dance and was expecting to observe the symbolism informing the choreography. Although she now knew that she had some Chinese ancestry from this region, her focus was unreservedly on traditional dance. Don, however, was developing a very different perspective as he foresaw levels of intrigue in this ancient and isolated community together with possible biological oddities that were yet to be documented. *A Chinese St George? Do dragons still live in the hills? Would this trip turn out to resemble the hunt for the Yeti or the Tasmanian tiger?* His mind flashed back to the metre-long water dragons that regularly looked down upon him like eerie premonitions from the roof of his shed back at 'Green Wattles'. His quest was now to reveal the mysteries that lay dormant in the rugged gorges of Hubei Province.

Chapter 33

Leaving Goslar. Mid-June 2007.

The weather was warming nicely in mid-June when
the four 'adventurers' left Goslar. Senta travelled
with them in Lihua's Mercedes to Frankfurt
International Airport. The estate car was packed to
the roof with luggage. Meike followed in a smaller
car belonging to the Academy. She was surrounded
by kitbags full of audiovisual equipment and
camping gear. Senta had offered to garage the car in
Hannover until their return. Meike would simply
unload and return to her work in Goslar. She had
been designated as the Academy's point of contact
for the team.

In the carpark there were embraces and farewells.
As Don lightly hugged Meike, she whispered
something disturbing in his ear.

"Goodbye Donny. Come back soon. The
professors have secrets. Be careful."

"Secrets?"

"Shhhh. Ask Annika. Goodbye. Have a lovely
trip."

The first stage of the trip was an eleven-hour
flight with Lufthansa to Hong Kong. They were to
spend three days there intensively planning before
taking the two-hour flight with Dragonair to Wuhan.
Lihua had made the arrangements for their road
transport and stay at the Hanshui River gorge area
and the others just had to trust that planning to her.

After that Annika had scheduled to visit dance establishments in a number of Chinese cities. All she knew for certain was that she and Don would mostly be travelling to some of those places without Lihua. Don had no real idea of how the plans might pan out.

The long flight was not totally uneventful. Annika leaned her head against Don's shoulder and took a half-hour nap. *Wow, she totally trusts me. Just this makes the whole trip worthwhile.* He breathed in her intoxicating scent, and several times ever so gently kissed her on the forehead. He looked at Lihua and Madam Long. Both had their eyes closed. *I wonder whether it might be a good time to ask Annika about the secrets. No, I'll let her sleep for now. She'll likely be a bit groggy when she wakes anyway. There'll be other opportunities later on.* As the plane approached Hong Kong, the sight of the dawn light on cloud over the Himalayas to the far south brought a tingle of excitement to the man who had seen so little of the planet.

On arrival, Professor Jiang and Madam Long were taken aside for questioning by immigration officials. Annika and Don waited helplessly, thinking the ladies may not be released. Their fears were unfounded as the pair appeared through a doorway about twenty minutes later with big smiles on their faces. It turned out to be a fairly routine passport check on German nationals who were ostensibly Chinese.

They caught two taxis to their hotel. Somehow the drivers were able to dovetail the passengers and luggage into their standard red Nissan sedans. The ride through the bustling street with towering skyscrapers somehow awakened Don from his jetlag stupor. *People everywhere. I've never seen so many people in one place before! Another new culture.*

The team spent the three days relaxing, checking gear and discussing strategies. Don and Annika swam together daily in the hotel pool. Here was an opportunity to ask about the secrets.

"Annika, Heike whispered to me to be careful. There are secrets. Do you know anything about secrets?"

"What do you mean? What kind of secrets?"

"That's just it, if it's secret I don't know what it is."

"I don't know any secrets. Oh, yes I do know one."

"Tell me … please."

"My grandmother might still be alive in China. I hope we can meet her."

"That's great. But why do I need to be careful?"

"She is a dissident. Communicating with her might get you into trouble I guess."

He found her manner a little evasive. Although he was seeing more of her these days, apart from little pecks goodnight and a little informal skin contact the relationship remained stalled on 'work associates'. He found that as the tour organisers, she and Lihua were becoming quite abrupt with him. *What have I done?* It was difficult for him to make any contribution to the planning. He just agreed with everything he was told. The time passed rapidly and before long they were again packed into taxis and heading through the crush of cars and trucks, bikes and carts to the airport for yet another round of travel red tape.

Their arrival in Wuhan set off some alarm bells. They were met by four men who were to accompany them during their visit. Professor Jiang explained to the group that these men were appointed by the government to travel with them and ensure that Chinese interests were not compromised. Don was not allowed to photograph the men and he very quickly twigged that they were minders. The group was led to a waiting minibus and then given a guided tour of Wuhan city.

They stopped for drinks and the youngest of the men ran into a shop, unfurling a wad of banknotes, and returned with a box of bottled water and soft drinks. For Don and Annika, this tour was a bit of a mystery as the two Chinese ladies chattered away with their newfound travelling companions. They were probably just nattering away to establish a good rapport but there was an air of secrecy as they travelled.

That evening the minders left them in their hotel rooms at about nine o'clock. Lihua checked the hallway and knocked on the doors. She gathered the group into a huddle in one of the three rooms.

"Get all your things together, we will be leaving at midnight."

"But we only just arrived," said Don, frustrated that everything was out of his hands.

"We must go. There is no other choice."

Lihua was not prepared to give further details apart from the fact that an employee of the hotel would knock on their doors, assist with luggage and lead them down a service lift to the rear of the building where their transport would be waiting. *This is ridiculous. It's like a spy movie. What have I gotten myself into?*

At the appointed time there was a very soft rap on each door. A handsome young man wearing a busboy uniform noiselessly piled the bags and equipment onto a trolley and without a word beckoned to them to follow. They took a lift down to a sub-basement and transferred to a larger service lift that was battered, smelling of fish and obviously in daily use.

When the doors opened at street level the four stepped out. The busboy unloaded the luggage without once leaving the lift, the doors closed suddenly and he was gone. His job was probably on the line if he was caught. It was a forlorn sight as the four stood with their stack of bags in a dark and smelly back alley, wondering what would happen next and fervently hoping that nobody could see them.

After about half an hour a blue flatbed truck with high sides but without lights came backing towards them. A short middle-aged man jumped out and embraced Lihua and Madam Long, shaking hands with Annika and Don. The man slung the luggage onto the truck. The Chinese ladies donned blue overalls and climbed into the cab. Annika and Don were then directed to climb into the back with the luggage and lie down under a tarpaulin. Fortunately, there was some foam rubber to make that more comfortable. Unquestioningly, they followed their instructions as Lihua whispered translations and confirmed their actions with nods and grins. There was no further clarification of the need for this midnight departure.

The truck lurched forward into the darkness and was apparently circling around narrow unlit back streets. The two ladies in the front wore workers' caps low over their eyes and stayed down. The two bouncing around in the back wrapped their arms around each other for support. When the truck left the winding streets and proceeded onto a more major road with street lighting, Don and Annika did not release their grip but held each other mainly for emotional support. Then the unimaginable happened. Their lips met momentarily in a kiss. Despite the darkness they both looked into each other's eyes and smiled.

"Tell me about the secrets you've been hiding."

"I'm not hiding any secrets." She pulled away.

"Well why are we lying in the back of a truck in the middle of the night?"

"You would have to ask Lihua. I'm trusting her for the visit to the community. She knows what she's doing. Just go along with it."

Don was far from satisfied with that answer but the bumps in the road caused them to smile and hold each other once more. Finally the headlights came on and they were travelling at a bit higher speed along a much smoother road. They sat up with their backs against the cab holding hands, the noise of the road and engine making conversation near impossible.

The journey turned out to be slow and tedious. After about three hours they turned off onto a gravel road and stopped in a clearing in a forest. The driver ushered them out for a toilet break. Lihua then explained that the minders had to be given the slip. She believed that the government had some warning that two dissidents were returning to China and that they would have to keep a close eye on their activities, possibly arresting them and their associates. Their driver was from the river gorge community and would take them there via some rough and mountainous terrain. Annika and Don looked at each other in stunned amazement. One of the secrets had been partially divulged.

"We're breaking the law. We could be arrested," whispered Don as they climbed back into the tray.

"She never shared with me how we would visit the community. It's news to me too. She just said it would be arranged by her and Madam Long."

"Can we trust them?"

"Donny, you know them. Of course we can trust them." Don was very unsure but he zipped his lips. *You have to step out, but this could be a step too far.*

The Chinese ladies sat up in the cab again for the remainder of the journey. They would not look out of place. It was best that the two westerners not be seen but they could sit up in the back and be ready to slip under the tarpaulin if another vehicle approached. The truck moved off deeper into the forest along an undulating track. *I hope this doesn't end up like the Six Mile Creek Road. We couldn't lever this thing out of a ditch.* At one point they stopped for the driver to remove an obstacle. Lihua stepped out and checked the rear. They were not being followed.

"How much further do we have to travel?" sighed Annika, now slightly disturbed that she and Don might be accessories to some highly illegal activity.

Lihua asked the driver and translated.

"It's about one hundred and fifty kilometres and it will take about six hours."

This was becoming a true adventure. Annika and Don sat close together in the back. Eventually they decided to lie down and have some rest. They lay on the foam with arms around each other from time to time, hoping for a little sleep. But it did not come. The tracks were very rough and at one point the wheels seemed to slip over a precipice causing the vehicle to pitch sideways before recovering. During that time there were no further kisses but in the growing dawn light each could see in the other's face smiles of contentment emerging from their mutual support through this astonishing predicament. As the first rays peeked over the horizon, they sat up and admired the spectacular panorama. Don shuffled around the tray, carefully opened one of the bags, took out a movie camera and began to record. There were three short breaks for ablutions and stretching of the legs, but they had to keep moving. The route became rougher. They seemed to be bush bashing over saplings. *The*

Peugeot wouldn't be able to tackle this.

It must have been approaching midday when they finally saw their first signs of civilization. The old truck rolled to a halt on a flat, cleared area surrounded on all sides by tall trees with straight narrow trunks. The understorey was dense with glossy-leafed bushes and arching ferns. It was a relief to stand up and walk around once again. There before them was a huge barn and some outbuildings.

"The dance school," shrieked Annika. "Bring the video camera." Don climbed back into the truck and emerged with two cameras.

They looked around. It was indeed an eerie sight to see movement in the undergrowth in all directions. At least one hundred people silently emerged from the surrounding forest and formed a circle around them. The driver spoke and the crowd erupted into joyous shouting. Lihua and Madam Long had tears streaming down their faces. There was a great deal of hugging, sobbing and handshaking.

Minutes later the crowd fell completely silent. They parted like the Red Sea and two old men, one looking particularly frail, slowly walked up to the women and embraced them.

Annika and Don looked on in awe. Amid her tears of joy Lihua was able to say to them, "My grandfather and my husband. They have been waiting for us forty years. We cannot express how glad we are to be home again. I cannot tell you our real names. It must be kept secret." The old men shook their hands and they all bowed several times.

The enormity and the illegality of the situation was not lost on the German and Australian adventurers.

After a time the people all moved into the barn. At least a hundred more silently drifted in. They all took up their places on the floor, but six chairs were set up to the side for the guests of honour and husbands. There was a lot of scurrying around. Children were being ushered to a stage area at one end. As he took his seat. Don looked up his mouth fell open. There it was. The very same gold-on-red wall motif that had originally led him to Annika and this amazing quest.

A squeal came from a speaker and a grey-haired man appeared on stage. He was wearing a dark blue velvet cap and monk's robes, the kind you might see on an altarpiece from the middle ages. His words, in a dialect peculiar to western ears, were greeted with cheers from the crowd. Lihua leaned over and whispered that he was the head priest and leader of the community.

Recorded music began to play from very tinny speakers and about twenty young dancers in traditional costume tiptoed in through a stage door. Annika nudged Don. He took the hint, lifted the camera and commenced filming.

This was the beginning of an afternoon and evening of celebration and sheer exhaustion. There was more dancing. Plates of food were offered to the guests. Beautiful young children ran up wanting to touch the strange-looking people, who were like nobody they had ever seen.

Sensing the fatigue of the group, the village

leader, now in simple shirt and trousers, quietened the assembly and spoke briefly. Lihua and then Madam Long gave short tearful replies. The husbands also made short responses. There was a lot of applause then the community leader motioned to the group to follow him.

They walked past the truck where willing hands grabbed and carried the heavy luggage then turned into the undergrowth where there was no discernable track. Several young men lit the way with powerful torches. They must have walked for about fifteen minutes before coming to what appeared to be a house front hewn into a low cliff.

The door was opened revealing a single room with two wooden slat beds, a small bench with a gas cooker and an ablutions area comprising a half barrel and a bucket. *Two beds?* Lihua explained that this would be the guest accommodation for Annika and Don. She apologised that they had to share but knew they would manage. The ladies were going to nearby homes to be with their husbands. Ever so quietly the luggage was placed in the room under Lihua's husband's direction.

The door was closed. They were left alone. Don and Annika looked at each other in absolute amazement and then embraced and touched cheeks. They felt a little abandoned and wondered whether the villagers thought they were a married couple. Not knowing what would happen next, they were there for each other and the bond between them had never been stronger. Don put aside for the moment his growing displeasure with the ladies who were now so obviously keeping who knows what back from him. *I need Annika right now.*

There were gentle knocks on the door ten minutes later. Visitors came with food, water and a lantern. There was no electricity in the accommodation. Fortunately they both liked camping and had some comfortable bedding in their bags. The journey had taken its toll and they would go to bed shortly. There was power at the barn, so Don thought about how he needed to make arrangements for charging batteries as a priority next morning.

Trying to keep their relationship as professional as possible, the two judiciously carried out their ablutions. A modesty blanket was suspended from some overhead timbers. They hugged good night and laid down on the hard beds padded only with bedclothes and some of their own clothing. Quickly they drifted off to sleep, facing in opposite directions.

The next thing they were aware of was the crowing of roosters accompanied by an intermittent and blood-curdling horn sound.

They jumped out of bed and dressed discreetly but without delay. Don slipped behind the screen first then waited outside the door. Annika emerged elegantly attired in khaki fatigues.

"Have you been in the military?"

"No. Lihua told me to tone down the colour. These people need to be inconspicuous. I got these at the army surplus shop."

"You look great. We match in our khaki gear."

"You look good in kakifaben also." Laughter was

their best antidote for the acute sense of insecurity they were both feeling.

Standing outside they stood awestruck at the silent beauty the mist rising past the tall trees. Everywhere they could see grey rocky outcrops. A slight rustling indicated that people were silently moving through the forest. Don loved the seclusion but he still had many nagging questions.

"How will we ever be able to leave the country when this research is over?"

Annika thought Don sounded unusually anxious.

"Stop worrying. I'm sure these people have worked out a plan. Let's go inside and get our gear. I think they're coming for us now."

"Who's coming …"

Chapter 34

Hubei Province. June 2007.

Looking out the door of the cliff house Don saw, in the misty dawn light, hundreds of dreamlike figures picking their way through the tall vegetation. He motioned to Annika to come and see. Her first instinct was to hand him a camera to capture the event on video.

They stepped out into the throng of people and were greeted with smiles and gestures indicating that they should follow. Picking up a bag each, they joined the flow of villagers. Don decided to begin filming as they walked. Two teenage boys ran up to carry the bags. People of all ages were converging on the barn and as they approached the sound of angelic singing could be heard.

Lihua was waiting for them at the door and led them to the chairs set aside for the guests of honour. There was no sign of Madam Long and her husband. Don was a little disappointed that he did not have his audio recording equipment ready but the soundtrack on the video would be quite reasonable, he thought.

With a little translation from Lihua, they understood that this was a daily ritual of worship. At least two hundred and fifty people were standing on the barn floor with arms raised. The singing was totally a capella and extraordinary in its range and harmony. Don would make sure he had his boom mike and sound gear ready for the next morning.

To the delight of everybody, four little ballerinas came out and performed a sacred dance that featured recognisably Christian symbolism of the Cross, acceptance and love. As they motioned towards the large dragon-tail symbol on the wall they stabbed and cut through the air, portraying the defeat of Satan. The piece ended with three dancers crouching in submission at the feet of one whose extended arms slowly enfolded them.

The village leader then spoke and the crowd erupted into spontaneous vocalisations, most likely individual prayers. Annika was thinking that the performance was not a traditional dance because it was quite Western in its structure. Lihua assured her that this dance had hundreds of years of tradition behind it but the story had European origins. Only the costumes were more modern. This was indeed a unique society.

Further explanation revealed that the community had for centuries been under threat from the authorities. The blowing of the horn of the ibex, an antelope once indigenous to the area, was used to signal events and alarms. Should the authorities raid the property there would be short blasts and everybody would disappear into the forest and caves. This was how the community had survived and maintained its distinctive culture, possibly for nearly a millennium.

The next two days were spent recording and documenting the customs and dances. Lihua organised a very full schedule for them but the various participants did not have the German concept of time. That really did not pose any challenges. Everything was taken as it came and it was all a total delight. The researchers were thrilled to observe men and women of all ages demonstrating their dances. Almost every person in the community was a dancer. Annika took copious notes as Lihua interpreted. Don filmed and recorded with the higher quality audio.

On their third afternoon a tour of the community facilities was organised. Don, in particular, was amazed at the ingenuity of their machines and electricity generation equipment. He observed an odd concoction of wires through the treetops, turbines in streams, a few solar panels, a very old diesel generator in a cave and a unique wind turbine built from scrap metal and a repurposed electric motor. Power was stored in an array of modern looking batteries below the community hall floor. The incredible thing was that it ran through an inverter and gave a near continuous 240-volt supply. *Now that is what physics and engineering are all about. And these people do it with next to no technical training, just the power of the human brain. Wow.*

He had no problem keeping his electronic gear running. The only thing lacking was Internet access so he was not able to securely store the videos and notes on a remote server. He backed up everything onto usb storage devices, which he carried around in the pockets of his cargo pants, just in case there was a raid.

Two twenty-something ladies, who looked more like teenagers, invited Annika and Don to come and see their home. They both spoke passable broken English and wanted to improve their command of the language. Their names were Mei Hu-a and Mei Le-in. Try as he might Don could not remember which was which. Annika, however, was able to correctly call them by name.

Thrashing through the bushy understory for at least half an hour they were approaching one of the hundreds of grey stony outcrops. There were no worn paths. To avoid detection the people always modified their routes through the prickly bushes.

"No picture please. Way is secret."

There was movement in the trees above.

"What's up there?" Annika pointed to the treetops.

"Ah. We have golden monkey here. Very rare. We feed the monkey and he do very well. He is a good watchman."

"And what are those?" said Don looking at some strange shapes above his head.

"I know that," said Annika. "It's called a gourd tree. Didn't you notice vessels in the barn were made from gourds?"

"I must have missed that. And those white things?"

"Handkerchief tree. Very useful." Mei Hu-a motioned to them to keep moving.

Between some dense thorny bushes there was a narrow cleft, barely visible to the unaccustomed eye. Using their dresses to protect their hands the women held the vegetation aside and pulled out a large plug of bark. A narrow portal could be seen. It was about one and a half metres high and only half a metre wide at ground level, tapering to about ten centimetres at the top. Dropping to the ground, Annika squeezed through with relative ease but Don had to lay down his equipment and wriggle along the ground on his side in order to just make it through. He had not paid much attention to the understory vegetation up to this point. To his astonishment the bushes he was slithering past had leguminous pods and fading cylindrical yellow flowers amid the thorns and deeply divided leaves. *Wattles?*

Inside was a revelation. They stepped down into a large space that took their breath away. The rock had been hollowed out to create a room. *That must have taken months of work.* Little shafts of sunlight from overhead illuminated what looked like a studio apartment with a polished timber floor, whitewashed walls and fairly modern furniture. It was spacious and comfortable.

"Welcome to home." Both women smiled. It was unclear whose home it was. They spotted two stretcher beds leaning against a wall. *Perhaps they both live here.*

"What a beautiful home," began Annika. The women were beaming now. Don had some practical issues in mind.

"May I film your home?"

"Of course," said Le-in with a sweeping hand gesture.

"Do you have electricity here?"

"No. No wires. The 'die' find us if they follow wires."

"Oh. Of course, who are the 'die'?"

"Sa dan shizhe." One of the ladies crouched and pretended to fire an automatic weapon. They immediately understood.

"And you have running water?"

"Yes. Come." Le-in was almost falling over herself to show them.

They walked through a basic kitchen with tidy timber cupboards and plenty of utensils. To one side, under a counter was a conventional brass tap. A cup was filled to demonstrate that it worked.

"Where does the water come from?"

It was to them a very silly question, so they responded in unison, both laughing and making hand motions like falling rain. Annika gave him a disparaging look. Don was really none the wiser. *These people have a water reticulation system. Amazing.*

"Hu-a, how do you cook food?" Annika asked.

"Come." She pulled out a saucepan, ran in some water and then placed it on a modern portable gas camping stove. Donald wanted to know where the gas came from, he had expected wood fires.

"You don't burn wood for heat."

"No. No want the 'die' to see smoke."

"Where does the gas come from?"

"We make. You see. Near Dà huìtáng."

"That's the barn, Donny," said Annika as if she expected him to know that. *You have an amazing memory but don't treat me like a child.*

"What food do you eat?" A little curtain was swished aside and there were two small sacks of rice, preserves in jars and leafy vegetables in gourd baskets. *No packaged supermarket goods. These people are truly self-sufficient.*

"Hu-a, that is a wonderful pantry."

"Thank you. We very blessed. I make the tea. You sit here. My sister must go now." *Ah, sisters living together.*

They sat on lounge chairs and drank green tea with an earthy taste and perhaps a hint of peppermint. There were many more incredible features to be explored but after about half an hour they got up to leave.

"May I use the toilet?" Annika said hopefully.

"Yes. Come." Hu-a motioned to them both. Donald gave Annika a quizzical look.

Behind a little curtain there was another smaller cavern. A white marble vanity with a mirror adorned one wall. Opposite there was a white porcelain western toilet with a beautifully crafted wooden seat, not the usual squat. There was no cistern. The wooden bucket standing beside it was for flushing. Don spotted another tap beside the vanity as he was ushered out and the curtain drawn. *I have no idea how they got all this in through that little crack I guess they dismantled everything and reassembled it in here.*

Crawling out through the narrow portal, Don wanted to photograph the wattle. Close-up. Hu-a shook her head violently. He had to just pluck a leaf and flower for later identification. The young woman led them back to the barn via a circuitous route that seemed to have never been taken before. It was time for some lunch followed by and the next round of dancing. But the barn was empty and no dancers materialized. Hu-a ran inside and returned a minute later shrugging and handed Don a bowl of seed pods.

"Thank you. What is this?"

"We plant seed in forest. It very sharp and make us safe. You see." Don peered down into the gourd dish. *Wattle seed pods. That's it. Amazing. Maybe a wattle species endemic to China? They're cultivating it like a hedge of protection. Wow. That gives another level of meaning to my place.*

Her faced beamed with delight as she took the bowl and turned to go.

"You please wait. I find somebody." She was gone.

"Sit over here. Somebody is certain to see us." Annika motioned towards an adjacent forest clearing.

Sitting together on a log in the communal area, they heard only the gentle breeze wafting through the treetops. There were no bird calls. Everything was eerily quiet. An opportunity for some romance? Don shuffled over a little closer and reached out for Annika's hand. She withdrew immediately.

"Don, we're at work now."

"But it's a beautiful setting and I just thought …"

They looked around and suddenly became aware of about twenty young children watching them.

"They've been taught to move with stealth, but this is ridiculous. I didn't hear a thing."

"Get the video camera. I'll ask them to dance."

"They won't understand English or German."

"Watch me."

She rose and began to twirl around. The children immediately started copying. Don rummaged around for the camera and quickly commenced filming. Annika clapped as she sat down to let the children entertain her. Don captured them snaking around with hands on shoulders. It seemed the first child was trying to catch the last.

"Is this a dance or a game?" he asked.

"Probably both."

"It is a game." Lihua was standing by watching. "It's called dragon tail. The head must catch the tail. I played it right here as a girl."

"Lihua, would you ask them to dance for me please? Don are you ready?"

"As I'll ever be."

"Emu Dao"

The children looked around at each other then ran to Lihua for some guidance. She organised them into three rows of about seven. As she began to clap, they jumped, hopped, swayed and commenced a complex series of graceful arm motions. Dust rose from beneath their bare feet. Even without music, the whole performance was beautifully coordinated. The delight on Annika's face was unmistakable. Don made sure she appeared in shot as much as possible.

Following the applause from the three adults, two

older children appeared, said some words and spirited the little ones away silently into the undergrowth.

"Lihua, what happened? Our afternoon dancers didn't show up?"

"No. I'm sorry. You were visiting a home and I could not tell you. They were all called away to harvest red berries. Weißdornbeeren. I don't know what it is called in English but they have to pick it today or it will be ruined. My husband is there."

"Hawthorn berries." Annika translated for Don.

"Can we go and film?"

"Yes, I will take you. First I wanted to tell you that tomorrow morning we will be going to see the quarry where the family crest was made."

"That's wonderful. I can't wait." Don had regained a little of his enthusiasm. But how long would it last?

"Will you please remember to bring the family crest to the gathering tomorrow morning. We will present it at that time."

"Sure, no problem."

Chapter 35

On the morning of the fourth day of their stay, as requested by Lihua, Don brought the copy of the cartouche to the barn. The whole community was present except for Madam Long and her husband. *They must be in hiding.* The package was unwrapped and the people gathered around while some elders examined the object. It was unclear whether they understood it to be a replica but that mattered little. Lihua said a few words, most probably about the find. Don was asked to stand. He waved to acknowledge their cheering. One of the elders rose and made a pronouncement and another great cheer went up. This was something that had gone from the community a long time ago and was now back. Three older men ceremonially lifted it onto a shelf near the door and stood back bowing their heads. They turned and motioned to Don to stand one more time. As he did so, many of the people rushed in and hugged him. He had never experienced anything like this sense of community in Australia. Once he would have been fazed by the attention, but things had changed. He really appreciated it.

"Did they say how it left the community? he enquired politely of Lihua.

"They said there have been many of these but this one is special. It is covered in gold. We never cover family shields with gold. There is no gold here. This one was taken far away and worked on. It is like a message from our relatives of the past telling us they found wealth. It brings a very good feeling to us all."

"So the miners in Australia gilded it with gold they had found and worked?"

"I think so."

A time of worship and prayers followed. Some food was distributed and a celebration was underway. The golden cartouche was certainly important to them. Everybody moved past to look at it more closely. After about an hour the rasping tones of the ibex horn signaled that they should depart to their daily activities.

With Lihua along for translation, two wiry little elders took Don and Annika on a longer trek through the deepest part of the forest. Everything was dark and dank until they suddenly emerged into glaring sunlight. They were standing atop a precipitous cliff overlooking the surging grey waters of a river far below in the gorge. This was their first sighting of the Hanshui River and it was truly spectacular. They stood at the top of a landslide of grey slate. *The quarry from which the stone for the cartouche was obtained. What a special place.*

Many minutes of video and dozens of images were taken as they picked their way down the forbidding slope. The flakes of stone were treacherously loose and slippery. One false step could have resulted in a three hundred-metre slide into the water. At one point they reached a ledge and their guides showed them a concealed cave entrance. *Yet another narrow squeeze? It doesn't look as narrow as the one yesterday.*

Two or three stones were quickly removed and the five of them squeezed through a small hole into an amazingly cavernous gallery. It was lit only by a sliver of sunlight reflected through the entrance from the stark rock outside. These people had mastered building rooms by hollowing out the soft rock. But this one was different. The walls appeared more naturally weathered and it was quite dark inside, unlike the well-lit sculped home they had visited the day before.

Lihua whispered something and one of the guides walked to a bench and lit an old oil lamp that had been skillfully carved from the soft stone. The smoking lamp gave off an eerie golden glow and produced a pungent herbal aroma.

"What kind of oil is that?" Don waited for a translation.

"It is not oil. It is honey and spices. It is also a good medicine. You put it in a room with a sick person and they get better."

Traditional medicine. Interesting. But the sick person would get less oxygen. Guess they didn't know about that when the tradition started. I won't ask.

The cavern was about thirty metres long. As their eyes became accustomed to the dimness, they could see more benches hewn from the rock. They were strewn with unfinished carvings, mallets and chisels. This was a masonry workshop and it was obviously in current use, but nobody was working there today.

"Film this Donny." He recoiled a little from her

explosive command.

The camera light illuminated sections of wall that were covered with Chinese characters and images reminiscent of the Cro-Magnon cave paintings in central Europe.

"This gallery has been used for many generations," Lihua translated.

"Are there any other caves?"

"Yes. We have hundreds. Everything here is done many times over. We have to have many secret places."

Don wandered about with his camera light on, studying the long rear wall. One rendering particularly attracted his attention. It was a large lizard. Standing back, he could see it was about five metres long and resembled a Komodo monitor. The lizard was extraordinarily large in proportion to the man holding a sword above its head. He asked Lihua about the painting and kept his light on it while she questioned the guides.

"This is a dragon of the type that lived in this area one thousand years ago. The smaller ones were used for food but the larger ones were very dangerous. This picture shows the largest dragon being killed by our ancestor. The painting is around eight to nine hundred years old and has been carefully retouched by descendants."

"So, it is a painting of a real animal?"

"Yes." She mumbled to one of the guides. "He can take you to see little ones. Tomorrow?"

"That would be fantastic."

"I like the way the man's legs and arms are

displayed. Is he dancing?" Annika moved in for a closer view.

"Wait." More mumbling. "Yes. He says this is a dragon dance."

"Oh my! This is exactly what we came to see. Donny, get plenty of photos and video. Here I'll stand next to it."

Moving in with his camera, the video light bathed the wall and the brilliant colours came to life, black outlines and glittering fill of intense reds and oranges. Positioned so her shadow was not interfering, Annika began a short commentary. She pointed to features of the dancing figure.

The intense light revealed that there were many, many more wall paintings in a variety of designs and sizes. There were no ceiling paintings. *It would only be possible to see the true colours in sunlight. Why did they colour them in the cave?* Don asked the question. He could not believe the answer he received.

"This is not a cave. It is a gallery on a cliff face. It only seems like a cave because rocks were stacked to make it secret. So the Red Guard could not find it. He will show you."

A guide jumped up onto a bench, raised his hand and pulled out a tiny plug of rock from above his head. Daylight streamed in onto the bench. He quickly replaced it, plunging them back into relative darkness.

"Ah! A skylight. Brilliant."

On the floor against the walls sat a large number of partially completed slate carvings. Don picked one up. The texture was identical to his cartouche.

"Can we see how the carving is done?"

The other guide picked up a mallet and began hammering. The noise was deafening as it echoed around the rocks.

Don turned on the camera light and diligently filmed the timeless craft. With a documentary in mind, he panned the camera around the walls to capture the ambience of the studio. He gave a fairly amateur description of how the stone was held and how it gave way easily under the chisel blows. *Annika can dub this later. I won't be doing any commentary in the documentary.*

After an amazing time of cultural immersion, they came back out into the glaring light and the stones over the entrance were replaced. Annika pointed to a boat rounding a bend in the river. Suddenly the two guides took off and scrambled to the top of the cliff.

"Where are they going?"

"To get a better view. Not many boats come here. The river is too dangerous."

Some words in dialect were heard from above. Lihua's face turned a brilliant shade of crimson.

"Police with guns. We are in danger!"

In alarm they looked around for an escape route from the slippery slope.

Chapter 36

One of the guides came racing down, slipping on the slate while trying to stay upright. Desperate words were exchanged in dialect.

"We must go to a safe cave. He will take us."

The man led them across the loose rock to a large stony outcrop that provided some cover. A minute later the short blasts of the ibex horn echoed around them.

"It's a raid! It is really a raid!" Lihua shrieked in a high-pitched voice that startled Annika and Don.

"Where will we go?"

"We must remain very quiet behind this stone." Something was whispered. "You wait here. They are taking me first. You will be safe. Stay out of sight."

With that Lihua and the guide were gone. It was the last time they would ever see her.

"They've abandoned us." Don was shaking. *Hell, I don't know what to do. Where can I run to? They'll see me if I make a run for it. God please help me.*

"No. They wouldn't." *I thought I could trust Lihua. Now she's left me. Don's no help. But why this?* "Lihua's in much greater danger than we are. The police might shoot her." Annika tried unsuccessfully to bring some logic to the situation.

"They might shoot us too. Just keep quiet."

They laid low peering down at the river. Don continually looked around for a place to run. He was visibly scared and in his panic he was not offering her any sense of security. That upset her. *He's no Indigo Jones. Why did I ever choose this wimp?*

The boat was a large inflatable. It slowed and four men stood up on the deck. They were carrying weapons. The pair watched as they landed and began to pick their way up the slippery slope. One of their guides crept down to them, scaring the living daylights out of them. He quietly moved some stones and without words motioned for them to empty their pockets. The notebook and cameras along with the hard drive and flash drives were rapidly extracted. The man silently placed their things into a rocky niche and covered them with flat stones. By the time this was accomplished, the armed men were slipping and sliding their way up the slope less than one hundred metres away. They did not appear to have seen them.

The guide put his finger to his lips. He gestured to them to stay down. With remarkable stealth and speed, he clambered up the slope and quickly vanished over the top. This left Annika and Don to face the raiders. Both knew intuitively that moving would lead to certain capture. They clung to each other and laid low.

Three soldiers in camouflage uniforms and one in street clothing were close now. Don recognised one of them. The man was not carrying a gun. He was the youngest of their minders from Wuhan. The other three were grabbing his arm at times as though he was their prisoner. Don suspected that the young man was in trouble for having lost his charges. Now he had turned up with soldiers to find them and save face.

The anxious pair huddled against the rock. The men were only metres away. One of the soldiers turned and saw them. They immediately stood with their hands in the air. The gunmen surrounded them. The cold steel muzzles were thrust into their sides. Not a word was uttered.

They were prodded towards the river. The treacherous descent to the boat took ages. Loose stones tumbled down under their feet. Each one slipped over at times. Knees and elbows were cut and grazed. One of the men slid at least twenty metres on this back. He jumped up, trained his weapon on them and laughed. Consternation showed on Don's face. *They're playing with us.* There was a metallic click. *No, they're serious!*

Clambering into the boat, they were handcuffed and made to lie face down on the deck. The outboard motor roared into life. With a violent jolt the vessel turned and raced against the swirling waters. Annika and Don felt gun muzzles banging their ribs as they were bounced up and down in the turbulence. Ploughing through the narrow gorges the boat eventually rounded a bend into a calmer stretch. On one side there was a narrow shingle beach. The bow lowered and the boat was brutally rammed up onto the shore. At gunpoint they stood and were unceremoniously hustled onto the stony ground.

Before them stood an eight-wheeled all-terrain military vehicle in camouflage colours. A machine gun was mounted in the centre. They were roughly manhandled over the sides into the back seats and driven away over very steep and rugged ground. In other circumstances they would have enjoyed the exhilaration.

After an hour the vehicle came to a stop at a familiar place. Two soldiers grabbed them by the arms and they were shoved out onto the ground. Picking themselves up, they found themselves standing outside the dance school barn. The building was deserted. Another vehicle was parked there too. It was white with a blue stripe, an insignia and red, white and blue lights on top. *A four-wheel drive police van.*

An officious looking policeman in a blue uniform approached the group and shouted orders. He sprayed out a mix of Mandarin and broken English. It became evident that they had been arrested for breaking the law and engaging in activities considered detrimental to the state.

Without any opportunity to collect their things, they were taken to the van and made to climb into the rear cabin. That was difficult in handcuffs. *I've never been in a paddy wagon before. What is going on?*

There was no sign or mention made of Lihua or Madam Long, so they appeared to have avoided capture.

"Have the ladies abandoned us?" Don was a little angry that his dream had suddenly come to a dead end.

"I don't believe so. They would probably have been executed if they'd been captured. In hiding they can still help us. Lihua knew we would be okay." Despite their situation, Annika was showing a clarity of thought. Don felt quite humiliated and tried not to show his angst.

"And I missed out on seeing the dragons!" This was his pathetic attempt to break the tension of the moment. Annika frowned.

The uniformed officer stood at the rear doorway of the van. A younger one appeared behind him.

"Where is the woman? You tell us or you go to gaol." They shrugged.

"We really do not know. We are European visitors. We do not know this area."

The officer took an aggressive stance. Feeling the need to appear manly, Don began to make a move. Annika stopped him.

"Don't."

The policemen spun around as two soldiers appeared with a child of about six from the community. There was a lot of shouting. The child was being shaken. It quickly became apparent that the young one did not understand and as they released him, he ran off into the undergrowth. Don could just make out the three soldiers picking through the thorns after him with guns at the ready to look for others who might have information. The minder came walking towards them, a slight grin on his face.

There was a loud verbal exchange between the police and the minder. Somebody was not pleased. In frustration the younger policeman, now brandishing a pistol, jumped in with them and the door was slammed shut. He insisted they get down on the floor. Both front doors slammed, and the engine started. Don and Annika tried to sit comfortably shoulder to shoulder. They started to speak to each other in code, but the young guard intervened. Annika turned and gave Don a very long kiss on the mouth. The guard laughed and from that point on he did not prevent them from talking. Don found it objectionable that she kissed him for a purely pragmatic reason when she had never attempted to do so for a romantic reason.

"I love you, baby," she bluffed.

"Me too, baby," he responded in a dejected tone.

"You can do better than that. Ham it up a bit."

"Okay, if you say so."

"Never mention the long lady."

Donald caught her drift. "Yes, that lady is immaterial."

"That's better. Little boy blue can't understand us. See the facial muscles smile but the eyes exhibit no comprehension."

The long and arduous drive took most of the day. The boredom was frequently broken by the quest to see who could come up with the more creative yet unintelligible turn of phrase. They were in an enclosed rear compartment of the vehicle. The day was hot. The tracks, if they existed, were rough. There was no view out and two narrow slits provided seemingly little air circulation. Huddling together on the floor, they tried to calm each other, but it was to no avail. The man in blue was watching their every move and laughing.

There was no toilet stop and both were in a deal

of pain holding on for so many hours. When they ultimately emerged, they saw that they were in a city, which they presumed to be Wuhan.

Chapter 37

The police lockup was dark and filthy. A strong smell of urine hung in the air. The concrete floor was black with mould and the brown painted bars bore evidence of many desperate hands. They were placed in adjacent cells which appeared to be a little better appointed than those of the other wretched inmates, although the squat toilets and hard bench beds were decidedly uninviting. Thick concrete walls were painted grey and imprinted with Chinese characters and sketches carved out by previous occupants. Clumsily mounted on the wall outside was a decrepit old camera. They wondered whether it still worked but the thought of constant surveillance made them nervous about trying to communicate.

This became their home for the next few days. Plates of rice with a few black specks were passed through to them twice a day. They very quickly gained skill in the use of chopsticks. Don thought he could hear Annika grunting at times. *I hope she's exercising and not being tortured.* Each saw the other only fleetingly as they were being escorted to another room. They could exchange only a brief smile to indicate that all was well.

There were interrogations but they were not harsh. They were carried out in an untidy office with papers all over desks and piled on the floor, not at the stereotypical single table with a glaring overhead light. The English was not totally decipherable, but Don was able to communicate to them that he was a research assistant, did not know that he had broken the law and had no knowledge of the whereabouts of the Chinese woman. Annika had a very similar experience. *Madam Long was never mentioned. She's not really a threat to anybody.* Their stories tallied so the police were satisfied the truth had been established.

Generally they were treated well. One officer in particular attended to their needs with a constant smile. He could speak a little English. They were suspicious of his motives but still thankful for his care and attention. After a couple of days he let them know that their baggage had arrived. This was rather amazing news. They found out later that their bags with clothing, notebooks and travel documents had been deposited on the police station steps during the night, almost certainly by a member of the community.

The authorities dealt with them swiftly. The Chinese obviously did not want any international controversy over the detention of an Australian and a German citizen. On day five he saw Annika being taken away by two men in dark suits. Despite watching all day, he never saw her being returned. He sat on the bed in his cell for another twenty-four hours, totally bored but also distressed that he was never given the opportunity to say goodbye to Annika.

Next morning before dawn he was whisked away in a police car to Wuhan International Airport where he was interviewed by immigration officers. They were able to tell him in English that he had breached his visa restrictions by visiting a forbidden area and he was consequently being deported. *Deported?* It sounded like a shameful thing to happen to a fine, upstanding Australian citizen. His hope of becoming a researcher was taking a nosedive. He was ignominiously escorted onto a Jetstar plane bound for the Gold Coast, Australia. His passport with the cancelled visa was handed to him at the last minute as he entered the aircraft, along with a now battered case which was whisked away by a crew member to be placed on the floor in an empty row.

He found the flight to be very unpleasant. Most of the passengers were Chinese and they had obviously observed him being delivered to the door. They spoke accusingly to him although he had no understanding of anything that was said. Even the cabin crew seemed to treat him with disdain.

About four hours into the flight an Australian steward approached him and asked him to move forward to the front of the aircraft. He was placed alone in a first-class seat. The friendly steward sat down next to him and explained that the passengers were upset to be sitting near a criminal. Don then had the opportunity to explain his situation. For the remainder of the trip he was treated much more hospitably.

Chapter 38

Queensland, Australia. Late June 2007.

On arrival at Coolangatta airport, more than nine hours after leaving Wuhan, he was first off the plane and was immediately approached by waiting Australian Federal Police and an Immigration officer who took him directly into a room and asked him about his trip. They were quickly convinced that he was an innocent research assistant who became caught up in an elaborate ruse by Chinese dissidents to return under cover to their own country. No further action would be taken except to report to the Chinese embassy that he had been questioned and released.

"Can I travel back to my job in Germany?"

"You would be best to contact the German embassy in Canberra because your work visa may be affected by the deportation. A new application will probably be required, and they may not grant it just in case you break the regulations over there. And you don't want to fly over there only to be sent back."

"I'll have to go home and have a think about the future."

"You will. Don't try to go back to China for a couple of years. You're probably best to sit tight and start teaching again in Australia. The deportation shouldn't affect you teacher registration."

"I hope not. Well, thank you for your advice."

"Do you have somewhere to go for tonight?"

"Yes. My brother can come and drive me home. But I don't have a phone."

He was permitted to use the office telephone and he called his brother Angus to drive the Peugeot down to pick him up. He knew his call would be a surprise, but he offered to explain in full later.

Don sat patiently in the terminal until Angus arrived around nine at night. Gloria was with him. They all hugged, and he did not feel uncomfortable at all. Just last Christmas he would not have hugged his own brother in public but now it seemed important to him to be reunited with family.

"Hi Bro. What happened to you?"

"It's a long, long story. I'll tell you on the way home. You drive. I'm wrecked."

It was apparent from his voice that he was depressed. Gloria put her hand on his arm and came out with a little piece of wisdom.

"Don, you gave it your all. You had no more to give. You should be proud of that."

"Yeah. Thanks Gloria. But I guess when you give your all and it doesn't result in anything, it's pretty disheartening."

"What do you mean by 'it didn't result in anything'?" Angus picked up the tired old suitcase. They began ambling out of the terminal. Gloria's arm was now around his waist for moral support. He didn't mind at all.

"Well, I didn't finish my assignment. That upsets me."

"Don, we often don't finish things. I was in the middle of a big report on trends in consumer discretionary spending for the company. Another week and it would have been finished. But I took the opportunity to do this short-term swap to Brisbane. So I just briefed a colleague and left it with her. It's all fine. I made the most of the opportunity, but I'm not upset about not finishing the report."

"Everything in life has stages. You move on when a new one comes up. Never regret what you left behind. It was what got you to where you are. You'll find something new and exciting that you couldn't have taken on without that experience behind you." There was Gloria's wisdom again.

"Yeah. I guess you're right. But Annika?" He had a note of sadness as they climbed into the Pug. Don sat in the back seat and Gloria turned around to comfort him.

"What happened to her?"

"I don't know yet. They took her away before they came for me."

"Do you love her?"

"I wouldn't call it love. I like her. We did a lot together."

"Well, there you are. The experience showed you how to find the right girl. You were close but there wasn't that spark between you. So, coming home maybe saved you from making a big mistake."

"She wasn't a mistake. I want to see her again. It's just that she was a different person when I worked with her. Sort of rigid. Not overly bossy but sort of German business-like. Not much give and take. Know what I mean?"

At this point Angus interrupted.

"Bro, I'm just going to pull in here for fuel. Go in and buy three thick shakes. I'll have caramel and Glore'll have chocolate. What's your favourite?"

"Banana. But I've got no cash."

"Here." Gloria handed him a twenty dollar note.

"When you come back, start from the beginning and tell us the whole story."

Don did as instructed. As soon as they drove off he began his narration, starting with finding the stone. After half an hour he was lamenting his hopes of becoming a researcher cum documentary maker being dashed. Then there was the one woman who cared for him being suddenly taken away before he really knew her.

"Are you attracted to other women?" Gloria showed her psychologist side.

"Yes. I am."

"Glore's taken mate," laughed Angus.

'Her assistant Meike is really cute. She's super-efficient and always nice. Annika could get a bit cranky if things weren't done her way."

"Well there you are. You just identified that she may not be the one. Maybe you should step out and date some others. Do you know any?"

"Well yes I do. But they don't like me."

"How do you know that?"

"They don't talk to me."

"Do you talk to them?"

"Well. Not really. Just hello and how are you."

"Don, you know what you have to do. You tried it once and it wasn't right. Try, try, try again."

He sighed and changed the subject. His talk

became somewhat more optimistic about the future, suggesting a return to teaching or possibly a new occupation in a tertiary research institution. His desire to discover new things had been stimulated enormously by the whole experience. They arrived at his house around midnight. He never expected to be back at 'Green Wattles' so soon. Following the difficult phone call to his night owl parents, he went to his desktop computer that had been unused for a couple of months. Booting up the machine, he had to wait patiently while software and virus protection updates occurred. Then he checked his email. There were quite a few but as they cascaded down the screen he saw a recent one from Annika. It was fairly brief.

> *Hallo Donny,*
> *I am so sorry that our trip turned out like this. I was deported back to Germany. The Academy might fire me. I have to make my case to them. I am at my father's house in Delmenhorst. Meike is staying here as company for me. Lihua and Madam Long are still in China. If they get caught they will go to prison or worse. I don't know anything more about what will happen to them. Please let me know that you are safe. Meike and I have worried about you.*
> *Mit Liebe,*
> *Annika*

Don immediately typed his reply.

Dearest Annika,
I am glad that you have arrived home safely.
It was an adventure, but not the kind we
wanted. I was flown back to Australia and I
am now safe at home. Please let me know if
you find out more information about
Professor Jiang. Do you think we will ever
see our video files and notes again?
Lots of love,
Donny

For the next week there was no reply. Don felt very strange as he re-established his daily routines. It seemed as if he had had a dream that turned into a nightmare. Angus and Gloria stayed at the house to support him through this difficult time but finally they had to return to Sydney for work. Gloria gave a parting remark and they drove away.

"Bye Don. You step out and start dating. Good luck."

Chapter 39

Don was alone at 'Green Wattles' once again. It was a cool, cloudless day in late June. He had spent the morning wandering the paddock with Col Chalmers, watering the small wattle plants. They went into the house for morning tea. He popped into his home office while his friend washed his hands. An email had arrived.

Hallo Donny,
I have been busy trying to get my life back together. I am finally back in Goslar. I have explained to the Academy what has happened and they accepted me back. They are not happy that Lihua broke the law and has left them without a senior faculty member. I think they will not allow her to return to her position. You will be very surprised to hear that a parcel has arrived from China. It contains most of our hard drives and flash drives. Even the card from the camera is in there. I expect we have lost the cameras and sound equipment but the files are preserved. I have been looking through them. They are really good. There is also a letter in Chinese. Meike had one of the music students translate it. It seems Madam Long arranged for the drives to be posted to me. It is a miracle that the parcel was able to leave China. I have had

*only a little news of Lihua. She has gone into
hiding with her husband in Shanghai. I guess
she wants to meet up with her old friends.
Madam Long is still in the community with
her husband. I hope they both stay safe.
You still have your German work visa. I
would like you to come back over here and
help us organise the material and make that
television documentary. How do you feel
about that? If you agree please let me know
and Meike will book your flights from
Brisbane to Frankfurt. I am thinking about
you often. I miss you.
Annika*

Don was in two minds over the proposal. *A few
more weeks working in Goslar, then what? Does
Annika ever want to have more than a professional
relationship? I would really like to see her again;
we went through a lot together. And I like Meike
very much too. But, does my attraction to these
women warrant another uncertain and possibly life
determining step?* He began to pray silently for
guidance. The image of Peter stepping out of the
boat materialised in his brain. He immediately called
out to Col and showed him the message.

"What do you think I should do?"

"Well from what you've told me you took a big
step of faith. You had a strong conviction that you
should do it. But it didn't work out how you wanted
it to. And that's not unusual. Sometimes it's God's
way of redirecting things. It's a bit like those little

wattles out there. You put in fifty believing they'll all grow to be big healthy bushes. I can almost guarantee that a couple of them won't make it. Some will be healthier than others. If we have a cold snap and a frost, they might all die. You just have to keep watering them and giving them the best chance. Nothing in this life is certain."

"Yeah, but this is an unfinished project and I just have to go and complete it. I hate leaving things up in the air."

"I know. I know. We have to learn to trust that our life journey is in God's hands. All we have to do is take the next step. But, listen, don't be hasty about it. Give yourself a week or two to mull it over. Go and talk to your boss Len White. See if you could go back to work at the school. Knock on a few doors."

That advice was extremely difficult to swallow for a man who liked everything in his life to be neatly pigeonholed. The two men chatted on over a cup of tea. The talk was mostly about improvements to the property. That was now a topic close to Don's heart. *I do want to farm this little acreage.* Col had another commitment and had to leave around ten thirty.

Don found himself in a state of disbelief. He could not commit himself to any household task so for a couple of days he was mostly sitting around on the sofa wondering about the future and waiting for something to happen. *I should be taking a step out. But which way? I just don't know.* He was moping about the house one morning when his new iPhone rang. *Nobody knows my new number.* It was Len

White.

"Hello Donald, this is Len White from the college."

"Oh. Hi Len. I wasn't expecting to hear from you. How on earth did you get my new mobile number?"

"I bumped into Col and Mary Chalmers at the marina on Saturday. I've known them for years. I've just bought a twenty-foot sailing boat. You know, for my retirement. It's tied up, I mean moored, right next to their cabin cruiser. Got to get the terminology right. Anyway, they told me about your situation and Col gave me your number. I'd like to have a chat with you. Can you call into the office about four this afternoon?"

"Yes, I can come in then." His mood lightened. Things were moving.

The drive to the school was one he had made hundreds of times before but today it seemed strangely different. The playground was deserted. The ladies in the administration gushed as they welcomed him back. One of them accompanied him to the principal's office. He was ushered over to the little lounge area in the corner. *The naughty corner.* Len came in with a big smile on his face.

"Don, how are you?"

"Well thanks. I didn't expect to be back here so soon."

"Oh. I knew you would be."

"I wish I was so certain about things."

He related the tale of his German and Chinese exploits to yet another fascinated listener. When he paused, Len walked over to his desk, opened a drawer and produced a crumpled piece of paper with a sketched diagram on it.

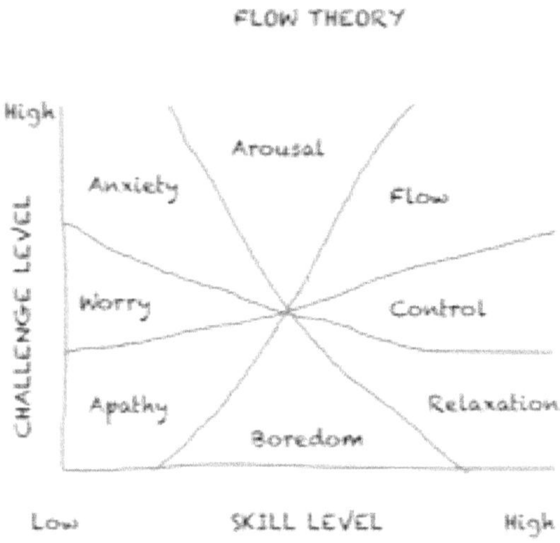

"Don, you might be familiar with this. It's the work of a Hungarian psychologist, Mihaly Csikszentmihalyi. I can't pronounce it properly, but it sounds like 'ma hayley chicks sent me highly'. Makes it easier to remember. Never mind his name, it's called Flow Theory."

"Yes, I came across it in my doctoral studies. Why do keep it in your desk?"

"I look at it a lot. And I show it to other people when they need motivation. I think having it hand drawn makes them pay more attention to it. I should redo it. This one's getting old. I'd like you to locate yourself on this."

Don peered at the sketch and put his finger on

'boredom'.

"Moderate skill and no challenge? I disagree Don. If I were you, I'd put my finger here." He pointed to 'anxiety'. "Low skill and big challenge. And I'm not talking about teaching or mathematical skill. You've got heaps of that. I'm talking about decision making skill. You have a challenge in front of you and you're hesitant to make decisions."

"Yes, I know. I want to finish my work, but I don't want to go overseas again if I don't have anything to come back to. And I'm not sure about my friend Annika. It isn't a really serious relationship. We were just getting to know each other."

"Don, I have something to offer you. It may help or it may not. But I hope at least you can get up into the top right-hand side of the diagram."

"Okay. I'm all ears."

"You know Alma Williams, don't you?"

"Yes. Not well though. She teaches social science, doesn't she?"

"That's right. Well last Friday she had an accident. She slipped down the C-block stairs."

"Oh no. Is she badly hurt?"

"She dislocated her shoulder and broke something in her knee. She has to have reconstructive surgery. I'm wondering whether you might come in as a casual and take her classes until she's ready to come back. That could be a few months."

Don looked down, deep in thought. Len gave him a moment.

"What do you think? Interested? It'd help us out."

"But I'm not a social science teacher."

"Don, you're a skilled teacher. Highly skilled. This will be a challenge for you. A high level challenge. Where will that place you?"

"Flow?"

"Yes, eventually. 'Arousal' at first then as you find your feet in the new area it will just start to come naturally and you'll flow with it."

"When would I start?" He was already planning in his mind.

"Tomorrow morning if you can. Her classes need a regular teacher. Oh. And I checked. Jessica Jones isn't in them."

They both chuckled.

"No, that's okay. Jessica actually apologised to me last year. I could do with a new challenge. So yeah, I can start tomorrow."

"That's great Don. Come over to the staff room. All the lesson plans are on her desk. It'll be your desk for a while. All the staff will be pleased to welcome you back. They've had a few rather strange bods in here over the past few days."

That evening he phoned Col to say thank you. His friend encouraged him to take the step and resign from the German contract job. He dreaded the task, but he carefully worded an email to Annika's professional address. *Direct, courteous and professional.*

Dear Professor Fluss,

I regret to inform you that I will be unable to

*return to Germany to complete my six-month
contract. I have had quite an experience
working with the Academy and I wish you all
the best for the future.*

Yours sincerely,
Dr Donald I. Kirk

He then wrote to her personal email.

Dear Annika,
*It has been wonderful getting to know you. I
think you are a very special person. At
present I am pretty confused about the future.
I have been offered work at my old school.
They really need me there. I want to see you
again sometime, but I just can't come over at
present. I need time to think. I've sent you a
more formal resignation. Please pass it on to
the administration. I'm so sorry it has come to
this.*
Love to you and Meike. Till we meet again.
Donald

He had no idea how sorrowful she would be when
this was received. But he stepped out and pressed
'send'.

Chapter 40

Redcliffe, Queensland. Early July, 2007.

The next morning turned out to be cold and wet, a challenge for the Peugeot wipers and demister. Len welcomed him back at the 8.10am staff briefing. He alluded to Don's adventures and suggested the other teachers may like to ask him about it. That would have previously caused him anxiety but now he welcomed the attention. Over lunch the Social Science staff gathered around him and listened to his jaw-dropping account.

The classes that day were also glad to see him. He had three Civics and Citizenship, two Economics and Business and one history class. He spent a little time with each telling them a sanitised version of his overseas experience. Hands shot up but their inquiries were not about the geographical or historical side of things. Not even the flights and hotels. Most wanted to know what the people ate and what young people did for entertainment in other countries. These were easy questions to answer, and he had two very different cultures to comment upon.

When the bell rang at three o'clock he was exhausted. As was his custom, he sat at the desk in staffroom, farewelled the other teachers and set about carefully preparing the next day's lessons.

After an hour there was a little rap on the door and somebody he had not seen all day appeared and asked to come in. She was dressed in a button-up blue top and army surplus pants. He swivelled around.

"Linda. How are you? Good to see you."

"Hello Don. It's really good to see you too. I'm a bit wrung out because I've been on a rock platform excursion all day. It was a bit cold and miserable. Not the best day for it but we managed."

"You can say that again. You look great."

"I knew you'd be here on your own. I need to talk. I'm actually having a bit of a hard time at the moment."

This was not the bright, vibrant Linda he had admired for so long from afar.

"Oh, tell me what's happened."

He stood and she rushed over and hugged him. Her eyes were now red and a tear trickled down her cheek. They stood clutching each other for at least a minute. She sobbed as he inhaled the beautiful perfume of her hair. He pulled over two chairs so they could sit to talk.

"It's Phil and me. It's over. We were even talking about getting married. But he broke it off. And now he's going out with my best friend Trudi. She used to be my best friend." Her lips were quivering now. "And I've been feeling sick every day."

"Oh no. That's awful". Rolling his chair closer, they hugged more tightly than before and he whispered in her ear. "I do know how you feel. When something you really believe in just doesn't work out it's really dreadful. I've found myself in that position in the past few days."

"Has your girlfriend broken it off with you too?" She sat back in her chair to see his reaction. "The dance teacher chick you kept telling everybody about?"

"She's not really my girlfriend. We kept it pretty professional. But I probably won't see her again because we live on opposite sides of the earth."

"You're not going back?"

"I don't think so. My place is here. Len said he needs me."

She hugged him yet again. A smile had crept over her face.

"I'm just so happy to hear you say that. You know when you were going gold prospecting?"

"That was ages ago. What I found changed my life, but it wasn't gold."

"I know. But I wanted to come too when I heard what you were doing. It was just that Phil the Rat and I were an item back then. Len keeps talking about your discovery, you know. I think he wants some credit for it. He'll give you back a job, I reckon."

"Really?"

"Yes. You wouldn't have heard. Garry Willcox is retiring in December. You're a shoo-in to get the job."

"Head of the Maths Department?"

"You'd make a great Head of Department. You're so smart and you really listen to people."

"Well, thank you. It would be a challenge,

wouldn't it?"

"You'd be up to it. All the maths and science staff think you should get the job. When we heard you were back, we all talked about it today after school. Garry wasn't there, of course."

"Thanks. That explains why I felt my ears burning. And I thought it was just the cold wind."

They both patted each other on the arm and laughed, then Don looked her in the eye and spoke from his heart.

"Look if there is anything at all I can do to help you, just ask."

He was about to stand when she put her hand on his knee to stop him.

"There is actually, Don. Um. That's why I came in to see you. Um. My little sister Hannah is having a big party for her twenty-first in Brisbane next Saturday. Phil and I were going but with the Rat out of the picture, would you like to come with me? Sorry if I seem too forward."

"Linda, I've always liked you. I'd love to take you there in my classic Peugeot."

She grabbed his hand and kissed him on the lips. *A genuine kiss. Wow.*

"Oh, thanks Don. I've always liked you too, you know. And I'd still like to go gold prospecting with you one day."

Author's Note

This novel is a work of fiction. The story and all the characters were created in the mind of the author. However, most of the events are based upon real happenings and thoughts in the life of the author. In a sense it is somewhat autobiographical, but not chronologically so. All people and the scenarios portrayed are fictitious. No similarity to persons living or deceased or to situations in which they have been involved is intended or inferred. Many of the locations in the story are real and have significance for the author but descriptions of them are only intended to give an appropriate location for aspects of the storyline and cannot be regarded as accurate. The important message of the book is that introversion is not a disadvantage and introverts may more readily be able to find purpose and fulfilment in life because of their abundance and depth of inner thoughts. For this to happen the author believes that the introvert needs to actively seek that purpose, overcome shyness and just step out and do it, recognising that overthinking has been holding them back.

Robert Flegg
Buderim Queensland
September 2020